MW00986390

BEAUTIFUL GHOST

Milana Marsenich

Published by Open Books

Cover image by Peter Oelschlaeger

Learn more about the artist at www.flickr.com/photos/thunderpete/

ISBN-13: 978-1948598613

Dedicated to my dear friend, the late Christine Dodson Kearney.

"How many times can a heart be broken? As many times as it takes."
— Frances Marsenich, my mother

THE WOLF DOG

September 1918

* * *

THE WOLF DOG WANDERS through the town where mining fumes singe the air, and tin shacks, thrown together in desperation, sit next to French mansions and yards flagged with cobblestone. He rambles past the Cabbage Patch, where bootleggers and criminals live in downtrodden shanties and the king of the Patch rules the poor with an iron club. The dog walks through Dublin Gulch, a rough bit of Butte, inhabited by stubborn Irish people and sour-faced old women, who rarely shop for fine china or cast-iron pots at the town's one department store. He continues his journey through Chinatown, past the opium dens, and down to the train depot on East Front Street.

He sits on the platform, under a center overhang, out of the rain, and watches the passengers disembark. Soot covers every surface of the depot, and, as the sky darkens, the wolf dog feels something coming. Something rising up out of the ground, on the wind, or perhaps in a blanket. Or maybe, a young woman carries it in her lap as the train roars across the country from the east to Montana. This tiny thing is barely a whisper. But it's there, wanting to live and live strong. It floats among the people hugging and kissing in the depot's large waiting room. It lights on jackets of men smoking, and hovers in the perfumed air where women tend to private matters.

When the travelers disperse, the wolf dog's great haunches carry him up to the black metal headframes. Butte miners cramped together in cages wait to be let down into the dark tunnels where they extract copper. Before work, they leave meat scraps and pieces of dried bread on a rock for the dog. At the end of the day, when they rise up out of the shaft, their faces grimed with dirt, they pat the dog's head and tell him he's good.

He lifts his large paws as he crosses Park Street and weaves his way through the people who haven't yet recovered from last year's fire on the hill. The town still spins from the dark mass of men who hung Frank Little. They hung a man for trying to do good, for daring to lend his voice to justice. They hung him for his words, for speaking out against those who oppressed the miners.

The fortunate in town have money and food and hold their loved ones tight. The fatherless children cuddle into their mothers' skirts. They know loss and they know love. They know meatless stews and crowded boarding rooms where there are plenty of other children to play with. With their fathers taken by the mining accident and the town swirling just outside of grief, the kids pull water, carry wood, and take care of the younger children. Their mothers work in shops, cafes, and the mansions on the hill, and bring home a meager pay.

The wolf dog loves one of these children, a boy who never had a father or a mother. Someone dropped him off at The Polly May Home for Kids, and never looked back. Now the boy has a new family—a mother, a grandmother, a young sister, and a father who is off at war and writes glorious letters to him. "Be good, my boy," his new father writes. "Take care of your mother and sister." Almost ten years old now, the boy has grown tall. He works keeping the bakery clean, supplying wood for the bread ovens, delivering food to the sick and elderly.

The boy has heart and gumption. He has a good mind. Somehow, he learned to love. Maybe from the woman at The Polly May where he once lived. He misses her. Some good things happened there. The wolf dog found him there. He loves the wolf dog, and the dog feels it in the very center of his ancient being.

This speck of something that has entered the town, maybe

on the train, or the leather straps of a trunk, or in the cough of a miner, worries the dog for the boy's sake. The dog wants him safe. This tiny thing, this unseen element, hovers nearby, ready to pounce and steal the boy's breath.

The thing is so tiny the dog can't even tear it to shreds with his great teeth. His claws are nothing against it. He can't find it so he can smash it into the dirt, or bury it. He can only feel it out there. Waiting. Lurking.

Chapter One

MARIKA JOVICH LOOKED AROUND Dr. Fletcher's office at the folded laundry and the clean desk, savoring the quiet satisfaction of a job well done. The late afternoon cooled. Smoke wafted out across the street. She had wanted to be a doctor, but her father had promised her in marriage to Michael Jovich, and marrying him had interfered with her medical dreams. Instead, she ran trivial errands for the doctor, and cleaned up the rooms at the end of the day. This day was over and she was glad of it. Pushing her long black hair back into its fallen bun, she turned to go. As she grabbed her coat, someone knocked on the door.

This knock shifted the air in the room. Smooth and quiet as silk, the joyful moment fluttered away, taking the breath of it and leaving not a trace to recall later. A soft pulse, deep in Marika's stomach, twitched. At first, she ignored the knock, hoping the person on the other side of the door could wait until morning. She wanted to get home to her family and Mama's good cooking.

Fighting the urge to sneak out the back, she opened the front door. A pale young woman, about her own age, dressed in a gray dress, pulled a brown wool coat tightly around her shoulders and shivered. Thick strands of blond hair straggled around her face. Her heavy lids shielded milky green eyes. She was lithe and thin, a wisp of wind, blown to the open door without direction or purpose. A crow sat on the porch railing and cawed. Pink clouds stretched out toward the Highlands, dusk barely forming a thought in the sky.

"May I help you?" Marika asked. A pure wave of urgency

flashed at the back of her brain. This woman needs a doctor, a real doctor.

"I have a headache," the woman whispered, barely seeming to register Marika standing there. Her droopy green eyes looked out across the waiting room. Marika followed her gaze. The empty chairs welcomed her. A skeleton picture hung down one wall and waved hello. A picture of a dissected arm showed its muscles and pointed toward a map of human body organs.

Dread crept into Marika like a tiny sick animal. Generally, a headache was no call for a doctor. She disregarded that bit of fear caught in her throat and said so. "Go home and drink some water. Rest. If you don't feel better in the morning, come back."

A small man appeared from the shadows just in time to catch the girl as her knees gave out. Cool gray eyes looked up at Marika from under the brim of his fedora. He held the girl up like a question, as if she were a bag of grain for the livery stable. Where should he put her?

Marika checked her fear and cursed her luck. She couldn't very well send the girl home, wherever home was, when she couldn't stand. She led them both to a bed she had just made up in the sick room. The man carefully put the girl on the mattress, making sure her personal parts were covered.

Without a word, he turned to leave.

"Wait," Marika called after him.

He stopped and turned toward her.

The girl sat up suddenly. "Louisa came back to work sick," she said. "She was weak. You know how weak. You helped her carry the material bolts to the cutting table."

"Shhhh," the small man said. And to Marika, "She's delirious."

"And Stella never came back to work," the girl yelled. "What did you do to her?"

"You don't feel well," he said. "You know Stella got sick. But she didn't rest. You must rest and get well." He pushed his hat back on his forehead and turned to Marika again. "Can you make sure she rests? I've seen this sickness before and the more rest the better."

2

"Who is she?" Marika asked. "Who are you?"

He cocked his head, tipping the hat sideways. "I found her in the street like that, ready to die. The sign says 'physician.' Are you?"

Ready to die. The words sent a cold ripple through Marika and she crossed her arms tightly.

"Am I what?"

"A physician?"

"Yes," she lied.

He nodded and walked away, vanishing into the dusk's pink glow.

"I'm sorry to call so late," the girl said. She coughed into her hand and leaned forward. "I don't feel good. It just came on me. I'd gone to the dress store and then to the market. I chose some good apples." She pulled a small bag of them out of her large coat pocket and set it on the bed. "But now I couldn't eat an apple to save my soul. And seeing that man didn't help anything."

The girl's face was flush, perspiration lining her forehead. She had a blue tinge around her lips. Marika was suddenly hot. She hung her coat and hat on a hook.

"Can I take your coat?" she asked.

The girl shook her head. "It's like I'm in an oven and then frozen solid. Right now, I'm freezing. Do you have a blanket I can wrap up in?" She was shaking and could barely sit up.

"You'd better lie down," Marika said. And this, right here, is why I want to go to medical school. There were other women doctors in Montana. Why not her?

The girl fell onto the bed. The room thickened with a sickly-sweet smell, alternating with a sour smell, sending off tendrils that reeked of the body trying to rid itself of something foreign, and failing. The girl wasn't going to make it home for dinner and neither was Marika.

Fortunately, she'd told Michael she'd meet him at Mama's house for dinner. At least he'd get fed. Would anyone think to come looking for her and bring her something to eat? She could eat one of the apples. No. No apples. The girl had touched them.

Marika pulled the blanket up over her.

"Thank you," she said through chattering teeth, the blue tinge at her lips spreading.

Marika turned away to get the thermometer. "Were you around anyone who was sick?"

"My landlord wasn't feeling good this morning. But he said it's just the change of seasons making his bones ache." She started coughing, a harsh full-chested cough that looked like it hurt. When she could continue, she said, "Plus, he's got my boy with him. That kid could run the sickness out of anyone."

Marika shook the mercury thermometer down, put it in the girl's mouth, and busied herself with folding some towels Miss Parsons had washed and hung to dry. She'd need them since she couldn't get the girl home. Sickness should be weathered in one's own bed whenever possible. We grow strong in the presence of love, her grandmother had said. A few days and the sickness would pass. In the meantime, she'd be in a familiar place with her son. Her landlord could help her. But that was impossible now.

She took the thermometer out and looked at it. One hundred four degrees. Way too high for an adult. Heat decimated the body at that temperature. She needed to get some water into the girl to get the fever down and prevent a trip to the hospital.

"How old are you?" Marika asked.

"Twenty-two. But I feel like a hundred and two. I hurt all over."

"It's no wonder. I don't know what you've got, but it's serious. You can't go home tonight. You'll be okay, but you should be where someone can watch you."

"Oh, I can't stay," she began. "I need to get home to my son." She tried to sit up, but it was no good. Her arms shook and collapsed under her. Her lip trembled and her eyes filled with water.

"Wait here," Marika said, as if the girl could do anything else. Marika tried to quiet her mind, staring out a window as the clouds turned dark and stormy. A soft sprinkle of rain pattered on the roof and she inhaled the aroma of wet dirt. She felt her grandmother's wisdom in her blood. Baba had known things, seen things, felt things in the air, on the rocks, when the leaves whistled and fell.

On another night the clouds might've parted for the moonlight to flood the streets. But tonight, the dark sky shrouded a secret, an omen read by candlelight in a shadowy room far, far away. The crow cawed again. Even the black bird knew that nothing good would come from this tiny whisper that had landed in Marika's life.

She went to the office pharmacy above Miss Parsons' desk and got some morphine for the girl. It wasn't much but it was all she could offer. Outside, a group of boys yelled at each other. The taunts faded as they moved on. Music and raucous laughter floated out of a nearby tavern until the door closed and the air went still. The rain stopped, leaving the evening silent and waiting.

Marika returned to the sick room. The girl had dark, blueish spots on her cheeks and was struggling to breathe. The morphine would help with that, too. It would open up the passageways to her lungs and relax the constriction. Marika steadied her shaking hands as she gave the girl the medicine.

She should call Dr. Fletcher. That thought set her jaw on edge. If she'd been trained, she could count on her own authority, without having to call the doctor in. She'd be the doctor!

Never mind that, she told herself. Tend to this girl.

There was a bit of blood at her nose and Marika wiped it away and noticed something dark and crusted lodged in the girl's ear. She thought of her that way: a girl. Maybe that was because the sickness made her look so young and frail.

Suddenly, she raised her knees up and held her stomach. "I'm sorry. Can I use the bathroom?" She was up off the bed before Marika could point the way, tripping over the cotton sheet, her gray dress flying out behind her. The bathroom door shut fast.

After a while Marika knocked. "Are you okay?" She had a bad feeling sitting in her chest.

No answer.

"Do you need some help?" Marika was afraid of what she'd find. The sickness had hit this girl hard and fast. The grippe could come on like this, and leave a person struggling to walk for weeks.

Knocking again, she leaned her ear against the door. "Talk to me," Marika said. The soft whisper of angel wings floated through the air.

Gathering her courage, she pushed the bathroom door open. The girl sat slumped on the toilet. Marika helped her clean up and walked her back to the bed. Once there, the girl shed her coat, pulled up her knees again, held her stomach, and moaned.

"What is your name?" Marika was hoping to distract her from her pain until the medicine kicked in.

"Amelia," she said, barely audible.

"Where are you from?"

"Philadelphia." Her voice was a hushed whisper.

"Okay, Amelia from Philadelphia." The words had a cheerful ring to them that fell flat. "I've got some water I want you to drink." She held the glass up against her lips, pressed the bottom lip down, and poured water into her mouth. The water ran out both sides of her mouth, down her cheeks to her chest. When she finished, Marika wiped Amelia's mouth and chest with a towel.

"Now, you rest," she said. The little man was right about one thing. Amelia needed a good rest. "I'll be right here. If someone comes by, I'll send word to your landlord about where you are." And I'll send word to my husband too, she thought.

But Amelia was already asleep.

The evening passed in bits of peace followed by fits of agitation. During the fits Amelia kicked off her blanket. Marika pulled it back up over her and felt the heat coming off the girl. At other times the girl looked peaceful enough, sleeping for long moments and waking with a start, sitting straight up, disoriented, worrying the blanket with her fingers. She would look around the room, terror clouding her eyes, turning them dark green. Did she see the sour, wrinkled face of illness coming toward her? Or was it something else?

Marika poured more water for her and held the glass for her sip. The girl tried to drink, but again, the water spilled down the front of her gray dress. She lifted her eyes to Marika and tried to smile. A sound came from her throat, something guttural and eerie, as unnatural as a trapped animal.

"What's your name?" Amelia had managed to ask.

"Marika," she said, silently cursing herself for forgetting the first rule of etiquette. She hadn't introduced herself.

Amelia nodded, fell back onto the pillow, and closed her eyes.

Outside, the moon tried to break through the clouds. A mine whistle signaled the end of a shift and a pack of stray dogs howled. Marika heard the howl like the crow's earlier warning. Her belly rumbled and she drank a glass of water. Michael would know that she was still at Dr. Fletcher's office. Maybe he would bring her food.

He'd done it before. One night when a woman had been poisoned, Marika had waited with her for the ambulance. Michael had brought a chicken thigh and mashed potatoes. It had taken the ambulance forever to get there that night. Once the woman was gone, Marika had gone right to Michael's chicken and potatoes. He had also brought bread and cured ham and a couple of oranges that were heavenly.

Tonight, she wanted to hear his voice, his laugh, the soft rhythm of his breath. She wanted to feel his hand touching hers. She wanted him to appear in the doorway with a hot plate of Mama's dinner. And cake. What she wouldn't do for a warm stew and a piece of Serbian rhubarb bread.

But she wouldn't ask him to bring dinner. She didn't know what had Amelia in its grip. She only knew it was bad and she didn't want him, or anyone she knew, getting it. Had Amelia been exposed to something horrible before she left Philadelphia? And it took this long to catch up to her? Most likely the girl had a simple flu, a slightly altered version of the one that came through last spring.

Marika wanted to help Amelia pass from this illness back to the life she'd known with her child. She wanted to protect her, rescue her dignity, and preserve the brilliant, radiant smile that Marika had imagined for her.

Ready to die. The man's words came back to her and she pushed them away. Amelia would not die. Not if Marika could do anything about it.

Finally, she called to tell Michael that she wouldn't be home and Mama answered the phone. "Should I have Michael bring dinner? Some roast and carrots?"

"No, Mama," she said, her stomach twisting a little. "I'm not hungry."

"He worries when you are late."

"I know, Mama."

"Marika," her mother said gently.

Marika could hear a spoon stirring a pot and the whisper of a fire. "Yes?"

"Papa would have been proud of you."

"Thank you." Marika said with a little laugh. "I'm only half as stubborn as he was."

Mama laughed too. "Get some rest," she said.

Marika hung up the phone and looked over at the girl on the bed. A vague mist surrounded her, her spirit rising half up out of her body and laying back in again. Marika could see the fragile threads of her life beginning to unravel, like a slow undoing of her birth so many years ago.

She bowed her head in prayer, asking for guidance on how to help her.

Dr. Fletcher kept four unused sleeping mats folded up in the closet. Patients usually went to the hospital or they went home. The sick room—with its gray walls, and plaster cracking over the logs, a couple of old sailboat pictures, a broken vase, long empty—was not exactly an invitation for comfort.

Marika pulled out a mat. Dust came off it in tiny gusts. She grabbed a sheet and blanket and made a bed for herself on the wood floor. Her hips would hurt by morning, but there was nothing for it. Fate had tied her to Amelia with a thin silver string, light and airy, but as strong as any good rope.

She closed the door between Dr. Fletcher's main office and the sick room, glancing at Amelia. A breath of air escaped her blue lips. Marika could expose herself and take care of Amelia. Or she could leave the girl alone and take care of herself. She couldn't do both.

The business of medicine was a gamble sure as any hand dealt up at the tavern that night. With a bit of Slavic luck, Marika picked up the hand, ready to play every card.

Chapter Two

KALY SHANE. KALY MONROE. Mrs. Monroe. It all seemed ridiculously funny. She, a whore, had married a decent, upstanding man—a soldier who'd gone off to war. But he would be back. He'd promised. And Kaly knew Tommy Monroe to keep his word. She had known him since she was five years old. That was when he'd moved into The Polly May Home for Kids, with Kaly and her twin sister, Anne Marie. And Bert Brown.

Coral Anderson had taken Tommy in without batting an eye, not realizing the trouble it would cause in Bert Brown's heart. Kaly hadn't known it then, but Bert was Coral Anderson's son. He might have been good at one time, but he turned mean long before his end. He'd died in the mining accident last year.

That suited Kaly. Dead, he could cause no more harm. At least two people would fervently disagree with her. Beth and Coral Anderson. Dead, he could cause no more joy.

A fierce storm homed in on Kaly, stinging her face as she climbed the steep uptown streets. It blew her brown curls into her eyes and she held them aside as she ducked her face into the thick edge of her coat. A crow cawed and swooped down to land on a tattered wooden fence.

The fence corralled a small yellow house that sat below the roadway, as if one of the mine tunnels had collapsed and it rested perfectly in the hole created by the fall, completely accepting its diminished stature. Dry weeds and long grasses punched out of the rocky ground in front of the house. Those ancient grasses fought to survive here long before miners came seeking gold and found the land rich in copper.

Dwarfed lilac bushes lined the house's long yard. At one

time, the bushes might have grown lush with lovely purple and white flowers. Now the leaves frazzled and fell. The smelter saw to the slow death of Butte's vegetation. The Copper Company was building a new smelter in nearby Anaconda. Sometime next year the smelting would move over there, taking much of the poisonous air with it.

Outside of the yellow house a tall thin woman with a sun-weathered face hung bed sheets to dry. Then she pinned diapers, a pair of men's trousers, and a soft yellow skirt to the line. She wore a pale pink nightshirt that blew sideways, revealing her narrow white legs. Another swift gust lifted her long hair off her shoulders.

Inside, a child cried.

Kaly wondered about the woman's husband and his one pair of washed trousers. She'd heard men talk about their mining partners. Down in the mines they were brothers. They saw each other day in and day out for years at a time. Strong bonds formed in the underground tunnels. They knew each other's thoughts. Survival depended on it. Hard rock mining was dirty messy work. She'd heard it said that the right kind of rock sang to the men. They dug blessings from God, trusting the luck.

When the luck went wrong, men stood by and watched while their partners hit a deep hollow or lit a fast fuse. A fast fuse could decapitate a man. Butte churches were filled with townspeople feverishly praying for men who had been killed in the mines.

Mountain Con. Moonlight. Moulton. High Ore. Kaly knew their names. As a child at The Polly May, she had memorized the names in a rhythm to calm herself, a momentary escape from a harsh world.

Even in good times, men lived with the fear that they would be put out of work if they didn't go along with the companies' politics. During last year's strike there was a war on and copper was needed for bullets. The nation needed the copper for electricity. The copper kings accused the strikers of treason. Frank Little had been hung with a stark warning pinned to his body 3-7-77.

Pay heed. Do not cross us.

Troops were brought in, and miners were beaten or shot. If more than three people gathered at a time they were told to move on. If they didn't, they got a little touch of the bayonet in the shoulder or side. Just a soft touch to start. But Butte men were stubborn and not easily pushed around, inviting the harsher end of the firearm.

The woman hanging clothes put the last towel on the line and packed her basket into the house, the door slamming hard behind her. Kaly feared for the woman. She knew that the child crying inside would grow up to wait at the gate each day, eyes fixed on the street until his father came home. And when his father didn't come home? He would get a paper route to help his mother pay the bills, beating up anyone who sold in his territory. Then one day he'd give the route to another boy, fix a work bundle, and don a hardhat. The woman would beg him not to work the mines, saying she couldn't stand the worry. But he'd go anyway, same as his father before him.

Kaly put the woman out of her mind. She was just stalling, killing time, avoiding that knock on Lottie Boyle's door. She wanted to see Beth. But she did not want to see Lottie Boyle. Lottie Boyle was one mean woman.

Kaly's simple blue dress hung loosely on her shoulders. She had lost her shape with the fat she'd gained and lost in the pregnancy with Annie and, a year after Annie's birth, the dress was still too big for her. Lottie Boyle would enjoy insulting her when she saw Kaly's frumpy style.

She pulled her coat even tighter against the storm and stepped up on the boardwalk. Wooden steps creaked and led the way to the large front porch of Lottie Boyle's Home for Girls, which was just a fancy, entirely deceptive, name for the woman's brothel.

Miss Boyle knew the cruelty of street life. She had taken up its mantle at an early age before becoming a madam and heavy handing the women who worked for her, getting rid of them when they showed wear, or cried, or got too drunk too often.

Kaly had sworn to never knock on that door again.

Yet, here she was.

A sour smell soared across the air and Kaly turned away

from it. The stern whistle of the wind filled her ears. When the gusts died down, a bird chirped a sound so sweet and pure that Kaly had to stop herself from hoping for something good.

Kaly had gotten pregnant and needed a safe place to live while she searched out a home for the unborn child. For a brief moment she had allowed herself to dream, to believe. She'd gone to Lottie Boyle in hopes of being able to spend that spring, while the child grew inside of her, at the brothel. Kaly had offered to do housework or cooking, but Lottie Boyle had no use for her.

She had humiliated her in front of Beth. Afraid to stand up to the Madam, Beth had turned her back on Kaly. That was crushing. If Dan McClane hadn't rescued her she might have ended both herself and her unborn child that night.

It turned out that Dan McClane was her brother. Her half-brother to be exact. Tara McClane's son. And that tiny-bit-of-something-grand growing inside of her? Little Annie Monroe was already a year old. The world that had been so harsh had finally offered her a hand, Tara McClane's hand. Her long-lost mother's hand.

She still didn't know if she could take hold of it.

Another large black crow soared past her; wings stretched wide and close enough to touch. He swooped down to the dilapidated wooden fence across the street causing a ruckus with the other crow already perched there.

Enough stalling. Enough thinking about the past.

Kaly lifted her skirt and climbed the stairs. From the top of the stairs she could see the whole of Butte's valley laid out against the clouds. The sky stretched south and east across the Highland Mountains. The first inkling of snow lined their peaks. No matter what happened in the tortured mining town, this sky and these mountains would go on and on.

The crows on the fence went quiet as the lilac bushes rustled. A small parting in the bushes widened to a cave-like opening where something wild lived. Kaly paused and moved closer, watching for the creature to emerge. To her surprise, Beth stepped out from that cave.

Her soft, blue velvet dress clung slightly to her breasts and hips and showed her anklebones just above her black shoes. Dried leaves were stuck in her dark, pinned up curls. Several curls had fallen out, framing her sharp boned face. The shadow of a cloud crossed Beth's cheek and her eyes glinted a secret in that dimming light.

"There's no harm in using a door," Kaly said with a laugh. She stepped away from the brothel, saved from that dreaded knock. "Don't tell me. She kicked you out?"

Beth laughed and Kaly's knees went weak. Beth had been her first love. The woman had rescued her from a life of drudgery and humiliation only to lead her to another life of drudgery and humiliation. But at least in the second life, Kaly had been in control. She had money and she could choose her customers. Except when she couldn't.

Beth had taught Kaly the principles of the skin trade— safety, money, and distance. Very simple. Very easy. Kaly still remembered those nights when they shared a bed before Kaly got her own crib. She'd felt the warmth of her friend's body through their soft gowns. Beth would throw an arm over her and pull her close, like Anne Marie had done when they were children at The Polly May.

"Naw," Beth said. Her sweet, calm face was smudged with dirt. "They're all sick up there. Someone's cold became everyone's cold. Do you still have your crib down in the Alley?" Her breath came in short, distorted gasps, and it made Kaly worry.

She pulled her sleeve over her wrist bone and nodded. She didn't know why she'd kept the crib. She now had a home and a job and a husband and two children and a dog. And a mother. But the crib had been her home for years. It had soothed her soul to have a place all her own, a place she could retreat to. Maybe she'd kept the crib as a little added security, in case things didn't work out in Tara McClane's upstairs apartment.

Kaly understood things not working out.

"Yes. But I haven't lit a fire in there for ages. The rats have probably moved in."

"You'd be surprised how fast I can get rid of rats." Beth winked. She ducked back into the bushes and came out with a suitcase. "Let's go." That ragged breath followed her to the boardwalk.

"You're running away," Kaly said in dismay. "You know Miss Lottie will never let you back in if you leave this way."

A soft smile crossed Beth's lips and she coughed. "I know. Let's go."

They walked hand in hand down Montana Street to Mercury Street, ignoring onlookers. Kaly's coat covered the abundance of her blue cotton dress. She felt dowdy next to Beth's elegance. "At least you got away with the best dress," she said.

Beth shook her head. "Miss Boyle will be spitting mad once she gets well. She's likely to come rip it off of me."

Kaly looked down toward the valley's flatland and felt Beth's hand pull against hers. She held tight, steadying her friend.

"I never forgave her for not taking you in." Beth said the words so quietly that Kaly felt, more than heard them. Something nearly alive and yearning spun in the copper gilded air around them, some dusty hope that every life haunting the dark tunnels would find its way back home.

"I know," Kaly said. "But it's time to forgive. We've all lost so much."

A siren blew on the hill, signaling a shift change. Miners would soon flood the taverns and the Red-Light District. Some would go to the opium dens, or to an upstairs booth for Chinese food.

Kaly and Beth would borrow wood for the stove and light a fire in the potbelly. They would then dust and sweep the small room, and Beth would be working that night. Kaly didn't want that for Beth, any more than she had wanted it for herself. But Beth had nothing else. And Kaly had nothing to offer.

When they reached the Alley, they waited for a woman in a red dress and a man with a chained pocket watch to pass by them. The woman laughed at the man's joke and tucked her tiny, gloved hand into his elbow. Once they had passed by, Kaly reached under a nearby rock for a key. But she didn't need it. The door swung open as Beth pushed a flat hand on it. They looked at each other and laughed.

Inside, the air smelled stale with a tinge of mold. Tan paint streaked the mottled wall, peeling in places. The iron stove sat cold and dusty and a blanket still covered the small bed.

Kaly reached over to the nightstand and turned on the lamp. It worked, sending a shiver down her spine. She looked over her shoulder as if she could see the imposter watching them.

Beth threw her suitcase on the bed, sending the dust flying, and opened it. She pulled out a pink satin dress with an elaborately embroidered hem and hung it on the wall in the same place where Kaly used to hang her red satin dress. Beth tucked a white lace nightgown under the pillow. In the suitcase, a plain brown skirt sat next to her brush. Underneath it a few green dollar bills peeked out. When Beth lifted the skirt to hang it, silver dollars clanged to the wooden floor.

"You are not hurting for cash," Kaly said. "Maybe you don't have to set up shop right away."

"That won't last a minute," Beth said. "I have doctor bills."

Kaly waited. They all had doctor bills.

"Yeah," Beth finally said. "Bert was diagnosed with the pox before he died."

"Syphilis?" That dirge of old mining air swirled around them, ghosts lost and found, spirits sailing the wind to some greater place. Kaly lost her footing. Her knees slipped and she sat down. She petted Beth's suitcase like it was a stray animal.

Beth nodded a slow, distant nod.

Something ungodly screamed in the Alley and Kaly felt it deep in her chest. That ghost of an enemy wind. "You have syphilis?"

Beth nodded again.

"No Bethy. Are you sure?"

"The doctor said there is nothing much that can be done about it, but they are searching for a cure." She sat on the other side of the suitcase and winked at Kaly. "I might get lucky."

Kaly went sick in the stomach. Syphilis was a slow, miserable death. Pammy, another prostitute in the cribs, had been infected. She went crazy when it touched her brain. She'd wandered half-dressed through the cribs, terrified, hiding from invisible villains, attacking anyone who tried to help her.

Beth was far too beautiful for such a brutal end.

"Beth?" Kaly felt her forehead lift, like worry could stop the future.

"It's okay," Beth was saying. "I'm tough as nails."

"Does anyone else know?"

Beth shrugged, and her fallen curls touched her shoulders. The smell of smoke came from down the alley. Horses pulling a wagon clopped through the mud, the wagon wheels making a smooth rolling sound. Through a frayed curtain Kaly could see that the sky had turned a pale pink. She opened the window.

"You can't work," she said. Beth would pass the syphilis along and soon every strumpet in town would have it. And half the men, too. And some of their wives, making for a very mean, very sick gathering of citizens.

Beth nodded at the suitcase of money.

"You stole it?"

"Borrowed it. I don't steal." She smiled that brilliant smile at Kaly. "I can do something with it. Set up a sewing business, or baking. Or I could make sandwiches for the miners over at the rooming houses. Or a liquor delivery service. I'll pay it back as soon as I can."

A wild animal crawled around in Kaly's stomach. Her chest would explode with fear. A cold, dark panic sat hard on her back. "Miss Lottie will send someone after the money. She won't have any trouble finding you here. And whoever finds you will not be nice."

That slow nod again. "Well," Beth said, drawing the word out like the beginning of a dance song. "If she does, I won't have much to worry about after that, will I?"

Something slow and dangerous slid through the air outside, shifted the light, and floated down like dust. It caught in Kaly's chest, and she knew, sure as the rich veins of copper running through the town, that Miss Lottie would never tolerate the betrayal. "She'll have you killed," she said, her words like the whispered wings of a moth.

"Shhuh," Beth said. "Butte does have laws. That old biddy is too sick to have anyone killed right now. Maybe the sickness will take her before she even misses the money."

Kaly shook her head, that enemy wind coming through the window strong and powerful, the ghosts outside demanding their due.

Chapter Three

MARIKA WOKE UP TO a foul smell in the room, her whole side hurting from sleeping on the thin mat on the hard wood floor. Slim rays of the sun pushed through the clouds and soot-filled sky, chasing the early morning miners and newspaper boys to work.

Amelia sat up, her legs hanging over the side of the bed, staring at a wisp of something in the corner, her eyes red and wet.

"You've been crying," Marika said.

"Everything just hurts so bad and I'm worried about my son. I have to go to him." But she didn't move.

"Is your child safe?" Marika asked. She didn't like getting personal. But, how could anyone doctor without asking personal questions?

Amelia nodded, her sad eyelids drooping over the spidery red veins in her eyes. This was beyond exhaustion. Besides her blue lips, she had those dark patches on her face and she looked terribly confused.

"Do you remember coming in last night?"

"Yes," Amelia whispered, a dark, foreboding sound.

Marika felt it quiver through her body. She again followed the girl's gaze to the gray walls. What was she seeing? The plaster cracked where the walls met the ceiling. Dust strings hung in the corners. "We should get you to the hospital."

"My eyes burn," she said. "My head hurts."

Marika moved closer and put a hand on her forehead. Amelia shivered at the touch and didn't stop shaking. "You're still burning up with fever," she said.

Amelia curled up in a fetal position, holding her stomach

tight, shaking. She moaned and tried to say something. It came out as a soft haunting sound, maybe a vague memory of the life she had left somewhere in Philadelphia.

"What is your son's name?" Marika asked.

"Tony," she said, her voice raspy. "He'll be wondering where I am." She closed her eyes and, just that quick, fell into a restless sleep, kicking the covers off.

When Marika put them back on, Amelia tossed and turned, wrapping herself in them until she could barely move. She twitched when Marika put a cold rag to her forehead, the twitch settling into a reckless, uneven breath. She had a sour smell to her. Had her fever climbed? No wonder she had a headache.

Amelia screamed and Marika jumped. The girl tossed and turned, moaning as if something were strangling her. Marika looked closer and saw fresh blood in her ears.

She opened her eyes. "I hurt so bad. Every muscle hurts."

"I'm pretty sure it's just the winter flu. I guess it's already started in the east." She didn't mention the caution she had read yesterday in the medical journal that the flu would be back with a vengeance.

The girl moaned again.

"You'll be okay," Marika said, not quite believing it, but wanting to offer comfort, nonetheless. "It's just going to take a couple of days. Let me take your temperature while you are awake."

Amelia closed her eyes and nodded.

Her temperature was 103, lower than last night but still really high. Too high. Marika put another cool rag across her forehead, trying desperately to break the fever.

Amelia needed the hospital. Marika just didn't know if she should make the call or wait for the doctor. But, of course, she should make the call. The doctor wasn't there to do it and she could do nothing more for Amelia.

She called for the ambulance, but they were out. They'd be there as soon as possible. Marika hung the phone in its cradle. Better to be safe, she thought. An explosion on the hill shook the roof tiles in a quick fierce tremor. Last night's rain clouds fought the sun for the sky and threatened ominously.

The girl coughed a light and easy cough that turned violent. She coughed up blood, her face turning a dark brownish purple. She clenched her stomach. Marika gave her more morphine, just enough to take the edge off, and help her breathe.

"I know it hurts," she told her. "Just hold on. The ambulance will be here soon."

"I have to go home to little Tony," she said, her voice a whisper, blood bubbling out of the side of her mouth and down her neck. She kicked the blankets off again, this time with purpose, and swung her feet down over the side of the bed. Her feet had turned completely black. She lay back down, gasping for breath, a bitter smell coming off her lips. Her face had turned blue, the black patches increasing both in size and number. She clenched her fists, holding onto something that she wasn't quite ready to let go of.

Life.

Marika could see her belly convulsing. Blood came out her nose and her ears. Small pink bubbles came from her lips. If only the emergency workers would come!

"You are not alone," she said to Amelia, trying to calm her own breathing, making her voice soft and firm. "I'm right here with you. I'll be here as long as you need." She sat by Amelia's side and held her hand.

Amelia opened her eyes. "Mother?"

"It's me, Marika."

"I'm going away."

"No. Stay here with us. We'll take care of you." Marika wanted to run after the girl's spirit, capture her and keep her here in the Copper Camp. Amelia hadn't had the chance to see the pansy gardens in the springtime, to dance in the big pavilion, to be driven around town by Fat Jack or someone like him, to read about Mary MacLane courting the devil. It was unfair.

"Tell me about your son. What does he like to do?" Marika asked. When Amelia didn't respond, she tried again. "Where does your mother live?"

"She lived in Philadelphia."

Lived. That word did not escape Marika. "Tell me about her."

"She was a seamstress. Like me. We worked together until

she died." She looked across the bed at something Marika couldn't see. "You are right Mommy. I should have let some-one else take care of it. There is nothing I could do to stop him. I thought my papa might help." She seemed suddenly calm.

Baffled, but pleased, Marika wanted her thinking easy thoughts. Pleasant thoughts would help her. That much she knew. "Tell me how to make a dress," she said.

"What shade?"

"How about blue?" Blue was a soothing color.

"Okay." Amelia moved her hands as if pulling a bolt of material from the shelf, feeling the soft fabric, and cutting it, her fingers trembling. "Mommy loved the bright fabrics," she said. Her fingers went still and rested on her belly. Soon, she slept.

But she woke with a start, nodded, and grimaced. Sud-denly she looked panicked, turning her head and looking side to side. "Is he here?" she whispered.

"Just me," Marika answered.

"That man tried to hurt me. Hurt others." She coughed up a pink mucous. She tried to speak again, and the words came out a raspy slur.

"Try again," Marika said and leaned close. The sickly smell assaulted her and she pulled back, chastising herself for being so weak. Baba would never have pulled away from one of her patients. She kept calm no matter what. Even at the young age of ten, before they left Montenegro, Marika had won-dered at her grandmother's strength. She'd sit by men whose burned skin was crawling with gangrene, the smell reaching past the medical tent, sifting into their tiny hovel. Baba had sat with the sick and dying, those stabbed and shot, those with limbs half torn off. She didn't blink or miss a breath.

Marika tried to emulate her grandmother's calm presence. But with the girl turning black before her eyes, and the smell lifting and filling the room, like some dark secret rising up and leaving the world, Marika felt anything but calm. She needed the ambulance to arrive, for Dr. Fletcher and Miss Parsons to show up, for anyone to show up and take over.

Amelia opened her eyes wide, a faint white line around her blue lips, a secret danger right in front of her, the fever making her dehydrated and delirious.

"Water?" Marika asked. A pathetic, useless offer. The purest water could do nothing here. Nevertheless, she poured some into Amelia's mouth, who immediately spit it out, the water splattering across Marika's face. She wiped it off with a towel. Then took her flowered apron off and set it aside. She'd wash it later.

Feeling helpless, she willed the doctor through the door, or the ambulance near. But the only sounds coming from the streets were the footsteps of a few early shoppers, and the crows. She looked down at her stained skirt. It wasn't a uniform. And she wasn't a nurse. She was nothing. She'd been trained neither in modern medicine, nor in nursing skills. All of her training had come from her grandmother's wisdom. Dr. Fletcher reprimanded her, and she learned from that, or she taught herself. But nothing had been useful here.

Marika made the sign of the cross over Amelia, blessing her. She hoped that she'd live to see little Tony again. She looked out the window. Above the rooftops she saw the black metal head frames of the mines, stern and ominous, an omen of things to come. To the east, pink brightened the clouds over the Rocky Mountain Ridge.

Having experienced her father's death, Marika recognized the signs: the dark shadow at the girl's eyes, her faint and rasping breath, the slight rise of her chest.

Failing to make a difference, she sat quietly, and prayed for Amelia.

Please, comfort her in Your arms, hold her here in the Copper Camp. Save Your Kingdom for another day. Let her go to the hospital, come home, see her son grow into a fine young man. The prayer took flight on angel wings, a soft flutter, a whisper of air, a golden light filling the room.

Amelia's body went limp and she took her last breath, raspy and barely audible. Her soul rose above the darkened head frames, over the mountain ridge and into the clouds. She floated out over the land, the soft feather of a spirit looking for a home.

Marika called off the ambulance and sent for the mortician, John Hurt. She couldn't get the taste of the air around her out of her mouth. It was like breathing in a thick liquid that landed at the back of her throat and stayed there, sending her into a fit of disgust. It was the last thing a doctor's helper should feel.

The blanket had fallen off of Amelia. Marika pulled it back up. She waited. She opened the back door. Outside a flock of wild geese thundered above the town, their honking a seasonal good-bye. If Amelia had died of the flu, the flu was on them and it, too, would have its season. And then it would pass. Like the birds in the sky. Like all sickness.

The cool fall air stung her cheeks. She pulled the hem of her skirt up and crossed her forehead with it, leaving an oily smudge on it. She'd have to wash it out later. Down the alley a saloon door opened, and the janitor tossed a bucket of water into the dirt. He nodded to her and went back to his duties.

She felt the bad omen hanging in the air, the harbinger of death waiting for its next victim. It all seemed so wrong, so upside down, so...so full of self-pity. *Stop it,* she admonished herself. She should clean the room. She should wait with Amelia for her final departure. But she just couldn't drag herself back in from the alley. Butte's alleys and underground tunnels offered refuge full of danger. The opium dens, the back-door deals, the illicit sex gone wrong, all bloomed in these dark worlds.

Marika wished she could imbibe in some temporary relief; take off this edge of pain, if only for a little while. The year had taught her so much. Sometimes she longed to pull her innocence out of her wedding night trunk and try it on again, if only for a night, knowing it would soon slip through her fingers and be gone.

When the dead wagon arrived, the sun lit the hearse's tracks in the mud. The undertaker opened the door slowly and climbed out.

"Another one from the east," John Hurt said, as if they'd been having the conversation already. He wore a frayed brown coat. His brownish red hair stuck out from under a small brimmed hat. His nose looked like it might have been broken a time or two and sat crooked and flat on his small face.

Marika nodded. "Philadelphia."

He walked into the sick room and lifted the blanket off of her. "Bruising?"

Marika shook her head. "She didn't come in like that. The patches developed as the night went on."

"Were her lips blue when she came in?"

Marika thought back and shrugged her shoulders. "I think so."

"She wasn't getting oxygen. Her lungs had already been affected." He paused, took out a small magnifying glass and looked closer. The strong smell of embalming fluids came from his clothes and filled the air. "Not much you could've done for her."

A flutter crossed Marika's heart and she shivered, the tiny hairs on her arms rising. Alley dust swirled through the open door, sending cold air through the building. She felt Amelia's slow rise to eternity. What had taken her breath? And what had hastened it?

Marika felt her cheeks get warm. If only she had the knowledge that she'd learn in medical school, she could be of use. Instead, she blindly searched the doctor's big medical book or his discarded journals for answers.

"Help me get her into the wagon," John Hurt was saying. "Then go home and get some rest. I'm sure you've been here all night." He wrapped the blanket around Amelia, trapping her arms to her sides. When Prince Ivan Tzrnoyevitch was shot in front of a tavern in Montenegro, a large wild goat shook the water from his fur and a great river flowed. River of Tzrnoyevitch. No goats would come for Amelia, no great rivers would be named for her.

Amelia's child would wonder one day who had buried his mother. The girl she'd been had already fled for the sky. The star that had followed her from her youth had already flamed out. Only flesh and bones lay on the sick bed, no longer sick, no longer dying, only bits of earthly dust now and forever silent.

Marika lifted the girl's legs as the undertaker took hold of her torso. Moving her from the sick bed to the dead wagon was easy.

Amelia, light and airy, was barely there.

Chapter Four

KALY WENT OUT FOR a walk hoping to see Beth. When Beth wasn't at the crib Kaly returned to the bakery and the upstairs apartment. The dog greeted her, wagging his tail and pressing his nose into her legs, a little howl escaping his lips.

"Hey boy." She reached down and rubbed his ears, accepting his welcome and trying to calm herself. She felt—no, she knew—that Beth would never be safe at the Alley crib by herself. She had tried to talk her into coming back to the bakery with her. But had she tried hard enough? Life on the street was wild and dangerous and hard to escape. Yet, here she was enjoying the luxury of Tara McClane's upstairs apartment while Beth started her certain demise at the cribs in the Alley.

"They're great," Tara said, waving a hand at Annie and George as she walked out the door. The smell of fresh baked bread filled the hallway. "They're all yours. I've got work to do to prepare for the week's rush and George's birthday party. Hard to believe he'll be ten! Holler if you need anything. I'll be in the kitchen."

Annie sat in Kaly's lap as she fed her Tara's ham and green pea soup. Her darling little girl ate a spoonful and a bit dropped on her pink dress. Annie frowned at her, her wide brown eyes in shock, as if Kaly had just betrayed her. She whimpered and reached for the spoon.

"Mine," she said. Closing her tiny hand around the silver handle and pulling, she insisted Kaly give it to her. Kaly relented and put the bowl of soup down on her tray, sitting Annie next to it.

George shrugged his shoulders. "I told you she's stubborn." He sat on the floor braiding the dog's tail. His bare feet stuck out from his trousers, his anklebones visible far below the hem.

"Well, she comes by it naturally," Kaly said. "Have you met her grandmother?"

George laughed and Kaly laughed with him. "Fetch me a rag, will you? I have a feeling this will not go well."

He got up slowly and sauntered over to the kitchen sink. As he wet a dishtowel, Kaly marveled at how he'd grown over the last year. She'd first met him in Miss Anderson's kitchen. Winter sunlight had poured in through dirty windows as large snowflakes fell outside. He and Julian fought over a knife to slice cheese for crackers.

Tempers flared and the boys wrestled. George got hold of the knife and stabbed Julian. With deft precision Miss Anderson separated the boys and pushed George into Kaly's arms. She'd sat on the floor holding him next to her pregnant belly, keeping him from going after Julian a second time. He calmed down in her arms, and she felt her first inkling of love for him.

Never did she dream he'd end up living with her. Never did she dream that he would end up her child. Never did she dream she'd ever be a mother to anyone, let alone a near ten-year-old boy and a one-year-old baby girl stubborn enough to take the spoon from her mother's hand and try to feed herself. Annie put the spoon on her face and laughed, smearing the green soup across her cheeks. She held the spoon out to the dog, and the dog inched closer to the little girl, as if no one could see him.

George crossed his arms and leaned against the kitchen counter, the wet rag dangling from his index finger.

Kaly shook her head. "That's enough. I guess you are not hungry." She took the spoon from Annie which sent her daughter into a fever-pitch scream.

The dog cocked his head.

George walked over and picked up Annie. "Shhhhh," he said, coddling his young sister.

A powerful anger came over Kaly. She wanted to reprimand both children, covering her ears to stop the onslaught. And to keep her anger from exploding out of her. She had no idea why she was so angry. After yesterday's evening with Beth, the injustice of all things crashed in on her. George an orphan, Annie born to an old whore, Beth down in the alley dying of syphilis. And nothing Kaly could do about it.

George held his sister and looked up at her.

She turned away from him, not wanting her anger to spill over to him. When she turned back, he was crying. Kaly dropped her hands and took a breath. "What's wrong?"

"You don't want me here," George said quietly.

It was the very thing she had felt a hundred times at The Polly May with Miss Anderson. She understood quiet rejection. "Oh no, Georgey," she said. "I very much want you here. We'd be no family at all without you. It's just that something happened last night that broke my heart. But it has nothing to do with you or your sister."

He tightened his hug on little Annie. She stopped crying and reached up and squeezed his nose in her chubby palm. He looked away from Kaly, taking the tiny fist with him.

Kaly thought about last year when Tara finally revealed that she was her mother. Kaly's heart broke a thousand times in that minute, the minute stretching forward and back through her life. For so many years Kaly had wondered where her mother was and why she had left Kaly and her twin sister, Anne Marie, at The Polly May Home for Kids. She had spent years longing for her mother.

And then there she was, sitting across from her in the up-stairs room at Miss Anderson's Big House. Rain had poured and the heater clanked through the night, as if nothing had changed. But something had changed. Something in Kaly shifted, bitterness watering the seed she'd kept buried all those years. It sprouted like an angry, tangled bush.

Tara hadn't even come for her. And that made it worse. She had come to ask her to talk Danny, her son and Kaly's half-brother, out of joining the army. The rain had splintered the sky, relentlessly pelting the empty streets, and Kaly felt the chill in her bones. She felt that cold darkness crawl into her chest, a bad rhythm pounding in her head that she'd never quit.

Later that night, George had slipped into her room and offered to take care of her if her mother wouldn't. Even a young boy like George knew how wrong her own mother had been. He offered her comfort, a young boy like George had offered comfort where her mother had failed.

Now, her mother was trying to right the losses of the past. Kaly still felt the primal sting of rejection, a cold moss growing on the wrong side of her heart. Tara had told her she'd been poor, with no help, and unable to feed her and her sister. She had feared they'd die in her care.

Kaly wanted to understand. And she did. After all, she herself had tried to find someone else to raise Annie, knowing that no good life could come from the child living in the tenderloin while her mother tried to eek out a living. The thing was, Tara had raised Danny. That was the part that Kaly couldn't put right. She had tried to forgive, but failed.

Then everything had changed again.

She didn't know how. She'd made the decision to raise Annie. Tommy helped. But it wasn't that. She'd spent years with her mother's rejection running through her blood. Somehow Annie, this little creature of a girl, found her way into her veins and righted the wrongs in a way that neither Kaly nor Tara McClane could.

So, here she was, in her mother's upstairs apartment. She looked around the room. A soft brown couch with crocheted arm covers sat against the wall, a yellow knit blanket, spread across the back of it, with matching pillows at both ends of it. A large painting of pink peonies hung on the far wall. Tara had painted it when she was pregnant with Kaly and Anne Marie, when she still had dreams, before Kaly's father, Vuko, was killed in a mining accident.

Kaly struggled to let Tara's love reach her. She breathed in the smell of the freshly baked bread, letting its warm essence fill her lungs.

"Do you understand how much I love you both?" Kaly asked George.

He sat quietly for a bit before he nodded. "I'm scared," he said, removing Annie's hand from his nose and batting it away when she tried to reattach. "You said that you and Tommy are my parents now. But Miss Anderson said that too. What if people keep giving me to new parents?"

Last night's heartbreak swelled and Kaly hoped she could be brave enough to hold the sorrow for all of them, especially for the boy. "We are not going to give you to new parents."

"But what if he doesn't come home from the war?"

"Tommy will come home," she said. "And do you remember when I told you I'd share my mother with you?"

George nodded.

"My mother, your grandmother, is right down there baking. Whatever happens she will make sure we have a home." She ran a hand through her brown curls. "So, clean your sister up for me and we'll make some hot chocolate."

He wiped Annie's face with the dishrag, moved her off of his lap, and set her next to the wolf dog, who had watched the whole exchange, tail wagging, front paws flat against the floor, bottom up, ready to help.

Kaly heated milk in a pan at the edge of the stove while George spooned cocoa and sugar into it and stirred. "Watch it carefully so that it doesn't boil over and the sugar doesn't burn," she said, while dressing Annie in her green sleeper. Her little bare feet poked out under it and Annie held them up in her hands.

"Sock?" she said quietly.

Kaly complied. She pulled two gray socks out of the drawer, checked them for holes, found none, and put them on Annie's feet. Annie kicked her feet over her head and said, "Sock?" this time with a whole new meaning. Or maybe the same meaning. Kaly really didn't know. She just made it up as she went along, hoping that her relationship with the little one got her close enough, often enough, that Annie would grow up strong and fine.

She did not want Annie living the life she had lived on the street. She would beg, borrow, or steal to keep that from happening. Or, as fate would have it, go to work for her own long-lost mother.

Late at night, when the taverns closed and drunks stumbled through the alleys, Kaly understood Tara McClane. On certain moonless nights, a cold wind would blow the sour smell out of the town and laughter would rise up from the streets below. Kaly would forget her grievances and feel a deep gratitude to Tara for taking her from the cribs, both children and dog in tow. But in the daylight hours, Kaly's heart shrank. She only had room for the children and dog, no matter how she tried.

She blew on the hot chocolate and put the cup to Annie's lips. Annie drank a sip and reached for the cup. This time Kaly was firm. Hot chocolate burns on the child would not do. The child fussed but finally accepted her mother's will. After she drank the chocolate and Kaly washed her face, she put the girl to bed in her crib, hoping that she would fall fast asleep.

"You've barely touched your drink," she said to George when she came back out.

"I know. It smells weird to me. Is it sour?"

Kaly hoped not. Annie drank nearly half a cup. She didn't need the girl throwing up. It smelled fresh. "I don't think so. Maybe it just doesn't sit well with you tonight. Why don't you wash up and get ready for bed too?"

George pushed himself away from the table, went into the bedroom, and returned with his pajamas on. "Will you read to me?" he asked.

"Go lie down and I'll be there in a minute."

He nodded and went back through the door. Kaly pulled the pan with the rest of the chocolate mix from the stove and set it on the counter, ready to read to the boy. She knew her affection for him could hardly make up for his first ten years, but she had to try.

Early the next morning, Kaly slipped away to the market-place. Tara needed supplies. She returned with a bag of apples, potatoes, flour, and cinnamon, which she left downstairs at the bakery. She quickly changed places with Tara, taking charge of Annie and George. They quietly drew pictures in the corner. George drew the dog. Annie drew something. A mess of lines, here, there, and everywhere.

"Dog," she said, her tiny voice firm and confident. George smiled at her and nodded. Kaly shrugged her shoulders.

"That's some kind of dog," she said with a gentle laugh.

She felt the familiar pang of missing Tommy. She kept his letters carefully tucked into a cotton pouch that she had made just for them. His letters soothed her in a way that surprised her. She wasn't used to being loved.

Tara hollered up the stairs at her. "Coffee's on. There are biscuits on the counter."

"Be there in a second." She turned toward the couch. She had no idea how someone got that stuffed brown cloth monstrosity into her tiny apartment. "Watch your sister for a minute?"

George nodded. He looked sleepy. She could see the bundle of blankets on the couch where he had spent the night.

"Are they feeling okay?" She asked Tara when she gathered the biscuits and coffee.

"They both seem to be a bit under the weather," Tara said.

"School is probably getting to George," Kaly said.

"Well, he can rest and sleep in. School can wait."

A quick shimmer crossed Kaly's chest. "I've heard that the flu might come back strong this fall."

"The flu comes every fall," Tara said.

"Some people are saying this flu is different. They are saying that people in the east are dying quickly, within a day or two."

"I heard that." Tara wiped her forehead with a cotton handkerchief. "I don't want to worry, but I am worried for you and the children."

A high-pitched gale blew through an open window. The soft tone of Tara's voice reached into a small part of Kaly's heart that she didn't know existed and tears spilled down her face. Tara worried about her.

Who was she? Kaly Shane, Kaly Monroe. This woman who cried at tenderness? She turned away to hide the tears. "Did I get any mail this week?"

"A letter from someone overseas. I just don't know who that could be." Tara held the letter out with a smile and a mischievous glint in her eye.

Kaly smiled back. She put the letter in her pocket.

Upstairs, she spread honey and butter on the biscuits and

gave one to Annie and one to George. She drank her coffee and slid her fingers over the ears of the big dog. The dog pushed his nose into her thigh and rubbed his head against her dress. When he finished, he went over and lay down next to George.

Of course, her mother had known who had sent the letter. The only person they knew overseas that sent letters was Tommy, her husband. She still hadn't gotten used to that idea. She had a husband. The world had turned so upside down after the Granite Mountain mine fire had killed 168 men. So many had lost their lives. But she had married and found hers.

And then one little girl was born. A girl with precious brown eyes and a stubborn will, both like her father's. Tommy left for Europe right after their daughter made her way into the world. All smiles, cries, and sleep. She'd so charmed her father that he almost didn't leave. But by then he'd had no choice.

It was too late to back out. Plus, he wouldn't have. He'd do anything to make the world a safer place for little Annie. He'd do anything to make the world a great and beautiful world for his little girl and this sweet boy with his dog. And it was a great and beautiful world now that they were in it. Kaly just hoped that Tommy would make it home to watch them grow up.

He will come home, she said to herself, turning the letter over, and feeling the warmth of it in her hands. She would savor the slow opening of it, ready to read every word twice.

Chapter Five

THE SEPTEMBER SUN WENT crimson behind a veil of smoky mining vapors. Marika Jovich studied the large display windows of the Silver Bow Bakery, where mannequins in lively green gowns held out pies and cakes. Enter here and you'll be pleased, they promised. She tucked a wild strand of her hair into a hairpin and stood in the doorway a moment too long, letting her eyes adjust to the sultry air and catching her breath.

It was noon and the packed café danced with good-living, life-loving miners. End a shift alive and the world shines. Every miner's wife knew the gift bestowed each night when her husband's face appeared. Good times boomed when the mines ran well and the Silver Bow Bakery brought in both the refined and the riffraff, the two just a breath apart. Marika took in the scene and felt a familiar surge of love for the mile-high mining town of Butte, Montana. Over 90,000 people lived there and the town was still growing.

She had come from Montenegro with her family when she was eleven, terrified and begging to go home to the mountain village where her grandmother lived. Now, that was all done. Baba had died, Marika had married, and the dark winds of Butte had thoroughly stolen her heart. She might well have been born from the copper-filled earth.

Marika still wanted to be a doctor. It was a desire etched into her bones, going back to when she was just a girl. She felt it in the rowdy streets, down at the Tenderloin, at the doctor's office, and at home with her husband. Having her own kitchen in her own home with her own man tethered her to the mining camp with a force far stronger than any childhood dream. Deep in her soul, at the center of her being,

Marika knew she would never leave Butte's sparkling lights and sour air. Of her own free will, she had chosen to marry Michael Jovich, even though her father had chosen him first. It was a marriage arranged by their fathers, a promise she'd had no intention of keeping…until she did.

Her brown skirt grazed her ankles. She tucked her hands into the tan sleeves of her sweater and walked into the Bakery's smoky haze.

George ran up, wrapped his arms around her waist, and hugged her. "I'm ten!" He looked up at her with wonder on his face. The bakery party wasn't only for his birthday. The town revelry had begun this summer when the strikes had simmered down and the mines ran again—when people had a couple dollars in their pockets and some food on the table.

George let her go and ran to a group of men sitting at a card table in the back room. They laughed at some joke tossed across the cards and he laughed too. Marika smelled pasties, those wonderful meat pies from Cornwall and Ireland, and realized she was hungry. She could almost taste the light crust and hearty meat-and-potato filling.

From the other side of the room Michael smiled at her. Her heart went wild. A band was playing and an older woman in a slim glowing dress was singing "When Irish Eyes Are Smiling." She had a low and throaty voice and a soft gentle wave filled Marika's chest with awe. Her hips flowed in a quiet tender rhythm. The woman's calm sure presence welcomed Marika into the bakery and the mining town's kinder world.

She needed this after Amelia had died in her care, needed this tenderness, this rich engagement with the townspeople. Looking across the room at her husband, her spirit swelled and she could barely breathe. She loved him so much, it made her warm in parts of her body she barely knew existed before she'd met him.

She respected the work he did. He cared about people and had worked hard for the miners, especially after a cable caught fire in the Granite Mountain Mine last year. Fire and poisoned air had poured down the mine shaft and into the underground tunnels, killing over a hundred men.

It broke the town's heart.

Michael was trying to get the miners safe work conditions and fair wages. He worked even harder since that group of masked men had hanged Frank Little, a labor organizer who'd traveled the west speaking up for the rights of miners and laborers. Those men had dragged him along the rocky streets to the hanging trestle. It was a horrible death.

Frank Little was courageous. He wouldn't be quiet about fair pay and safety, not even when threatened with a whip and bullets, not when kept in a wet hole with no food, not when facing the grave.

Marika felt proud of Michael, that he had vowed to carry on and try to fulfill at least a portion of the man's work. The town had gone on strike after the accident. Frank Little had come to help the cause. After his hanging, anger grew to rage, and rage shut down all operations for a while.

Michael waved Marika over. She walked slowly, assessing the curve of his chin, his near black eyes, the way that his dark hair fell lightly across his flat forehead. Even though she loved him, she had been hot and cold with Michael since the beginning. She hated herself for it. Why couldn't she just settle in and accept her choice to marry him?

Every time she was in Michael's arms, her restlessness evaporated and all the world went right. Today, with the salty red sun and warm fall air outside, she wouldn't let herself be uncertain. She wouldn't let herself be wishy washy. She would love him with all the good she could muster.

Kaly Monroe stood in the crowd, holding little Annie on her hip. She wore a green taffeta dress that Tara McClane had made for her. Her spirited green eyes caught Marika's for a second. "Just go to him," she said, as if reading her mind.

Marika knew Kaly was right. Still. She hesitated. She wanted to be a doctor. And Amelia had just died in her care. Marika's heart tightened at the thought of the girl dying so far from family and leaving her son without a mother. If Marika got too comfortable with Michael, or, heaven forbid, got pregnant, she might forget her dreams, and never become a doctor.

Kaly leaned in close, tilting Annie back on her hip, those brilliant green eyes looking into Marika. "Please. You are sulking again. You will learn medicine. You're too stubborn not to. Now just go enjoy your husband."

Marika wanted to explain that she wasn't sulking, she was grieving. A woman had just died and she could do nothing for her. But it wasn't the time to explain so she kept quiet, biting her lip, a slight scar forming on her bottom lip from silencing herself.

Dan McClane stood next to Michael. Her face turned warm and her heart beat fast. Before she married Michael, she loved Dan. Dan almost died in the fire. It had been a long recovery for him, but standing there, he looked strong as any good ox. She smiled at the two of them. Both good men. Just one too many to love well.

"Welcome to the party," Dan said, his green eyes—so much like Kaly's—glorious and full of mischief. His light brown hair dropped across his forehead.

"How is it?" Marika took Annie into her arms. The little girl laughed and freed Marika's hair from the hairpin. Annie wore a soft green dress made from the same bolt of taffeta as Kaly's dress.

"George is happy," Kaly said. He ran in circles on the dance floor with his dog barking and chasing him. The table of gamblers cheered them on.

Annie smiled at Marika and Marika felt herself shine. Love welled up in her for those sweet brown eyes, her dark hair, her tiny eager hands. She wondered what her uncle Vuko would have thought of his little granddaughter. What would Papa have thought of this little creature? She knew what Mama thought. Mama just couldn't get enough of Annie. And she kept asking Marika and Michael when they were going to have children. Marika always shrugged it off with a joke.

She kissed Annie and handed her back to Kaly. Annie frowned and Marika felt even more love for the child. It was crazy how much she loved this little girl. Children indeed, Mama. But Mama was not joking. She was serious about her quest for grandchildren.

And Michael? Michael looked at her with the same questioning eyes as Mama. Send me to medical school, she wanted to say, and then we'll talk babies.

Those were the very words she had shouted at Papa before

he died. There had been no money for medical school, and Marika knew it. She had been selfish and then Papa died. She felt deep regret remembering the ire she felt toward him in those last weeks. And how he never got to see her marry Michael. She'd given Papa his dream, but she hadn't given up her own.

She'd spent hours sitting at Miss Parsons' desk scanning Dr. Fletcher's heavy medical book for bits of knowledge, taking notes, focused and determined. Then the sun would shift and a quiet light would fill the town and she'd find herself playing with Miss Parsons' scissors, or twirling a pencil in her fingers, and daydreaming about Michael. Or sometimes, when she let herself, daydreaming about Dan. Her damned imagination was about to drive her wild, especially now that she had time to think. The town had slowed down and found an even keel, and, except for Amelia, few people had been sick.

But again, she and Michael had no money or means to send her to medical school. Settle down and enjoy the life you have, others said.

Medical school or not, Marika vowed to be of use. Fate itself had conspired with her. Experience, the best teacher, had heard her calling and found her at every turn: the women of the streets; the miners and their accidents; the constant brawls that broke out after Frank Little's hanging; a drunk with one too many drinks; a prostitute with one too many violent Johns; someone's last dose of opium. Syphilis, botched abortions, rapes. And now, Amelia. She may not be a doctor, but she had plenty to do.

Children would have to wait.

Outside the bakery the mountains glowed, the glow breaking through the soot-filled air, the East Ridge turning pink. Inside the people laughed and shouted over the music, telling stories. Michael pulled her close and she melted into him, her whole body tingling. "Things must be slow at Dr. Fletcher's office," he whispered, "for them to set you free so early."

She put her head on his chest and put her hand in the pocket of his blue vest, wanting to get as close to him as possible. She wanted to feel his hand on her hip pulling her tight. She wanted to forget all about Amelia. At moments like this her ambivalence disappeared, a dove set free, flying into the sun, looking for another home. She'd found her home and it was right here with Michael. "Except for the other night, it's been a quiet time." She took his hand in hers. "I'll go back in a bit, but for now I can join the party."

Dan smiled at her and she felt her heart miss a beat, just like old times.

But it was wrong. She turned her smile from Dan to Michael, including them both. She breathed in the steamy air of the bakery as the band started a new tune, one she'd never heard before. It was a lively song about a "Raggle Taggle Gypsy Boy." A rich woman leaves her whole rich life and family behind just to spend one night with the "Raggle Taggle Gypsy Boy." She would give it all up for his just one kiss.

Marika understood that desire for escape and love. But in the end, Papa had been right. She needed someone to watch over her and her family. She needed Michael. And in some deep way, that made her love him even more. She'd leave it all for his just one kiss. Except, of course, for her medical dreams.

"Let's sit down," Michael tightened his grip on her hand and led her to a booth.

Dan came along. "A year has passed since they hanged Frank Little and the town is still spitting mad," he said. "It may seem quieter, but you can feel the rumblings of unrest just under the surface."

"Just like the mines," Marika said.

Dan's face went slack, a dark memory crossing it. He'd been caught underground in the Granite Mountain Mine fire. Tommy Monroe had found Dan, put his oxygen mask on him, and pulled him to safety. Marika and Dr. Fletcher worked on him until he started breathing again. Together they had saved his life

"I'm sorry," she said, watching Dan's face. His reaction surprised her. It had been a year, and it wasn't as if Butte went all hush about mining accidents. It wasn't that the mention of an accident jinxed the next man down the shaft.

No.

Butte did not lie down quietly. The townspeople demanded that men be given safe work, and that common folks benefit along with the copper bosses.

"I shouldn't have brought that up," she said. Her cheeks flushed hot.

"It's not that," Dan said with a determined smile. "I am one of the lucky ones. I feel guilty that I'm here and so many others aren't. I'm grateful to see the milky sun come up over the East Ridge. And there is good work to be done."

"Doesn't have to be done by you," Marika said.

"It's all I know." He shrugged.

She knew that he'd wanted to escape the mines by joining the military. But after the accident, the military passed on Dan.

Mining was dangerous. It put them all in peril, but they talked about it like they talked about roasting a lamb for Christmas, with the same casual tone. She worried her thumb on the booth's wooden table, thinking she should eat something and get back to the clinic.

Michael seemed to read her mind and turned the conversation toward illness. "There is some sickness hitting the military back east," he said. "Ill soldiers are cordoned off from the others."

"Have you heard much about it?" Marika asked.

"Men are turning blue and dying. It comes on quickly and spreads easily. The tents are full of sick men. No one wants to go near the sick ones except the doctors. Then doctors get sick and die too."

"The flu?" It sounded so much like Amelia.

Michael shook his head. "They think it's a gas attack, that German stealth soldiers snuck in carrying vials of the stuff and uncapped them when they got close to the camps."

Marika didn't believe it. "It could be that the same flu bug from last spring coming back through. It hit people hard the first time." She couldn't get the image of Amelia out of her mind. The dark patches on her face. The sour smell. The high fever. She hated sounding like a know-it-all. But she did know some things. She felt Michael loosen his grip on her hand. Still, she had to ask one more question. "Why would the Germans come here when the war is in Europe?"

"German U-boats were spotted in U.S. waters last May,"

Michael said, as if that explained it.

Marika remembered that the word of the U-boats had traveled slowly to the west, finally arriving and scaring the town into a week of hiding behind locked doors. All for naught. "Why now, though?"

Michael cocked his head at her question, letting go of her hand.

"Why would they send boats here now, when they are talking about peace?"

"I agree," Michael said to her. "It doesn't make sense."

"Maybe the talk of peace is folly," Dan said.

"Also, wouldn't those who released the gas get sick too?" she asked. Pipe smoke from a nearby booth wafted over, stringent and sweet, stirring the memory of her father. She inhaled the scent, and Papa seemed close enough to touch.

Michael shrugged and pointed at Marika's hands, which were drawing circles on the wooden table. "You think it's the flu?"

She settled her hands on her lap. "It makes more sense."

"Maybe Dr. Fletcher knows. With his office slow you have more time to study. Perhaps he can spend time teaching you."

Marika smiled and lightly touched his hand, ignoring the fury she felt at having to defer to the doctor. She wanted to be the one who knew.

"Hello," a woman with dark brown curly hair came up to Dan. She wore a soft pink skirt with a waist coat to match. She smiled at Dan and her smiled seemed sweet and full of confidence.

"Elizabeth!" Dan stood and turned his attention to her. "I'm so happy you could make the party." He took her hand. "Marika, Michael, meet Elizabeth. She is a teacher over at Washington School."

Marika suddenly forgot about the flu. She forgot about Amelia, and her husband sitting right next to her. Her very dark brown eyes turned suddenly green. Bright, devil green, she was sure.

THE WOLF DOG WANDERS

October 1918

* * *

THE WOLF DOG LEAVES the boy at the bakery with his new family. Earlier that week the boy slept so much that the dog refused to leave his side, fearing that some primitive devil crashed its way into his lungs. The boy is up an playing now and the dog strolls through the town, mystified by the boy's fatigue and the altered weather, the light behind the black headframes shifting and changing, a sure sign of the coming winter. He watches for the devil, smells for a trace of the odor trailing him.

The odor comes from the sick people, grasping their stomachs, falling suddenly to their knees, passing the gesture to those nearby, until the whole house smells odd and sad moans escape. The odor comes from the dead wagons as they carry people to the morgue. The odor, the whisper of a spirit, that untouchable devil finds the strong and fine, and turns them weak.

The wolf dog sniffs it out and finds the scent of it everywhere, this tiny enemy soars on the wind, digs into the earth. It reaches down from the icy cold sun crossing the sky. It has found a tunnel to burrow into and lodges in a copper vein deep in a dark hole where dynamite could blow it to a million little pieces, each piece landing anew on some unsuspecting creature, driving the scent deep and taking the breath. And the life.

In just one day the men who drive the black wagons carry so many bodies down Montana Street to the cemeteries that they end the night exhausted, looking for comfort in each other, and a stiff drink or two. Over and over the dead wagon arrives at a home and leaves. One, two, three, ten, twenty bodies, until the men stop counting. When the dog gets close enough, he smells their mouths and their noses. No air comes out, not even the slightest ruffle of a breeze. Only the dead smell wafts off of them and the dog knows they have gone from this world. But they have not taken the devil with them. The devil jumps to someone new and vibrant and full of life, until that life, too, goes beyond.

The people left behind cry and scream, or go stone cold quiet. Soon cloth masks cover mouths and noses. Soon people wear garlic at their necks and lock their doors. Businesses and churches shut down. A group of men and women sit in a room and wonder what to do about this tiny bit of a germ.

If the wolf dog could travel back in time and cross the continent to Philadelphia he'd see the girl. She works at a garment factory that pays little, and since her husband lost his job, she must work twice as hard to bring in enough money to feed her son and husband. For long hours, she sits at her sewing machine and pushes the pedal up and down, lost in its metallic rhythm.

She feels the flow of material under her fingers as the lovely textures graze her skin. The girl loves making women's clothing. Like her mother did, she loves the colors of the bright cloth, the lovely lace trims, the soft satins, the beautiful buttons. As if they have a mind of their own, they spin out before her and turn into women's dresses or brightly colored tops, an occasional spring cape. She loves the smell of the machines, the constant hum of stitching, the women's laughter when they work the beautiful soft velvet, her son's quiet breathing as he sleeps in the crib next to her machine.

If the wolf dog could travel across space and time, he'd see the girl when she first meets the devil. He is a short, handsome man who always wears a topcoat and a hat, except at work. At work he wears old pants with patched knees, a stained front button shirt, and an apron. He combs his hair back in dark brown waves with a touch of gray at the sides. When he smiles his mouth turns crooked, his left lip a tad higher than the right.

If the dog could travel across time to protect the boy, his fiery essence would flare at the sight of the man with the crooked smile. His great thighs would hold tight and ready to halt the danger. He'd watch the girl quarrel with that feeling in her stomach that tells her to stay far away from the man. Something is off in him, something dark and unmanageable.

The man disappears for a week and returns slow and frail. Some gloom creeps out from under his nails, oozes out from his pores, a ghoulish, murky mist. He had been sick. When the girl returns home with her son, she learns that the man visited her husband. Her husband is sick in bed, sicker than he's ever been. She brings him water and blankets. When he doesn't get better, she calls a doctor. But the doctors are too busy and, before they can get to him, her husband dies.

When she returns to work the man in the patched trousers turns that crooked smile on her. He snickers under his breath. The next day her son takes sick. He turns blue and his breathing is shattered. She calls a doctor right away. And, this time, she begs. A doctor arrives and her one-year-old baby lives. The crooked smile seems sad and down turned when she makes her next shift. And the devil pedals his machine slowly, moving the material in a nonchalant, careless rhythm.

With the mismatched smile, he says he is sorry about her husband. He brings her flowers, offers to clean her machine, and brings sandwiches for picnic lunches. The other girls barely wait to hear the gossip, prodding and curious. Being a woman with a kind heart, who just lost her husband, she is not a fan of gossip, the girl keeps a closed lip. When the man takes a train west with a promise to return soon, the girl follows him, a tiny seed of suspicion sprouting in her brain.

She and her son board that same train west and sit in the middle of a dozen rowdy soldiers from Boston. They are being moved across the country. They laugh and joke with her, insisting she drink with them. They drink and the loudest soldier falls suddenly quiet and retreats to his cabin. By the time the train crosses the eastern plains to the Rocky Mountains three more soldiers have taken to their beds.

If the dog could crisscross the nation, he would feel the quiver in his skin. His silver fur would stand tall on his back to watch the girl. In the reversing of time, he would see her in the week before she takes her final breath.

If the wolf dog could have gone through the ethers, past the heavens, or read the clouds, he might have stopped the girl from boarding that train with the soldiers. He might have kept her safe. He might have kept that vague essence out of Butte and contained the enemy, keeping that slender speck of a germ away from the boy. By the time the girl and her son step off of that train at the Front Street station in Butte, Montana, that flick and whisper is already doubling in the soft folds of her skin.

Chapter Six

KALY WALKED OUT OF the bakery and left the children with Tara McClane. Her mother. She would accept the woman in her own good time, just like Mrs. McClane had done with Kaly. Turnabout being fair play and all. Kaly's heart being the mess that it was and all. Still, almost against her will, her heart welled up with gratitude to Tara for providing a home for her children. And for watching Annie and George with no complaints.

Tara had taken the dog too, since George exploded into fits without him. The dog kept him calm. A calm George kept Annie giggling and laughing. Tara seemed to enjoy them all. "Nonsense," she'd say, when Kaly apologized for asking her to watch the little ones. "George is a great help in the bakery, and not a lick of trouble. And Annie simply watches every move anyone makes. A real detective, that one." And then she'd laugh at her own joke.

Kaly was glad. Even if she felt bitter, there was no sense in poisoning the young ones against their grandmother. To-day she was especially grateful that Tara would keep the kids while she went on an errand for Marika. No good would come from dragging Annie and George down West Broadway look-ing for Amelia's husband. If Amelia had a husband, he was sure to be grief-stricken once he heard the news that she had passed, and there was no need for the children to witness it.

On her way, Kaly took a detour to the Tenderloin. No harm in trying to check on Beth again. She felt the warm wind blow the soft cotton dress against her thighs as she walked down to Mercury Street. The warm fall day had brought out everyone. Lovely women with tasseled hair filled the streets. They called out to the miners just off shift, "Come close, see what you can see. Come to me and you'll be happy." The women wore taffeta and satin dresses in bright reds and pinks. Some wore scanty gowns with black silk stockings and elaborate jewels, hair draping over their shoulders.

They fluttered fans in front of their faces and laughed at the children running up and down the streets, chasing and tackling each other. Two young girls sat on a doorstep head-to-head, telling secrets. A girl and a boy played a game of marbles at the end of the street. Young drink runners stood ready to sprint to the nearest tavern and back with whiskey or gin for a tip and a kind word. All the world was right that afternoon in the Red-Light District.

Kaly sauntered into the Alley, enjoying the warm air on her face, clicking her boots on the boardwalk. She looked at the East Ridge and allowed herself to breath in the beauty of the land hidden behind Butte's gray and soot-filled sky. Butte held no vegetation. But the hills around Butte would be splendid with autumn color.

As she approached her old crib, Beth opened the door and stepped into the doorway. She wore the velvet blue dress, her dark hair falling from a pile on top of her head to ringlets around her face. The sun left the clouds and Beth's face brightened, her eyes shining in mischievous wonder. "Boo!" Beth said.

Kaly, relieved that no harm had come to her friend, pretended to be startled. She laughed and hugged her, feeling the soft velvet against her skin. Behind her, she could she Beth's other dress, the soft pink, hanging on a hook on the wall, the only decoration in the room. "How is crib life?" Kaly asked.

"I am wonderful here." She lifted a hand toward the alley. "Fit right in."

"Is there anywhere you don't fit right in?" Kaly meant it. Beth belonged everywhere and nowhere. She had a way of transcending time and boundaries, like air, like sunshine, like the stars of a thousand heavens. "Have you heard anything from the hill?"

"Oh, you know. Miss Lottie's girls only do this and not

that." She feigned the indignation of her madam. "Meaning that none of them have ventured this way. So, no, I've not heard a peep of the mouse from the brothel."

"It doesn't seem right, not with Miss Lottie missing money," Kaly said. "I was sure she'd send someone for it."

"I told you. They have a cold."

"They can't all still be sick, can they?"

Beth shrugged, a smile edging her lips. "They've no call to come after me. Any angel could've taken it."

"You worry me," Kaly said. Beth's laissez-faire attitude had gotten her through some dangerous scrapes, but it had also gotten her into some dangerous scrapes. She didn't worry like Kaly did. She'd never had a sister die on her, never felt that fear take hold. Kaly realized she didn't even know if Beth had siblings. How could she have known her all these years and not know about her family? Beth knew everything about Kaly.

"Not everyone has the luxury of her mother showing up and taking her in. Some of us still must work for a living." Beth gave Kaly a sweet smile.

The worry doubled in Kaly's chest. "That's not fair, Bethy."

"Life and fairness do not go hand in hand. How is the little one?"

"Come back to the bakery with me and you can see for yourself. Annie doesn't even know I exist when you are around. You can stay with us. You'll be safe there." Kaly heard herself echoing a sentiment Beth had once professed to Kaly. "Come stay at Miss Lottie's," her friend had said. "You'll be safe there."

This was different. Kaly looked at the ground. "Besides, we talked about it. You can't work the line now." Beth had agreed. The syphilis would infect others, eventually killing them. "Maybe Tara would put you to work."

Kaly worked hard in the bakery. At first, she'd waited tables, but soon learned to cook good wholesome food. She cleaned tables and swamped the place at night, shopped, and stocked supplies. Still, she would not be able to make ends meet without Tara's help and Tommy sending home his army money.

Beth shook her head. "You know I can't live on that kind of money. I've got a scheme brewing and as soon as it's ready, you'll be the first to know."

Kaly couldn't help but feel that she had betrayed and abandoned her friend. So many didn't have the means to retire that profession. Old prostitutes often died cold and sick on the streets, or at one of the hog ranches for old whores. Those with syphilis did even worse.

She couldn't stand to think of that fate for Beth. Beautiful, bold, vivacious Beth. Kaly missed their camaraderie. Beth had been her best friend since she was fourteen. If Kaly had her way, she'd never give her up. But Beth had distanced herself from Kaly since she'd moved in with Tara McClane, and there seemed to be nothing Kaly could do about it.

"To answer your question, Annie is good," she told Beth. "She has a little cold, nothing that won't pass quickly. She's a trooper, that one. Butte tough."

Beth laughed, and Kaly was glad to see her light-heartedness again. When they first lived together in Beth's crib, the tiny room just big enough for a bed and stove, they'd had many late-night conversations about how strong a person had to be to survive the west. Whiskey, violence, disease, men mean from some slight or another, all took their toll on the working woman. When the women stuck together, they warded off the danger. If a woman found herself alone in a hovel or at the edge of a back street, she could find a world of hurt.

"I'm headed over to West Broadway to find a woman's husband, if she has one. The woman's name is Amelia. She's from the east. I don't know her husband's name so I'll be knocking on doors. Do you know of a man married to an Amelia?" Women of the line knew all of Butte's hidden secrets.

Beth shook her head. "Doesn't sound familiar. A lot of men live in the boarding houses over there."

"Married men?"

Beth shook her head. "No. Not a whole lot of those guys go for shift beds." She wrinkled her nose. "I don't see how they can stand to sleep in the bed another miner just crawled out of, just in time for work."

"They are dead tired from the long hours underground. They don't care. They could fall asleep on a rock."

"Not known for their hygiene," Beth added.

"Don't we know it," Kaly said. "Come with me, Beth, please?" Her voice was too pleading, but she couldn't help it. She missed her friend. "Then we can go back to the bakery and eat some good bread and soup, compliments of Tara Mc-Clane." Kaly heard the bitter tone in her voice and she needed her bitterness, to seal the bond between her and Beth—the very bond that unraveled when Kaly's mother showed up and took her in.

The wind tossed a stray paper at their feet. Beth reached down and picked it up. She put it in the crib stove. She hid her face with her hands. When she looked back at Kaly, she had tears in her eyes. "It's a crazy world. You should be grateful that you have a mother," she said. "I'd give anything to see my mother again."

Kaly's heart broke. It wasn't that long ago that the two of them had sat on the front porch of Miss Lottie's Brothel and talked about how wonderful it would be to find their mothers, to have a mother hold them, and tell them it—life—would be okay. They'd had so many things go wrong, so many wrong things in common. But then everything changed. Kaly had gotten pregnant and married Tommy. Tara McClane gave them a home and good work. The Granite Mountain mine disaster killed Bert Brown, whom Beth had loved. He was a forbidden topic for Kaly and Beth.

"We never talked about it, but do you have brothers or sisters?" Kaly asked the question it had taken her years to wonder.

Beth shook her head. "I think I was hatched from an egg, pushed out of a nest up in the Highlands somewhere. A hawk picked me up, half wild and half grown, and dropped me in the Mining City."

Kaly smiled and shook her head. "That's about right," she said. "So, you could be part hawk."

"Vulture, more like it."

"No. You're too kind to be predatory."

Beth rolled the blue velvet sleeve between her fingers and let it go. She leaned against the doorframe and looked away from Kaly.

"Come live with us," Kaly said again. "You can help at the bakery. We can help you make it on the slim wages," Kaly pleaded, promising her mother's love. Life had so reversed itself.

Just a year and a half ago, when Beth had begged Kaly to come live at Miss Lottie's, Miss Lottie wouldn't take her in, saying Kaly was too old to be one of her girls. And that she wanted *less to do with that bastard child than the dirt on the mister's boots.* The words had burned into Kaly's brain and she fled the brothel, looking for comfort in Dan McClane and a late-night cup of tea. And then to find out that Dan was her half-brother. Crazy world, indeed.

Tara McClane was not mean like Lottie Boyle. She would take Beth in. She'd do anything to make up for leaving Kaly and her sister with Coral Anderson. In spite of her own bitterness, Kaly could see the thousand cracks in Tara's heart. She believed her when she said she did the best she could. Kaly was beginning to think that the thousand cracks in her own heart might just break wide open toward the woman someday.

Beth was staring out toward the valley where new houses had started to crawl down the hill and sprawl out. She shook her head no. "It's no good," she said, "I've got this life to the end."

"It'll be a short end."

"Maybe."

"Come with me at least for lunch." Kaly smiled. She and Beth were so much alike, neither willing to be beholden to anyone. That had changed for Kaly once she found herself pregnant and decided to raise little Annie herself. Well, with Tommy. But Tommy wasn't here. He was overseas in the army. For Annie's sake, and for George, she would be beholden to her mother.

"I better not," Beth said. "You know Miss Lottie. Duty calls. I should at least poke my head in at the brothel, see if they need anything, keep the suspicion off of me about the missing money."

"She'll wonder why you left."

"I'll tell her I didn't want to get sick." Beth pushed her shoulders back. "I'll need to find another home soon. Do you think I can stay in the crib?"

"That would be up to Miss Lottie," Kaly said, a sick feeling welling up in her stomach. "She owns the cribs. I'm only surprised she's left this one empty for so long." Fate had materialized a mother for Kaly and left Beth alone in a sad, dark life as a syphilitic. It wasn't fair.

"You better go," Beth said, stepping back inside the crib. The dark day followed her. A rush of air lifted the pink dress lightly from its hook on the wall.

"Okay," Kaly said through the door frame. "But don't be a stranger."

"Sure, I won't be," Beth said. And then she said what Kaly knew but didn't want to admit, "It's difficult for you and me now. Our lives are so different."

"You've always have been my best friend. The only friend I've ever had." Kaly's heart beat fast, and her face felt warm. "Don't leave me now."

Beth's eyes softened. "I know, Kay. I won't. It'll be okay."

Leaving Beth there gave Kaly a sense of dark despair. It crawled up her legs to her stomach and chest. She walked fast, trying to escape it. She thought about Frank Little. No one had ever been arrested for his murder. It scared her to think of who they, or another mob, might go after next. If Little could be snuffed out that quickly, and no one held to account for it, what could happen to a woman like her or Beth?

Pushing the thought from her head, she knocked on doors asking about Amelia. No one knew of her or had even heard of her. One woman shut the door in Kaly's face, which Kaly didn't understand, but was sure she deserved.

She stopped at a rooming house where the landlady wore a lackluster brown dress and her hair fell in clumps around her head. She blocked the door, perhaps protecting her from whatever was going on inside. Kaly heard moaning coming from the rented rooms and figured that the sickness had found its way there.

"I have a friend who works with Dr. Fletcher. She might be able to help your renters." Kaly offered a weak smile to the bedraggled woman.

"What can she do that I can't? I give them water, keep them clean, and try to feed them soup. Good soup. But they won't touch any of it. They die anyway."

"They die anyway?" Kaly asked in disbelief. How could people die so quickly from a sickness? A terrible dread in her chest told her that the woman was telling her the truth. She'd seen people suffer from a variety of sicknesses, but normally they recovered.

The woman didn't answer, only fixed her pale, milky eyes on Kaly. She hadn't put her dentures in, so her lips collapsed on themselves, making a thin straight line across her face, waiting.

"I'm looking for someone who knows a girl, early twenties, named Amelia. She said that her son was at home with the landlord. Don't know if she has a husband. Amelia had brown hair, green eyes about as tall as me…" Suddenly Kaly felt like the whole thing was useless. Maybe Marika had made the whole thing up. Or maybe the girl had been delirious.

The woman nodded, and her tangled hair fell forward. "She wasn't here, didn't want a room here. Went somewhere else. She hasn't been in Butte long, but I saw her out walking. Don't know nothing about her family life. That girl looks to be carrying a secret she ain't gonna take to the grave."

Kaly cocked her head in a question.

The woman leaned in close and dropped her voice. "I feel things in my bones and damned if they ain't half true most of the time. She might be running from the law, or a violent husband. Or worse. Though, I can't think of much worse."

"You might be right," Kaly said, more convinced than ever that she was running the streets for a fool's errand. She shivered in the chill air, or maybe at the woman's premonition.

The woman dropped her chin to her chest and lifted it. "My husband hasn't come home for two days," she said. "I'm afraid he is sick. Will you keep an eye out for him in your travels?" Worry furrowed her brow.

"Sure, I will. What is his name?"

"Riley James. Works at the Orphan Girl."

"If I see him, I'll send him home." But Kaly knew that if he'd been able to go home, he probably would have gone home by now. "Otherwise, I'll bring back any word I hear about him."

After a few more inquiries, she came to a man hauling a cart of wood. He knew Amelia. "She lives across the street there in Jack Kelly's rooming house." He pointed to a white two-story house in need of a good painting. "No husband that I know of. Unless she's hiding him under the covers, which you girls are good at I hear," he said with a chuckle.

"No husband? You sure?"

"Sure as a snoop can be." He huddled over his cart, making himself small and round, as if his back had suddenly given out.

Kaly knocked on the door and a large burly man opened it. He had a full head of hair and full beard and kind green eyes. He wore a clean white shirt and brown trousers. She heard a young child crying in another room.

She introduced herself. "I'm looking for the husband of a girl named Amelia. Do they live here?"

The man shook his head. "Where is she? She left that kid with me. And I'm no good with kids."

"Are you her husband?"

"No. Name's Jack Kelly. No husband. Just her and the baby. She arrived from the east, Philadelphia maybe. She talked in circles. I couldn't keep the story straight. I'm not sure she could. Leaving for hours at a time, coming back just to sleep. My opinion? I'd say she was hiding something."

"The baby?"

"Indeed, hers. She needs to get back here." Jack Kelly rubbed his beard, his eyes wide and worried.

"Mama." The scream came loud and clear. A boy, about the age of Annie, stood in the doorway to the kitchen and sat down abruptly.

"Amelia's baby?" Kaly felt a sudden sense of protection toward the young boy.

"Yes, he's her son. Little Tony. I'll give him some cups to stack and he'll be distracted for a bit. But he keeps asking for his mother." Jack fumbled through the cupboard until he found several cups for the boy. "What do I tell him?"

Kaly watched Little Tony pile the cups, one on top of the other, and laugh heartily when they toppled over. He looked up at her with deep brown eyes, like Annie's, and rich black hair. "My mama?" he asked with a sweet light voice.

"Oh baby," Kaly said. "Someday we'll tell you all about her." And she meant it. She'd either learn about his mother or make it up. No matter what, Amelia would be good and kind and love Little Tony more than anything in the world.

"She hadn't been here but a couple of days. Usually, she took the kid with her, but for some reason this time she begged me to watch him." He pointed toward the boy. He wore a clean sleeper and socks that matched. "At first, I said no, but then she cried. What could I do?"

"You sure she didn't have a husband with her?"

That man tilted his head, like the man with the wooden cart had, and looked down at her, as if trying to figure what kind of creature had come to his front door. "Oh, I'm sure. No husband. She better get home soon. I have no clue, or inkling to find a clue, as to how to take care of a child. She said she'd be gone for an hour and now it's a week later. And, except for times like this, the kid has been screaming."

"Is he sick?"

"Did you hear those lungs? I'd say he's healthy as a horse. If you know where she is, tell her to get home now."

Something dark and unfathomable circled around Kaly's chest, something cruel and desperate. She felt it crawl up her arms into her neck. Amelia had left behind a young son, way too close to Annie's age. "I can't tell her. She passed away."

"Dead?"

"I'm afraid so."

"No, no, no. She was strong when she stormed out of here."

"I'm sorry."

"What am I going to do? I can't take care of him. I have to work."

"Welcome to a woman's world," Kaly said.

A train arrived from the east as Kaly stepped onto the platform. People chattered and bustled toward the train, holding hands and kissing, not wanting to let each other go. When the conductor got off, she walked up to him. "Excuse me," she said, "Do you remember a girl, Amelia, early twenties, with a young boy? She would have arrived from the east a couple weeks ago. Philadelphia, I'm told."

The conductor, a tall thin man with a thick lively mustache, nodded his head. "I do remember her."

"Did anyone disembark with her?"

He shook his head, put his thumb to his chin, and looked away. He pulled on his mustache. "There was a man, but he wasn't with her as far as I could tell. She might have wanted him to be, but he seemed oblivious to her."

"Wanted him to be?"

"She was never too far from him, a disjointed shadow. If he was in the food car, there she was. If he was down at the bar, there she was."

"And the boy?"

"A quiet, happy thing."

"You sure they weren't together?" He titled his head and gave her the same look that the man with the wood cart and Jack Kelly had given her.

"Yes, ma'am. If he knew she was on the train, he was avidly avoiding her."

Chapter Seven

MAMA FRIED POTATOES ON the cook stove. A rich onion and buttery aroma reached into the room and soothed Marika's heart. Good food made her happy. And after so many sick patients and the deaths these last weeks, Marika needed something good. Michael and Marko sat at the table playing cards with a stranger. Their work bundles rested on a bench at the door. The men had already cleaned up for dinner.

"Hello," Marika said, looking at the stranger and then at Michael.

Michael stood and kissed her on both cheeks. "Marika, this is Derrick Boggins. We work with him over at the Orphan Girl. He just got to town a couple weeks ago. Figured he could use some good home cooking, especially now with most public eating places either closed or with limited hours."

She smiled. "Nice to meet you, Derrick."

"Likewise. I'm grateful for the invitation," he said.

She cocked her head at him. "Weren't you with Amelia when she came in to Dr. Fletcher's office?" Marika asked.

Mama handed her a clean apron and she put it on, ready to help. The wood stove crackled and soft smoke rose up through the loosened door. Mama's small kitchen often made her feel claustrophobic. Tonight, though, she felt only comfort being here with her family.

"Amelia?"

"Yes, you brought her in and said you'd found her on the street very sick," she said.

"Aahhh, yes. You're the doctor," Derrick said. "Did she make it?'

"She didn't."

"I am sorry to hear that," he said. "She was so young."

"That, she was." Marika's heart broke again for Amelia.

"I thought a doctor could help."

"Well, I'm not really a doctor."

This time it was Derrick who cocked his head.

"I'm just a helper. But this sickness doesn't care two wits about doctoring skills. It's stopping at nothing," Marika said. "It sounded like you two had a spat."

"Aw, yes." He looked calm and thoughtful. "That was a simple misunderstanding. I'm sure she thought I was someone else. I didn't understand it either."

"But, she yelled at you."

"She was delirious. You saw how sick she was." He tilted his head toward her, a question in his eyes. It made Marika feel foolish.

"People aren't happy," Michael rushed in, "that the Board of Health has closed the town. Churches, schools, cabarets, bargain sales, anywhere that people gather."

"Saloons?" Mama asked.

"Not yet," Marko said. "But the churches are saying it's unfair. If they have to be closed, so should saloons."

"You'd have a mess of unhappy miners on your hands," Michael said. "They love their end of shift drinks. People find the daily news at the taverns."

Marko nodded. "That's how I know they've closed down the town, I was at the Copper Tavern."

The sudden shift of topic made her dizzy. "That's the point," Marika said. "People are getting sick and dying by the dozens. The thing spreads anywhere people gather. It's dangerous. Several people died every day last week from this illness." A great heaviness overtook her. It was mid-October. Influenza had been in town less than a month and an estimated five hundred to six hundred cases already plagued the city. Well over a hundred people had died. "Promise me you will stay away from the taverns."

Marko must have seen the worry in her face because he nodded.

"Seems to me that at least half of the town is blatantly ignoring the order," Derrick said. "The streets were full tonight."

"Sheriff's only got so much power," Mama said, shifting the cast iron skillet of potatoes to the back of the stove to keep them warm while she fried hamburger steaks. The sweet smell of caramelized onions filled the air. Standing on her tiptoes, Mama brought down five white porcelain plates, motioning Marika to the silverware.

"They need to close the schools," Marika said, as she put forks and knives on the table.

"They have," Marko said. "And people are mad about that."

"The teachers lost the fight to keep them open," Michael said. "Dan's friend, Elizabeth, was there at the board meeting. She said schools are sanitary. If the schools stay open, the teachers will know where the kids are and they'll know if they are sick. She said the kids are in more danger at home. A good number of sicknesses and other maladies will go unaccounted for. The Board still said no. Elizabeth didn't take that well and left the meeting abruptly."

Jealousy shot right up Marika's back at the mention of Elizabeth. But what right had she? None. She calmed herself as much as she could, putting Elizabeth and Dan out of her mind and focusing on the conversation.

"I'm grateful they still let us work," Derrick said.

"Copper is essential for the war," Marika said, as she got glasses from the cupboard. "I think they should close the mines. It would be safer. They completely closed whole towns when the plague crossed Europe. No one went to work." She looked at Michael. He came over to her, took the glasses from her hands and set them on the table.

"*Certza moya*," Michael said, pulling her close. "That was in the 1700s. Medicine has come a long way since then. You need to take care of yourself too. We don't want you getting weak and giving in to the thing."

Marika leaned into him. She wanted to cry, but her eyes were dry. She'd cried herself out over the last year. She could see Marko watching them carefully. He'd grown tall, almost six feet tall, with dark hair and bushy eyebrows that reminded her of Papa. "And the miners die of consumption," she said, moving the subject away from herself. "The dreaded black lung." She knew she was being melodramatic, but she didn't stop, letting an unfortunate rudeness overtake her. "You'll all face the same fate, as long as you're in the mines. Between that and this flu, what hope is there?"

Michael let go of her and stoked the fire.

She wanted to kick herself for spoiling the tender moment with him and ruining the mood for everyone. None of them had done anything to spark her sour mood. "I'm sorry," she said. "I'm sorry, Mama."

Every day this week, the flu had taken at least two of Dr. Fletcher's patients. And how many more across the city? She was powerless to stop it. The weight of it hit her full force and she found it hard to breathe. She hoped her apology would show a relief that she didn't feel.

"Sit and eat," Mama said. "You can tell us what has broken your heart. This sickness frightens us all."

"I know, Mama." Marika watched as Mama put a steaming plate in front of Michael. She served the rest of them and cut the cornbread into thick squares with butter. After Mama joined them at the table, Michael said the prayer. As the others dug in, Marika took an extra moment to gather her wits. What had come over her? The deaths. The stranger. The town closed up tight. All of it. "I'm sorry," she said again.

"Shhhh," Michael said. "Eat your food and then, like Mama said, you can tell us."

"This flu is so bad. I don't know enough to help. I need medical training."

Derrick spoke up. "You said the doctors don't know how to stop it. And they are trained."

She bristled at that, although she didn't know why. He had a right to speak. "I can dress a wound and set a broken leg. I can clean out ears, and offer medicine for pain. But when it comes to sickness, I'm always guessing at the answer, instead of knowing it. If I knew, I could be of use instead of sitting idly by my patients."

Mama looked up at Michael, who had been quiet. Marko looked from Michael to Marika. Marika had somehow silenced them all. All but Derrick.

"Well, then, just go to medical school," he said, sounding casual and innocent.

"Okay," she said, laughing. "Just like that. I'll wave a magic wand and fill the hope chest with money."

"And food," Marko said.

"Might as well throw in a cart and a few horses," Michael said.

"I'll give you the cast iron skillet," Mama said.

And just like that the angry spell was broken and their evening began in earnest. After dinner they drank *rakija* and Marika savored the warmth of her family around her. Even the stranger seemed a friend.

That night, back in their hovel, Michael chattered on about the great house he was going to build for them some day. "It'll have a grand kitchen with a big cook stove and a large tub to relax in. We'll have plenty of bedrooms for the children, and a giant bedroom for us. And a very large office for you."

"And what will we put in the kids' rooms?" She was only half joking.

"Oh, you know, a train set for the boys and half a dozen dolls for the girls. They'll have tool sets, and tiny dishes, and an ore car." He smiled.

"No ore car," she laughed. "And that big, glamourous office?"

"You'll do your best work there."

"And that giant bedroom?"

"Come here," he said.

Her knees went weak and she couldn't object. He touched that very special place just below her neck and followed the line down between her breasts. Her whole body went so mushy that he'd have to carry her to the bedroom, which is exactly what he did. That night she slept so close to him that she thought she'd meld into him, inhaling his earthly scent, feeling his skin against hers, his warmth filling her up, his sweet, gentle love being the only thing she ever wanted.

———

Marika stood at the back door of Dr. Fletcher's office as the dead wagon carried another casualty away. This time is was a miner, Riley James, who had worked at the Orphan Girl for five years. He'd worked hard to save a nest egg for him and his wife. They owned a boarding house where miners of alternate shifts shared beds. They had planned to sell the boarding house and leave next spring for the Yukon, in search of the elusive gold. Men usually took that trip alone. But he had a good woman, a woman he loved with all his heart, a woman he loved more and more every day, he said, and he was going nowhere without her.

But the flu swept in on him and took him on a quick flight to God, leaving his missus behind.

And that was that.

This demon devil, so small she couldn't see it, plagued her. She was starting to understand evil, to believe in evil. It could come out of nowhere and permeate a town. Or it could just sit down hard on one person. No good luck or good heart could fend it off. Nothing bad could fend it off. The flu cared nothing for good or bad or anything in between. Influenza had not one ounce of caring or discrimination.

The door opened and Dr. Fletcher walked in, light-hearted and full of morning sunshine. He wore a white shirt, a tan vest, and tan trousers. His glasses sat lopsided on his face, a crooked smile to match. "You're here early," he said, his hands twitching in front of him. "You make the boss look bad by arriving before him. Think of me, young woman. You don't want to sully my reputation."

Marika wanted to match his light-heartedness, wanted him to be proud of her, but another man had just died on her watch and there was no redemption in that. "I didn't go home last night. Another late-night patient came in." She fought back the tears.

Dr. Fletcher raised his eyebrows at her. "Where is this patient now? Did you cure him already with your magic spells?"

Her sadness flipped to anger. She did not like the doctor mocking her, not after watching Riley James die. Marika breathed deep into her lungs and let it go. Showing anger toward Dr. Fletcher would only hurt her. "A miner this time," she said, "Riley James. He was too far gone. I could do nothing for him. I didn't want to leave him alone and I didn't call because I figured he'd wait for morning when you could see him. I was wrong."

Now she saw the anger behind the doctor's glasses. "A very

sick patient, sick enough to die, came in and you didn't call me?"

Marika looked at the floor. When she looked up, his face had softened.

He shook his head. "Sorry I snapped."

Marika lifted her eyebrows. The doctor didn't usually apologize.

"The Board of Health says that influenza is epidemic. It is spreading quickly across Butte."

Marika nodded.

"It's highly contagious. Physicians all over the country report that patients contract it and quickly perish."

"The mines frighten me. The men work so close together, with little ventilation."

The doctor shrugged. "It's hitting them hard. Theatres, churches, movie picture shows, dance halls are all closed, but the mines are open."

Marika shook her head. "Germs spread quickly in those conditions."

Dr. Fletcher nodded. He straightened his glasses, pushing them up his nose. "The mines just became a lot more dangerous."

"What about the streetcars? They've been packed to the brim with people going to work, shopping, going down to the Flats and up to the Columbia Gardens."

"That'll slow down with the business closures. People will have to wait for another car if the trolley is too full. And the windows need to be kept wide open."

"Winter is coming. People will freeze." Marika usually walked, but others took advantage of the quick ride to work or the marketplace.

"The point is to keep good people alive to tour the town another day," the doctor said.

"How will they enforce the orders?"

"The sheriff's office has dispatched the news."

"Which people are ignoring."

"They had better rethink that."

At least the Board of Health was not laissez faire about the flu. They were clearly trying to take control. But Butte people did not like to be told what to do. She feared, any day now, all hell would break loose. The doctor was right. They had better rethink ignoring the Board of Health.

"I would have liked to have tried to help this miner." His voice softened again. "You must call me for each sick patient now."

The dark hole in her chest must have shown on her face because he explained himself, something he wasn't in the habit of doing.

"We have to try to stop the devastation," he was saying. "You cannot do this without me."

She nodded. "Then you have to teach me." *Rather than just giving me trivial errands to run,* she wanted to say. But the moment was too important for minor grievances. Instead, she said, "Because I have no one else to teach me about medicine."

Dr. Fletcher's face turned red. He rubbed his cheek, turning it even redder. She could see him fighting with himself. Could he truly respect her? Could he understand that she, too, could become a doctor someday?

"In this man the flu was deadly," Marika said, in a slow, modulated tone. "Maybe I could have done nothing at all to help. But I'd have a better chance to be of use if you would mentor me. Rather than repeatedly sending me on simple errands." Right away she wanted to kick herself for not holding her tongue. She hadn't meant to say that out loud!

"I've been thinking about that," he said. "Murray hospital has nursing classes. Perhaps you could attend them. Nurses are needed more than ever right now."

At first her face flamed red and anger filled her brain. But then, a swift calm soared in and lifted the anger away. A nurse wasn't a doctor. But a nurse had medical knowledge she didn't have. "Okay," she said.

The door screeched across the wooden floor and Kaly walked in. She wore a simple cotton dress and her cheeks flushed red and chapped from the cold. The paper skeleton on the wall lifted and settled as the door shut.

"Marika, Dr. Fletcher," she said. Mud clung to the bottom of her dress and her black boots were dusty from the streets.

"Did you find him?" Marika asked. The memory of Amelia's face came to her, her spirit shivering across the room.

Dr. Fletcher cocked his head. "Find who?"

"Amelia's husband," Marika said.

"No, no husband." Kaly looked from Marika to Dr. Fletcher and back again, a slight tilt to her smile, maybe not quite immune to the tension in the room. "I talked to Jack Kelly at her boarding house and to the train conductor. They both say she was alone with the child. The proprietor now has the boy and wonders what he'll do with him. He must work and has no way to care for the child."

"Welcome to a woman's world," Marika said.

"That's exactly what I said." Kaly smiled. "Someone needs to take the boy."

"Noble wanderer." Marika folded her hands.

Kaly's eyes widened.

"An orphan can wander from home to home, looking for a place to belong." She didn't mean to put Kaly on the spot. She was trying to acknowledge her experience.

"Beth stopped me from wandering in my early years," Kaly said, "and now, Annie and George keep me from fleeing to the coast. You're stuck with me."

"And glad of it." Marika laughed.

Dr. Fletcher looked back and forth between the women, a somber look on his face, clearly not getting their connection. "But the child," he said. "Who will take the child? You can't leave him to a grizzled old miner."

"Can you take care of him?" Marika asked Kaly.

"No room at the inn." She shook her head. "You and Michael could take him. He'd thrive in your family."

But Marika was at work every day. The danger of exposing him to a contagious sickness was too high to bring him to the doctor's office. Plus, she'd never make it to medical school if she took in a child.

Dr. Fletcher continued to look back and forth between the two women, a mild curiosity on his face. "What else did you find out?" he asked.

"The conductor said that there was a man on the train who wasn't with her, and that he seemed oblivious to Amelia. But Amelia was never far from him, following close behind him."

"Sounds like she knew him," Marika said.

"Maybe. But the man didn't know her. When the conductor

mentioned the girl and child to the man, he looked confused."

"Well, she is gone. Nothing for us to do but tend to the living," Dr. Fletcher said in his usual conclusive way. Except that nothing was resolved. The child needed a place to live. And, of course, there was *nothing to do but tend to the living*. That's what they were doing! He'd said that same thing to her when they waited on the hill for survivors of the Granite Mountain Mine fire to be pulled from the poisoned tunnels.

Marika looked at him, waiting.

Without another word, the doctor disappeared into the back room where he saw his patients. He was done.

Marika shook her head and turned to Kaly. "Promise me you'll be careful," she said. "This flu is really contagious." *And deadly*, she wanted to say, holding Kaly's gaze, wanting her to understand the dangers to herself and the children. "I shouldn't have asked you to find Amelia's boarding house. I didn't understand the peril I put you in when I asked. But now I do."

Kaly didn't say anything.

"You've got two children to keep safe," Marika continued. "And a husband coming home someday. You better keep healthy so that his return is joyous."

Kaly nodded, her brown curls shifted on her shoulders. "Speaking of children, I better get home and get some lunch into them." Kaly patted her stomach. "My mother will have them full on sugar cookies and caramels if I'm not there."

Marika smiled. "You look good with a little weight on you."

"It feels odd to have plenty of food and shelter." Kaly laughed. "I feel like an imposter, that any day I'll be found out, the world will crash down around me, and the children will be taken away. And things will go back to an endless dark tunnel."

Marika knew that Kaly had been through a lot, even if she didn't know all of the details. She remembered the cold stare in Kaly's eyes when she talked about Bert Brown. It had made the hair on Marika's arms rise. It was the look of a heart gone wrong, a look of pure hatred. It lasted a split second and fled, leaving a sooty slime in its place. Bert Brown had done something so wrong to Kaly that a twinge of evil had landed solid in her heart, and it stayed there, closed off and contained.

"Kaly," George suddenly said from the doorway, making both women jump. He held Annie on his hip. "She's hungry."

"What are you doing here?" Kaly's voice rose.

"Grandma got sick."

Marika and Kaly exchanged a glance. Ten-year-olds took care of their siblings all the time in Butte. If their father had been killed in the mines and their mothers went to work or died of the flu, some ten-year-olds even raised their siblings. Nothing new here. But Marika knew that Kaly wanted to keep Annie and George away from all that.

Marika took Annie and bounced her on her hip. "How are my two favorite kids?"

"Hungry." George smiled.

"Okay, I get the message," Kaly said. "I have to go. There is nothing like being bossed around by a ten-year-old. You were right to come and get me. Where else did you look?"

"The Alley."

Marika saw the look of pain that crossed Kaly's face.

"You stay away from the Alley," Kaly said. "You hear?"

Fright and confusion filled George's face and he nodded.

"If you need help, you come right here, to Dr. Fletcher's office. If Marika isn't here, Dr. Fletcher will help you."

George nodded again. Marika wanted to pull him close and tell him he wasn't really in trouble. That Kaly was just scared for him. She knew that a good time in the Alley could turn violent, the last of someone's life spilling into the dusty road. Marika bit her lip and remained quiet as she handed Annie to Kaly.

George looked away as Kaly wrapped an arm around him and pulled both kids to her side. Annie cooed and reached over to him. "You did a good job, George," Kaly said. "Now let's get you some food. You must be starving."

"She is," George said, this time leaving himself out.

Marika watched the cloud cross over George until he took a breath and leaned into Kaly, wrapping his arms around her waist, accepting her comfort in spite of her anger, in spite of his own.

When Kaly opened the door, Marika saw the wolf dog

standing guard. When he saw them, he pressed his paws to the ground and wiggled his hind end in the air, waiting for a hello or a pet or a scrap of food.

"Let's go, boy," George said, letting go of Kaly and running ahead. Marika yelled a good-bye to Dr. Fletcher through his closed door and heard a muffled grunt. She walked them to the bakery and then kept going. With the smell of sulfur in the air, she headed for South Idaho Street, dragging her weary body toward home.

Chapter Eight

AFTER FEEDING GEORGE AND Annie, Kaly put her daughter down for a nap. She marveled at the little girl, with her curly hair and her soft skin, her dark brown, nearly black eyes. She looked nothing like Kaly. Annie must look like Tommy at that age, or like Anne Marie.

She felt George watching her and looked up. He sat cross-legged on top of a green and pink quilt on the couch. He looked cautious and timid. She needed to learn to stop herself before reprimanding him, even if she didn't like what he did.

"I'm sorry I yelled at you," She said. The wood in the stove cracked and a small bit of smoke escaped, the spirit of a mountain fairy. "I was scared," she said. "Bad things happen down in the Alley, especially to children."

"I was scared too." He turned his head and looked toward the wall. "She closed the bakery and went to bed. Annie was hungry. I didn't know what to do."

"Next time just come up here. I'll make sure that there are some crackers and cheese in the icebox. Or, like I said earlier, go to Dr. Fletcher's. They'll find me." She walked over and sat on the couch next to him. Reaching out a hand, she tousled his hair. He smelled like the hot stove. "You are wearing the fire in those clothes. We'll wash them tomorrow, okay?"

He nodded.

George had grown up on the Butte streets, and knew them nearly as well as Kaly did. She tousled his hair again. "And you could use a washing too," she said. "Will you stay with your sister while I go check on your grandmother?"

He nodded and sat on the floor with his dog.

Downstairs everything was quiet and the air was cool. Kaly checked the doors and found the front door to the bakery unlocked. She clicked the lock shut and put wood in the stove. Tara must have been about to stoke the fire just before she took ill. It wasn't like her to let the fire burn down.

She lay quietly in her bed, dressed in her day clothes, her breath light and airy. Kaly put a hand on her forehead and felt the heat of a fever. Getting a cup from the cupboard, she filled it with water and put it on the nightstand.

"Mother," she said, the word still awkward in her mouth.

"Mmmm," Tara mumbled.

"Here is some water for you. You should drink some."

"Mmmm, okay."

"Do you want some soup?"

Tara opened her eyes and looked up at Kaly. They were bloodshot and milky.

"I have a bad headache," she said.

"I'll call the doctor," Kaly said.

"No, don't. I'll be okay. I'll drink some water."

"Can I get some soup for you?" Kaly asked again.

Her mother shook her head no and closed her eyes.

"We're right upstairs if you need us." Kaly didn't understand her own tender feelings but she meant what she said. She was right there if her mother needed her, and she wanted her to know. But Tara had already gone back to sleep.

"She'll be okay," she said to George when she got back upstairs.

He walked over to her and wrapped his arms around her. She would beat all the devils down just to allow a moment like this. A moment of honest affection. She hugged him back.

"Don't leave us," he said.

"I won't, buddy. I won't."

With that, George lay down on the couch and pulled the quilt up over himself, staring at his dog. "Hey buddy," he said. The wolf dog tilted his head, first one way and then the other, alert, a question, wondering, maybe, what the boy wanted.

George loved easily. Kaly had to work at love. She had to work at not running away the second she felt anything like fondness coming her way. She couldn't help it. She had walked the fence of wanting and avoiding closeness for as long as she could remember. Who could have known it would be so difficult to fall off the fence in the warm arms of her family?

Family.

Deep in her heart, she understood how much children needed love. For them, she would learn to love. Their pure affection made her feel even more sharply how much she had missed as a child. Their love shined a light where she had once felt darkness. Something inside of her had cracked and, like it or not, the light was coming in.

She had begun at the bottom of possibility at The Polly May to avoid being disappointed. Miss Anderson had tried to help the children in her care, but she was drunk too often and preoccupied with the one boy she couldn't help: her son, Bert Brown.

Now people loved Kaly. Tara, Tommy, George, Annie, and maybe the dog. She'd hit a copper-rich vein. How it happened, she still didn't know. One day she was alone and now this.

She sat on the couch next to George and patted his shoulder. The boy felt bone frail and thin.

"You hardly ate anything when we got back. Are you hungry now?"

He nodded.

Kaly could see the trust lingering behind his sad smile, his desire to come out from his shelter, a scared rabbit in its hole. She knew that feeling.

"Well then, let's get you something to eat." She pulled a cold piece of chicken and some potato salad from the icebox and served them to him. "Do you miss being at The Polly May?"

"I miss Julian. He was like my brother." George ran a hand through his dark hair, reminding her of Tommy at his age.

"I'm sorry," she said.

George nodded. He barely touched his food before he lay back down for a nap. It was rare for him to take a nap. *Must be the weather*, Kaly thought as she pulled out Tommy's latest letter.

My dear Kaly,

How are the children? Does George's dog still follow him everywhere? Is Annie growing like a weed? How are you holding up? A bad flu has hit some of the men over here. Several men died last week. I hope it doesn't hit our troops. More than that, I hope it stays on this side of the Atlantic. As if the war hasn't killed enough men already.

I'm strong and healthy. I hope you are too. I miss you so much and can't wait to see you again. They say that victory is ours any day. They'll settle for nothing less than surrender. But I hear it is soon.

Give my love to the Annie, George, and your mom. Pet that old dog for me.

All my love always,
Tommy.

Kaly put the letter aside and let the warm feelings rush through her. "All my love always." Tommy had been at The Polly May with her. He'd brought food to her room after Anne Marie died. He'd invited her downstairs for a game of cards. He'd called to her from the fire escape to come outside and watch the stars. Even though she often ignored him, Tommy never gave up on her.

Kaly wrote a quick note back to him, telling him that they were all healthy and that they missed him desperately. They looked forward to victory and his homecoming. She wanted to say more, to tell him she loved him, but she didn't know how. Sweat piled at her brow even as she thought it. Why couldn't she just say what was in her heart? Was she that afraid he'd reject her? So many times Tommy had stepped in to stop a group of kids from taunting her. After Anne Marie died, he kept Bert Brown away from her. When a lady pirate, who normally went after men, took a disliking to Kaly, Tommy drew her ire toward him.

Was she afraid he'd reject her, even after he'd married her? After he'd professed his love to her?

Yes. She was.

People lied. They lied all the time.

She sealed the envelope, put it aside, and took out her knitting. The yarn slipped through her fingers, rubbing her skin, as she knit it into the beginnings of a scarf. Kaly liked yarn. She could count on yarn. She really liked this color combination of red and gray, brilliant and muted. She'd send a couple scarves to Tommy with her letter. Maybe that would make up for the things she couldn't say. Knitting quieted her mind and gave her time to think. It felt good to make something warm for the troops.

The clicking sounds of the needles and the children's breathing filled the room. In that quiet space a deep, primitive sadness hit Kaly at the back of her head and it hurt, sending something icy cold down her spine. She thought of Tommy overseas, fighting for freedom, and Beth in the Red-Light District, sick, unable to work, and teetering on homelessness. Tears welled up in her eyes. Pushing the brown curls back away from her face, she wiped at her tears.

After the big fire last year, they all kept a stiff upper lip. One large communal stiff upper lip. They pushed their sadness aside and let their anger fly, especially after Frank Little was hanged, united in the wrongness of it all, half the town showing up for his funeral procession.

None of them had any time to get their bearings before the town went on strike and the fights became bitter. The working girls suffered too often at the hands of one angry John or another.

Beth took the bruises in stride. All in a day's work. Now, with syphilis in her blood and no family, no work, and a limited supply of money, a stiff upper lip was all that Beth had.

Kaly made a decision. She would bring Beth home with her. She'd go get her, and insist she come to the bakery. They'd fix up Annie's room, give her a safe bed and a place to hang a painting. Kaly would knit a blanket for her. And a couple doilies. Maybe she'd get brave and knit an entire sweater for Beth.

Bert Brown had done the ultimate wrong to Beth, giving her a death sentence. If he hadn't died, he would have killed Kaly, too. She knew it. One night he had pounded on Kaly's door, shoved his way in, and beat her. After he left, Tommy had knocked and she'd told him to go away. He didn't. Her lip had already swollen and she was pregnant with Tommy's child, and there was so much that she hadn't said. She figured keeping one more night of violence from him could only protect him.

And she'd wanted him to think well of her, not feel sorry for her. He'd pushed his way in and saw her bloody, swollen face. Kaly had watched his mind split in a quiet angry way. She'd seen his eyes turn dark before, but that night a deep chasm opened in them.

"Who did this?" he'd demanded.

When she didn't answer, he went after Bert and found his knuckles beat up. The next time Kaly saw Bert, he'd stared at her, a wild danger in his eyes that scared her more than his fists. Bert was dead now, but there were a dozen more like him out there, and they'd all be banging on Beth's door once they knew she was carrying the pox and staying in the cribs.

Kaly wanted to move Beth to Tara McClane's home. But she knew that Beth was proud and she'd feel even more the outcast than Kaly did at the bakery. Kaly at least had the children. And her mother lived right downstairs trying to make up for the past. It would take nothing on Kaly's part to accept her mother's apology, putting aside a little vanity and maybe finding a touch of forgiveness in her heart.

Beth had nothing but Kaly. Even if Beth didn't know it.

Disturbed by her own brooding, she put the knitting needles down. The gray and red scarf lay across the arm of the brown velvet chair, looking handsome and innocent. George slept soundly on the big couch cushions. Annie slept peacefully in her crib. Downstairs, everything was quiet.

Leaving her apartment door open, she went downstairs to check on her mother. She was still asleep, her breathing a little ragged. She had kicked the blankets off of the bed and they lay crumpled on the floor. She picked them up and put them back over Tara, feeling the heat come off of her. The cup of water that Kaly had earlier put on the nightstand sat undisturbed.

———

Back upstairs, the wolf dog lifted and tilted his head at her, and then at the door, as someone knocked. It was Beth. Kaly did not like what she saw. Disheveled and panicked, her friend walked through the door without waiting for an invitation. She looked pale and sickly, her black hair falling down around her face and her blue dress soiled and hanging limp to her ankles.

Beth set herself gently on the sofa next to where George slept. "I don't feel good."

A panic alarm went off in Kaly. Beth had said that everyone at Miss Lottie's brothel was sick. "What's wrong?" Kaly tried to sound lighthearted but already the fear gripped her throat and her voice came out harsh.

Beth tangled her fingers in her messy hair, her skin too transparent. "My throat hurts. Really hurts. And I have a bad headache. Every muscle in my body aches." Her eyes squinted nearly shut, as if the lamplight hurt them.

Wanting to comfort her, Kaly went into the kitchen. George's partially eaten chicken and potato salad sat on the counter. She put it in the icebox for later, and looked through her cupboards. She didn't keep much food up here, since they had immediate access to anything that Tara made for the café. The townspeople loved Tara's pea and bean soups, chicken noodle casseroles, pasties, and sarma. Earlier today, before she fell ill, Tara had made a huge pot of pasuli, that white bean soup the Serbs made with carrots and potatoes, onion and celery, and a touch of clove. Kaly's favorite. Just the smell could settle a stomach. She thought to go downstairs in the quiet and get some for Beth.

Instead, she found some crackers, a loaf of bread, and some soda water. She brought them into the living room on a wooden tray, feeling quite competent and with a bit of hope in her heart. "Try this," she said brightly.

But Beth, like the children, like Tara downstairs, was already asleep.

———————

The next day Kaly left George and Beth at the apartment. Beth was feeling better and had said she'd stay the afternoon and Tara, also feeling better, said she'd watch George when Beth went home. He'd be in good hands either way. She'd given George the option to come with her and he preferred to stay home with his dog.

Kaly carried Annie on her hip across town to her old home, The Polly May. She arrived just as the snow began. It was clean and fresh and made the town feel wholesome.

Miss Anderson had turned the now defunct Polly May Home for Kids into a boarding house. Late at night, when the wind blew hard, and sometimes in her dreams, Kaly could still hear the cries of children turned loose in the hallways. They were hallways overrun by heartbreak and violence, and too much grief. The children had lost parents in mining accidents, violence, disease, and sometimes suicide. Miss Anderson had taken them in, fed them oatmeal and corn mush. She had sent them out to collect coal that had fallen from the train cars. She had whispered kind words to them when they came back with their arms full.

Beth said the house was full of ghosts. The stairs creaked. The wind blew through closed windows. A flame might jump unexpectedly and die down suddenly. Those things scared Kaly, but not nearly as much as the dark things in her dreams. Too many nights she woke up paralyzed, shadows hovering over her, looking past her to Anne Marie. Kaly would try to scream to warn her sister, but not a sound came out. She couldn't move, couldn't speak. She could barely breathe.

She hitched Annie up higher on her hip and shifted the cloth shoulder bag with the pasuli in it to her other shoulder, careful not to break anything open. Annie cooed at the house, cooed at the street. Beth would say Annie was greeting the ghosts. The nice ones. Kaly knew about ghosts. The whisp of Anne Marie's spirit had only left once Kaly remembered all the events from that fatal day that her sister died, once her killer died in the mining accident.

Up until last year, she had the occasional visit in the smoke from fire or the rustle of tree leaves. Sometimes a lovely memory would come in so pure and clean, Kaly could nearly touch her face. But nothing since the mining accident. She hoped that meant that Anne Marie was at peace somewhere in the sky or deep in the clouds above the wild mountains.

The large house loomed before them, the rooms now full

of adult boarders. Miss Anderson fed them spaghetti or stew and cornbread, drinking while she cooked. Kaly stopped at the gated fence. Cold snow pelted her face, keeping her alert, warning her to keep watch, to sense the danger, to listen for the door opening, quiet footsteps on the stairs, arms that reached out to grab her, pulling her into a cubby with a hand over her mouth. The smothering hand had smelled like oil and didn't let her go until the other hand finished hurting her. She was twelve that time.

She shook her head, shaking off the phantom and wishing she had left Annie at home. She looked up at the second-floor dormers, turned into the yard, and climbed the steps to the covered porch. She lifted the heavy metal knocker and clanged it down.

A young child answered the door. She took in a sharp breath. A child should not be here! She looked around for an explanation and found only the familiar scene. The oriental carpet on the floor in the entryway was tattered and worn from years of use. The dark wood banister had long since been polished. She saw the photos of the children who had passed through these doors.

A young Anne Marie looked out at her, the tiny cross sparkling in the corner. Someone had painted a gold cross on Bert Brown's photo too. Kaly had the urge to dig her nails across his face, to mar his image, nearly forgetting that she had come in peace, at the request of her sick mother. Tara had started feeling better, but was still not well enough to venture out.

Annie squirmed on her hip wanting to get down.

The boy in front of her wore tan trousers too short for him, showing sharp bones on his bare ankles.

The boy shouldn't be here.

Annie shouldn't be here.

"Is Miss Anderson in? I've got some good hearty pasuli for the boarders, compliments of Tara McClane," she said.

"She's in the kitchen. You can go in." The pale kid looked like he was about eight years old.

"Where's your mother?"

"She's in the kitchen too. They're playing a game of cards."

Kaly lifted her skirt, shifted Annie, and stepped inside.

"Pa is too sick to play cards. Ma says I'm not to bother him."

"So, you're the doorman." She looked around for another adult, debating whether or not she should deliver the pasuli or put it in the hands of the boy. She did not like having Annie at The Polly May.

The boy cocked his head in a question.

"The door boy."

"What's that?"

"The person who answers the door."

He gave Kaly that cocked head question look again and she felt a little foolish.

"Never mind," she said.

Annie pushed away from her mother and whined, stiffening her body so that she nearly fell from Kaly's arms. She really wanted down. But Kaly would not put her down inside of The Polly May, or even in front of The Polly May. She had vowed to be Annie's safe home and she had learned too well, the hard way, that The Polly May was not safe.

Through the years Miss Anderson had looked away when Bert hurt the other children, minimizing his actions, and dimming her awareness with alcohol. Coral Anderson had done the ultimate wrong. Some of the children had died. Anne Marie had died. After last year's mining accident, Miss Anderson had agreed to close the home to children and Kaly agreed not to go to the authorities. The local churches and The Paul Clark Home had stepped in to fill the gap.

"Can you bring medicine for Papa?" the boy was asking.

"I don't know. What's his sickness?"

"He makes a funny sound and coughs up something pink. His lips are blue and he can't breathe. Mama called the doctor but he hasn't come."

"Sounds like he needs an ambulance."

"She's afraid they'll take him and not bring him back."

"And she's playing cards." Kaly reminded herself that this boy was very young.

"For a moment of sanity, she said. I'm supposed to be sitting with him. Can you get the ambulance? I have to get back up there to him."

Kaly was baffled. She wanted to shake the woman by her shoulders. And she wanted to let Miss Anderson have it. Kaly charged into the kitchen, where Coral Anderson stood at the counter, hand on her hip, her gray hair pulled up into a bun. She wore an ash green dress gathered at her waist that dropped in folds to her ankles. The sleeves puffed from her shoulders to her elbow, covering half of her pale fragile arms.

The commonplace nature of the dress was its own sleight of hand. Miss Anderson was anything but commonplace. She drank, lied, and disregarded the welfare of others. Was Kaly still bitter? It appeared so. "What are you doing letting the boy answer the door?" She demanded. Annie, still squirming, suddenly seemed terribly heavy.

"What are you doing coming in uninvited?" Miss Anderson threw it back at her, her voice edged in anger. "You've no right."

"He's just a kid and he's taking care of his sick father." Kaly wanted to explode. After everything that had happened to her, to her sister, she didn't care who thought she was hysterical. The women at the card table stared at her.

"I brought pasuli for your boarders. I came in peace, but peace can't last when you put children at risk."

Coral Anderson narrowed her eyes at Kaly. She pushed herself away from the counter and stood taut, a wild cat ready to pounce. Miss Anderson dropped her voice to a near whisper, the tight edge of it barely contained. "You be respectful." She said it, not as a reprimand to a child, but as an ultimatum to an adult, with the full weight of a threat behind it. The words hung in the air.

Kaly put the pasuli on the counter. Annie reached for Miss Anderson who took her out of Kaly's arms. Coral cooed at Kaly's daughter, making strange sounds, making her laugh. Trapped into a meager submission, Kaly fumed.

"The boy's mother is right there. Talk to her," Coral said while rubbing her nose against Annie's.

Slowly, Kaly turned to look at the woman. She wore a ragged dress stained with dirt. What might have been a bright pink at one time was now muted to drab beige from too many washings. Her brown stringy hair fell past pale skin to her shoulders. Pale watery eyes looked up at Kaly. She had a blue tinge to her mouth.

"It sounds like your husband needs to go to the hospital," Kaly said, the anger drained out of her.

The woman nodded her head, a slow nod, methodical, like she'd been nodding to people all her life, always a yes, never a no.

"Five more shifts in the hole to pay for an ambulance, when it's probably just a cold," she said. The words had a strange halting sound to them, like she'd forgotten each word as soon as she spoke it.

"It sounds like he is really sick," Kaly said.

"The doctor is on his way."

"Your son said you've been waiting a long time."

"Have we?" She looked up at Kaly, a lost child carried on the wind. Compassion welled up in Kaly and she reached for Annie, trying to hold back her tears. Miss Anderson let go of the child and Kaly swung her back onto her hip, where she belonged. Annie leaned her head into Kaly's shoulder and Kaly's heart burst. Against her will, tears filled her eyes as she looked from Miss Anderson to the woman. The heater in the hallway moaned as it spit out steam. The skin on Coral's face hung heavy and damp, wrinkles creasing her mouth. Something like resignation, the defiance drained out of her.

Holding Coral's eyes, Kaly said, "I'll go straight up the hill to the hospital and get someone down here to get him." She didn't say, "to get them," even though, by the boy's description of his father, she could see that the woman and the man had the same illness.

Chapter Nine

MARIKA WALKED SLOWLY OVER Park Street toward the hospital. The streets were empty and businesses were shuttered up tight. Tara McClane came out of the bakery wearing a long brown skirt, a brown overcoat, and a blue knit hat that covered her ears against the cold. She carried a large basket, filled to the brim and overflowing. She had the look of a woman on a mission.

"Mrs. McClane," Marika called and ran to catch up with her.

"You should be home with your family," Tara said, her voice tight and concerned. "The town is locked up."

Marika nodded. "I'm on my way to the hospital to sign up for nursing classes. I heard you were sick."

"Just a cold," Tara said. "I recovery quickly from colds."

"Where are you going and what's in the basket?" Marika was being nosy. But with her own purpose. She worried about things spreading germs. Things like baskets, cloth napkins, and food could not be trusted. Nothing could be trusted. This flu had gone through Butte so quickly. Now, they tried to stop its spread.

Every year the flu came and went. People got sick and people got better. Occasionally someone died from a flu—usually those who were weak and fragile. But this flu was different. It took strong, healthy adults, and it moved rapidly, razing the city like misplaced dynamite.

"Pasties that I made. I'm taking them over to Audrey James. Riley passed on and she's still got a houseful of boarders."

Marika nodded. She had been there when Riley James took his last breath. "And half of them sick. Be careful. People are getting sick and they aren't recovering."

Tara nodded. "How are things at your home?"

"Everyone seems fine so far. Michael is overworked. The miners are getting sick like everyone else. He's down in the tunnels with them. It worries me." She looked up at the head frame of the Orphan Girl. Puffy dark clouds sat heavy on the hillside. Another snow storm would hit before the end of the day. At least the cold might keep people from visiting their neighbors.

Tara pulled the dishtowel over the sides of the basket and tucked them in tightly.

"Kaly said that a woman from Philadelphia died a few weeks ago," Tara said. "Did you find anything out about her?"

Marika shook her head. "Amelia just moved into Jack Kelly's rooming house near Audrey James. Audrey said she had a son. Mrs. James thought she was running from either violence or the law. She kept to herself."

"No one to mourn her passing," Tara said. She lifted the basket slightly, seemingly anxious to get on her way. Her skin was pale and translucent, her eyes milky, the look of a woman not really well.

"Shall I take that food over to Audrey?" Marika asked. She didn't want to insult Tara but she didn't think she should be out wandering the streets. Especially since a cold might not be just a cold. As far as she could see, half the time the flu started with a cold.

Tara pulled the basket tight in a close, protective hug. "I can do it. You might ask Dan's Elizabeth about that girl. Elizabeth lived at Jack Kelly's for a bit."

The clouds darkened, the crow cawed and spread his black wings across the sky, and jealousy hit Marika so hard it took her breath away. Dan's Elizabeth.

"It was the flu with that woman, right?" Tara was asking.

Marika shrugged, like nothing mattered.

Tara lifted an eyebrow. It reached the top of the wool stitches on her hat. The crow had landed on a sign, twisting his head toward them, wanting in on a secret. It was a secret Marika held close. She would not think about Dan's Elizabeth.

Somewhere on the hill a whistle blew and bells clanged. A group of miners crowded into the underground cage and asked to be brought up to surface. Their shift had ended.

"She definitely died from the flu," Marika finally said.

"With a little shove in that direction?"

Marika didn't know.

That didn't stop Tara from guessing. "So, Audrey was right. She was running from something."

"Just not fast enough."

Tara McClane shook her head. "I better deliver these," she said. "How many do you have for the dead wagon today?" Her throat quivered and her voice cracked. Her eyes had gone quiet and narrow.

"Three since yesterday from Dr. Fletcher's office. Who knows how many showed up at other doctors' offices or the hospital?"

"Or didn't get out of bed in the first place."

———

The large room inside the hospital bustled with women signing up for the nursing classes. Dust motes hung in the small bits of sun sneaking through the windows. The last person Marika expected to see was Elizabeth Jordan, Dan's Elizabeth.

"Hello," Elizabeth said, a smile in her eyes. Dark curls bounced and touched her shoulders as she came to stand by Marika. She wore a pink sweater over a white blouse. A soft gray skirt hung halfway down her calves. A gauze mask covered her mouth and nose. "I met you with Danny at the bakery a couple weeks ago. You are Marika, right?" Elizabeth had an earnest sing-song voice. It must be the voice that she used with the children she taught.

And they must love her for it, Marika thought. Of course, it didn't mean that Marika needed to love her. It didn't mean that Dan loved her!

Marika pulled her mask up over her mouth and nose and ran a hand across her flat black hair. "Yes, I met you at the bakery," she said. She didn't say that Dan hated to be called Danny. He'd told her so on their one date to the Columbia Gardens, where the electric airplanes flew and the colorful carousel horses galloped in circles.

"You're married to Michael, right?"

Just blurt it out that I'm not available and Dan is all

yours, she thought. "Yes, I am." Her chest tightened in dismay. Ninety thousand people in town and she had to run into Elizabeth. Dan's Elizabeth. She had to run into the one person who, by doing nothing at all, could send her into a fury. Couldn't she please just grow up for once and for all?

"Since the schools are closed and I can't teach, I thought I'd get certified as a nursing assistant. That way I can still help those in need. I have so much to learn. Are you here for the nursing classes?"

"I am," Marika said, trying hard to find her tongue. What was wrong with her? She was married to Michael. She loved Michael.

The nurses at the front table called out a list of names. "Well, okay. That's me," Elizabeth said. "We might be in the same classes. I'll look for you there."

"Thank you. We have so much to learn," she said, repeating Elizabeth's earlier phrase. Marika felt a fool. Of course, they had a lot to learn. The town needed as much medical help as they could get. Elizabeth had already signed and left by the time Marika calmed her emotions. She had completely forgotten to ask her about Amelia.

When Marika walked out of the brick building heavy clouds had mixed with the soot filled air and she blamed the dark sky for her sour mood.

And her sour mood was perfect, because there sat Derrick Boggins watching the prospective nursing students leave the building. He stood and stepped in next to a young girl with short black hair.

"Derrick," Marika called out.

He turned abruptly. "Oh, it's you."

She pulled her coat tight and raced up to catch up to him. "I thought you'd come by to check on Amelia, after you dropped her off at Dr. Fletcher's office."

"No need. I barely knew the girl. I figured she was in good hands." He gazed back toward the short-haired brunette just as she turned a corner and disappeared. "I am sorry she didn't make it. I had hope for her."

"Which makes me wonder why you weren't just a bit more curious."

"I was. But it wasn't my business." His voice was calm, even. He tilted his head, tipping the fedora, and turning his cool gray eyes on her.

That stopped her. She'd been taking her bad mood out on Derrick. But feeling the fool seemed to be the order of the day. "No worry," she said. "Did she ever mention her father to you?"

"Like I said, I barely knew her."

"She mentioned him before she died."

His face was flat and still, betraying nothing.

It was almost enough to shut her up. But it just seemed so odd. Amelia had yelled at him. *What did you do to her?* Stella. It was Stella. What did he do to Stella?

Someone opened a window in one of the hospital rooms. An older woman stepped into an automobile that had been waiting for her. The streets had emptied out, the chatter of the nursing students moving on until nothing was left but the memory of their laughter.

Derrick shook his head and started to walk away from her.

Marika knew that she should be quiet, should let him go. But she didn't. "And who, pray tell, was Stella?"

When he turned those gray eyes on her this time, she felt something electric shoot right through her whole body.

"Leave it," he said simply.

And she did, walking home befuddled, feeling more foolish than ever.

———————

In the end, Marika had needed few qualifications for the nursing classes. No one cared that she'd been working in Dr. Fletcher's office over the last year. In fact, the only qualification she seemed to need was to be alive and breathing. And she had that mastered.

The classes were held in a school gymnasium and the classes were full. The instructor, a big boned woman who meant business and knew her business, rushed through crash courses on the body, germs, the psychology of sickness, family matters, blood pressure, broken bones, infections, common and rare. She talked about prison nursing for those who wanted to go over to Deer Lodge and work with the sick prisoners, of which there were many. Influenza had evidently taken its own prisoners and put several to rest. There were classes on attitude and demeanor, how to inspire confidence in your patient. How to convince your patient to rest. And how to keep yourself safe.

"Nurses are dying," she said, her cap pinned tightly to her bushy hair. "We need you to stay alive, so that others will live."

Marika looked over and Elizabeth nodded at her. It was a sisterly nod, like they were in it together. That they needed to stay alive. Marika smiled and nodded back. They were. And they did. Rule number one: stay alive. Jealousy, be damned.

"We are losing eight to ten people a day of influenza," the instructor said.

An eerie silence crossed the room. She let that small bit of information sink in before she spoke again. "You will wear your masks. You will wash your hands with soap and water every time you even think the word 'pee'."

The room did a collective gasp and giggle. Marika caught Elizabeth's eye again. They needed this information. Marika had been watching people die since late September, when Amelia first arrived at the doctor's office. According to Tara, Elizabeth had lived at Jack Kelly's boarding house. How well had she known Amelia?

When the class finished and Marika walked into the doctor's medical clinic, Dr. Fletcher and Miss Parsons were arguing.

"You can't go up to the hospital every day before coming to the clinic," Miss Parsons said. "That place is teaming with bugs. And you'll end up bringing every last one of them back here with you. If a person wasn't sick before they arrived here, they'll get sick the minute they walk through that door."

"You haven't. She hasn't," Dr. Fletcher pointed at Marika.

"I'm older. It isn't after me. And Marika," she said, as if Marika wasn't standing right there, "is too stubborn to get sick."

Marika smiled and nodded. True. She was her father's

daughter: strong, opinionated. Papa missed the changes in the town, the Granite Mountain fire, Frank Little, the anger, the strike, and now the flu. Papa, lucky Papa, he missed it all. His heart would have been broken in a thousand ways to see the changes. "Has the dead wagon come yet?" she asked.

"No. They should be here any time," Miss Parsons said.

"Has John Hurt said anything else about Amelia?" Marika wanted to know about the woman, find out what brought her to Butte, find family to take her son home.

Dr. Fletcher shook his head and then nodded. "Seems pretty obvious she died of the flu. Although, Hurt said that she had some marks on her neck indicating that she'd been in a fight before coming in to the office. The striations on her neck were not normal. She escaped death only to be taken by the flu."

A flash of light cool spirals rose and settled in the room leaving a vaporous red hue to the air. It sent icy shards down Marika's spine. *The striations at her neck were not normal.* Amelia had sat up fast on the cot in the sick room, asking about her son, wanting to get back to her son, trying to protect the one thing most important to her. She never did get back to him. And that thought, so potent and sad, nearly dropped Marika to her knees. She braced herself against Miss Parsons' large wooden desk.

"She had a son, but no husband. She mentioned her father. But even that's a mystery," she said, as if this simple bit of information would satisfy the ghostly squall in the room.

"Yes, has anyone taken the boy from Jack Kelly?" Dr. Fletcher asked. "The child needs a proper home."

"He does," Marika agreed. "Maybe his mother was a fugitive?"

"Running from what?" Miss Parsons sighed, a touch of irritation in her voice. "It's not our job to know everything about everyone. Patients have a right to their privacy. Maybe she had a husband in another town who got sick and died. Maybe she was looking for a good life for her son. It's her business, not ours."

Marika shrugged and went into the back room. She couldn't shake the idea that somehow it was her business to figure out why the woman had died and where she got the marks of a fight, and if it was a fair fight.

Amelia clearly had her secrets, like everyone, but her secrets had led her to Butte and ultimately to some kind of violence and death. The flu might have killed her, but strong hands stopping her breath were not far behind.

She hadn't been running from the flu. She'd been running to the flu. The striations on her neck had blended with the blue gray of her skin and, in the end, were barely visible. Amelia's coat had been left in the sick room, folded and put on a shelf. Marika covered her hand with a cloth and reached into the pockets to see if the woman had carried a clue to her identity, to her family in Philadelphia. Most travelers did. A piece of paper crinkled under Marika's fingers. She pulled it out and unfolded it. The scribbled lead of the pencil had faded and fallen into the folds.

Still, it was readable: *J.K., Butte, Montana.*

Marika wrapped the paper in the cloth and put them both on top of the filing cabinet. Thinking of the nursing instructor's command: wash your hands with soap and water every time you think the word "pee," she rushed to the washroom to do just that.

THE WOLF DOG CHARGES

November 1918

* * *

THE WOLF DOG PUTS his long nose toward the sky and sniffs. He can't smell it but he knows it is out there, landing on milk cans, on a woman's mitten, in the blond braid of the miner's girl, on his work bundle. That wisp of a thing that enters the nose or mouth and comes in blood out the ears. The town carries an eerie silence, like an old forest, like a cave deep in the side of the mountain.

And then, one day the cold sun shines and the miners come out of their hovels. The flu is gone, they yell. It has come and it has gone. The doctors breathe a sigh of relief. The stores open. And word comes from the east that the war is over.

Victory is here. The war is over. The flu is over.

People from the town flood the streets in celebration. Stools and chairs populate the taverns again. Women and men crowd to standing room only. Music and poker resume in the back rooms of saloons and cafes.

Somewhere in the crowded tavern a man sweats as he drinks a shot of old rye. He puts his glass on the bar and bumps shoulders with the man standing next to him. He wipes the sweat off his brow and shakes the man's hand in an apology. He orders another drink. He is tired, from all the work, he thinks. The mines have been dark and dirty and the work hard. One more shot and he'll go home to the boarding house that Audrey James runs. He'll claim his bed for the night and sleep hard.

He drinks a second shot. The heat in the tavern is sweltering. He can't wait to get outside where the cold air will pelt his face. He needs that cold air. He walks outside and tries to get his legs to carry him. They take him partway down the street until they won't go another step. He sits down on the boardwalk in front of the men's clothing store and rests his weary bones.

A tiny wisp of something rounds the air in his lungs and multiplies. That wisp of something finds its way to his blood and bones. He doesn't know he carries the fatal germ with him. He has no way of knowing that somewhere in the mine or on the street or in the newly opened taverns, the smallest of small creatures has landed on his shoulders, or his long fingers, or caught a ride on the hem of his pants or his bootstrap. He has no way of knowing he transfers the creature by the film his sweating lips left on the shot glasses at the tavern, the shake of another's hand.

The wolf dog saunters by the miner on his way back to the bakery. He lifts his great nose to the air and howls. He howls and howls and waits until finally the bakery door opens. People hoot and holler inside the bakery. They dance a jig, share bread, and toast to freedom. Their laughter hurts the dog's ears. He follows the boy upstairs. When the boy snuggles back under the rumpled covers on the big couch, the wolf dog settles his great body next to the boy and he sleeps.

Chapter Ten

PEACE HAD COME. VICTORY was won. People hugged and kissed in the streets. The war was over!

Not a mask in sight.

The flu had gone the way of the war and all but vanished from the land.

People laughed and slapped each other on the backs, sharing beers and shots of whiskey. Marika walked with Michael to Dr. Fletcher's office ignoring the gloom in the sky, enjoying the new vitality of the town. The flu, the war, all bad things coming to an end.

Her brown skirt swayed against her legs and she enjoyed the soft feel of it. She enjoyed the feel of Michael's hand in hers, skin to skin, his sweet palm pressed against hers.

She felt sorry for others that couldn't feel the warm heart of love toward the world. She felt sorry for her old self who fought against every new possibility that didn't exactly match how she thought the world should be.

People danced in the streets, as the last of the flu slid around the corner. Marika rejoiced, swaying to the music from a nearby band. Never mind that she'd spent weeks feeling worn down and harsh toward Dr. Fletcher for being left alone with Amelia while she died. If only the good doctor would have simply said "thank you." But he never thanked her for being with Amelia, or any of the others. By now, there had been so many.

She ignored the lurking dread in her stomach, the sense that every day brought a new heartbreak. To celebrate the end of the war, she would forget the flu's bleak trail across town, sometimes taking whole families.

But today was a new day with Michael at her side, tall dark-haired Michael, with his wide flat nose and strong broad forehead. He took long easy strides and sent her heart a shiver. He was about as fine a man as any woman could want for a husband, if a woman wanted a husband, which Marika hadn't. Nevertheless, here she was, married, and better for it.

He pulled her hand close to his chest. She swooned at the simple gesture, her desire growing with their closeness. If they weren't careful, Mama would be getting those grandbabies, and Marika would be looking for sitting services so that she could still work at the clinic. But she was careful. They'd been careful, her passion overruled by logic most of the time.

Most was a terrible word.

Marika enjoyed the simple comfort of this man her father had chosen for her. When her father died and the world had crashed at her feet, Michael picked her up. When they got word of *Baba's* passing, Marika cried and cried while Michael sat nearby, a silent holding and support. He didn't try to fix it, or tell her not to cry. He just stayed close and that closeness was enough.

They crossed the street in front of the men's store. She heard the men in the tavern next door singing: "Oh bring my gold, laddies. There is no gold, laddies. Then bring my silver, laddies. The silver is all gone, laddies. What is left, pray tell. Copper is all that fills the well. Then bring my copper, laddies. Here is your copper, laddies. And make me a drink of whisky of rye. Give me a cheer and I'll give my copper to thy."

"Do they just make it up as they go along?" Marika laughed.

Michael grinned. "That singing is a bit painful."

She nodded, letting the lightheartedness come over her. It was a welcome change, after the rough time with Amelia and the others. "A wee bit," she said. "But who cares? Things will be better, and this wicked flu is leaving us."

"Do you really think it's nearly done with us?" Michael asked. "Men who would never miss a shift haven't shown up for work."

"Men?"

"At least three of them," he said. "Three days of missing

shifts. It's unusual. Not many can get by like that. There's no shortage of workers. Miners flood in from everywhere."

Marika nodded, tried to hold her tongue and failed. "And one of the missing people should be you. Not that you should get sick. I just don't like you up there. Look at what happened to Papa. It wasn't even an accident—just a slow corrosion of the lungs. Even without the flu, without accidents, it's dangerous."

"We've been through this. No one will take me seriously if I am not involved."

"What about what they did to Frank Little?"

Michael drew in a breath and let it go, as if drawing in the great expanse of the mining city and setting it free. "Men like him will have worked in vain if we don't carry on the fight."

She knew that he was right, but she couldn't admit it. She hated it that both he and Marko were in the mines every day. The accidents hadn't stopped. You'd think the Granite Mountain Mine fire would have been enough for a century, as if the earth had exacted its toll and the sacrifice had been paid up for generations.

But the mines of Butte had bottomless bellies. They never stopped claiming men's lives. Few of the men caught in landslides, or fires, or poisonous gases ever made it to Dr. Fletcher's office or the hospital. They simply made it out to one of Butte's cemeteries where only the mountains stood guard.

"So, I was right," she said quietly as they turned onto Broadway.

Michael cocked his head and looked at her, his dark eyes catching her heart in a way that made her crazy, sparking a desire that made her yearn for his touch. She hadn't known that she could love like this.

"I fought with Papa about marrying a miner. I said he'd be lost to the mines and I'd be left alone to raise our children."

Michael exhaled slowly, nodding his head. "So, you do want to have children?" His smile lit up the sky.

She punched his arm. "Stop it. I'm serious." She didn't look at him because he'd see the glint in her eyes, her lips upturned and delighted.

"It couldn't have been easy for you, this arranged marriage.

You don't like to be told what to do. I've witnessed your stubbornness." He nudged her with his shoulder.

"Two of a kind, me and you." A crow landed on a nearby roof and tilted its head.

"I know you don't want me working up there," Michael was saying. "But it's the right thing for now." He pulled her into a fully public hug.

"Michael. People will talk." She leaned into him for a brief moment before pulling away, and hiding another smile.

"The horror," he said. "In the street in broad daylight. Of the Mining City."

She shrugged. "I guess they don't bat an eye at the Line."

"Which is right there." Michael pointed toward Mercury Street and the Alley. And he was right. Conscience was big, but morality was slim in Butte.

She stood on her tiptoes and kissed him, slow and sweet, for anyone to see. "There. That's settled. Let's go."

But he wasn't so quick. "You want children, right?"

"Yes, but not now. We'll talk about it another time. I need to be at the doctor's office."

He took her hand and they continued walking.

When they stopped in front of Dr. Fletcher's office, she could see through the windows that people were already waiting for the doctor. Another busy day. That was okay. Busy days went by quickly. She would probably learn a lot today. Dr. Fletcher had finally put her to good use. And the nursing classes had really helped boost both her knowledge and her confidence.

Now she needed to somehow get herself to medical school—with Michael's blessing, of course. He'd bristled at her avoidance of the one topic she refused to discuss with him: children. It wasn't fair to him. But having children before she got her doctor's training wasn't fair to her, she thought, feeling childish, thinking in terms of fairness. So much in Butte was anything but fair. This killer flu, the mines, the taverns. Not one of them took favorites.

"See you at dinner tonight?" Michael asked.

The crow had followed them and now sat atop of the doctor's roof. She looked up and it cawed, the pitch eerie and strange. When she looked back at Michael he was waiting, eyes on her.

"Hopefully we don't have another Amelia today," she said.

He nodded. "I don't think there was anything you could have done to save her."

"Like so many patients. Michael, if I had my medical training I could do something for them."

"You already do something. Your grandmother taught you plenty. And you learn every day. You've been in the nursing classes. You stay up late at night reading Dr. Fletcher's books. You're a natural for healing." He smiled that broad smile at her again, and her knees went weak.

"I'd better get in there to help. And you'd better get to work," she said. "Although, I wonder the wisdom of it, if men are still falling ill. You all work in close quarters down there. Even a good ventilation system won't help much."

Michael said nothing. He looked out toward the mountains. Clouds hung thick in the town, casting shadows, and trapping an acid smell in the streets, evaporating the hope she'd felt earlier.

"I don't want to lose you," she said, feeling shy and confused. They'd been married for a year and a half, and she was still getting to know him.

"I'll be careful," he said.

"I hope the flu really is almost over." She brushed her hair out her eyes. "It's hard to know for sure, with the way it just blew in on the wind by itself."

"Well, we have fresh air in the west," he said. "Where the wind can continue to blow it on its way."

She squished up her nose at his play on her words. Michael kissed her on that squished up nose and left for the hill.

Chapter Eleven

"HEY, HEY," THE LOUD knock and voice came from downstairs, where the doors had already been locked.

"We're closed," Kaly whispered to Tara. They were together upstairs in Kaly's apartment, where the children were sleeping. The wolf dog lay on the floor next to them. "Leave it and they'll go away. Probably someone who's been drinking too much."

"It's okay. I'll just shoo them away politely. No hard feelings then." Kaly and the dog watched Tara go down the stairs, smoke wafting in through an open window.

Except for the banging on the door, the town held an eerie silence. It had been lively just a week ago, the flu gone, the war over. Then suddenly a hundred citizens took to their beds and the town went quiet.

Tara opened the door.

Kaly could hear a man's voice. "I'm sorry to come calling after hours, but I've got instructions to shut this place down until further notice."

"Why shut down?" Tara asked. She'd been letting customers in to eat. Orders of closures had been lifted. She ran the handkerchief over her forehead. Her voice held steady and deep, a voice not many would want to challenge. "On what grounds? We've done nothing wrong. We follow the laws."

Kaly didn't like it. The flu had exploded in the town after the parades and celebrations of peace, and dozens of good men and women toasting to victory. But the flu was back. Those same dozens, thinking they were safe, had fallen prey to it. Kaly didn't believe in safety now. She didn't want anyone bringing the flu in to the bakery to infect her children.

"Nothing you've done. Except, the claim of victory over the flu was foolish. The board says the illness is back with a vengeance. We already have hundreds more sick in the county. We're just taking precautions."

"But it had all slowed down," Tara said, the voice of authority.

"Well, it's beefed up again. Shortness of breath, high fever, blue tinge to the skin, black patches on the cheeks. It's nasty and quick as ever. Stay home and tend the fires. Lock your doors. Take no chances."

"This is wrong. People can't survive if they can't eat!" Tara started to ring her hands, stopped and put them on her hips. Kaly felt a cold chill come up the stairs. The dog sat on his haunches and let out a soft moan.

"Saloons are shut to all but take out again. I don't make the rules. I just enforce them. And spread the bad word. Please do not open in the morning, not your front door, or your back door. Or you'll have five of me at both doors. And that won't be good." His voice grew instantly gruff and sounded weary, as if he'd been saying the same thing over and over.

Kaly smelled the bread baking. Good bread that people would want, to make their homes stays more comfortable. Good bread that they wouldn't get if Tara closed the bakery.

She heard Tara say good-bye and close the door. Annie cried and she went to check on her. George had wandered out and sat on the couch with sleepy eyes. The dog lay down next to him. Kaly smiled to think of what might happen if anyone threatened the boy with that dog nearby. The thought gave her comfort. They'd think twice.

The kids didn't feel good, but they had none of the symptoms the man had just described. No blue tinge to their lips. Slight fevers, but not bad. No shortness of breath. No black patches on their skin. Kaly let out the breath she hadn't known she'd been holding. Annie and George most likely had colds. It bothered her that they'd both gotten sick at the same time. But everyone said that this flu didn't go after the young or the old. It'd come for her before it'd go after her kids.

With the bakery and schools closed, she'd have plenty of time to take care of them. As she approached Annie's crib, she heard a stifled sound that strangled her heart. "Hey, hey now," she said in a sudden panic, leaning over to make sure Annie was breathing. If she could cry she could breathe. Kaly picked her up. Annie's head lulled back and her eyes fluttered. Her cheeks were flush and her little body radiant.

Tara came in the door. "Is she okay?"

"Her fever is up."

Tara put a hand on Annie's forehead. "We'll get it down with a sponge bath. Babies get little fevers at times."

Kaly knew that. Her heart beat so fast as she rocked Annie, humming quietly.

Annie tried to cry but it was barely a whimper.

Kaly knew her daughter had good lungs. She'd heard the girl cry when she was hungry or her diaper was wet, or last year when she had colic. The whimper scared her. "It's okay darling. We're here."

The dog whined at her feet. He looked at George and at her, throwing his head at the boy. He'd gone back to sleep. When the dog paced back and forth between George and Kaly, she hooked Annie to her hip and went over to George.

The dog pawed her. He usually didn't give her the time of day. She looked at George and she saw red splotches on his forehead. When she felt it, she knew his fever had spiked too.

"Better get another rag," Kaly said, motioning to George. Tara shook her head and went back downstairs. No questions asked. Neither of them wanted to say the unthinkable, that the flu had come into their safe home.

The next day, with the bakery closed and time on her hands, Tara fixed a big meal for lunch. Danny sat at the lunch table with Elizabeth, Marika and Tara. They all seemed to be waiting on Kaly. After tending to George and putting Annie in her crib to sleep, Kaly left the door open, listening for the slightest sound. She didn't want to but she joined the others at the table.

"You have to eat," Tara said.

"Elizabeth can't stay long anyway," Dan said. "She's needed for a family down on South Dakota Street. Two children and two parents. They're all sick."

No one answered Dan. Elizabeth looked down at her

lap. Marika had turned her head toward the open door. Kaly didn't know what Marika's problem was but Kaly felt bad, like she should thank Elizabeth for taking care of the sick. Still, she had her own sick children right here to worry about.

Dan said grace. He seemed especially edgy. But who wouldn't be with all the death surrounding them, and now with Elizabeth nursing the ill. Kaly didn't know Elizabeth, but she seemed nice enough, and Dan seemed to like her. It seemed her feelings were mutual, with how close she sat to him. What could possibly be wrong with that?

Tara served split pea soup and meat loaf. Marika pushed her meatloaf around on her plate. Wanting the lunch to be done, Kaly ate a bite of meatloaf. It felt dry and rubbery in her mouth.

"You lived at Jack Kelly's for a bit?" Marika surprised Kaly with the question to Elizabeth.

"I did," Elizabeth said. "He's a fine man, hears a lot of stories."

"Did you know a woman named Amelia?" Marika asked.

Elizabeth nodded. "We were there together for a couple of days. She had a young son. I was sad to hear that she passed on."

"Does she have relatives?" Marika got right to the point.

Elizabeth looked at Dan, as if looking for permission. But Kaly didn't think that could be the case. She probably just didn't feel comfortable with the tension in the room, or by being interrogated by this woman she barely knew.

"Marika," Kaly said. "Let her eat her lunch. She has to leave soon."

"It's alright," Elizabeth said. "She told me that she couldn't believe her luck. She'd followed a man she thought she'd loved at one time. He just happened to be coming to a town where a special person lived. 'A magical coincidence,' she had said."

"Magical coincidence? Did she tell you more?" Marika asked.

Elizabeth shook her head. "I asked, but she didn't want to jinx it. Said she'd tell me as soon as she could."

Tara had pot pies baking and the oven threw off a sweltering heat.

Elizabeth looked around, looking uncomfortable. Kaly felt uncomfortable too. She couldn't know if it was Marika's abrupt questions, or Kaly's own distraction, or a little bit of both. She didn't like to be rude, but she excused herself anyway.

As if on cue, Elizabeth also excused herself. Marika stood and thanked both Elizabeth and Tara, and said she wanted to look in on the children. Tara had a befuddled look on her face at the table of half-eaten lunches as everyone dispersed.

Dan walked Elizabeth to the door. He had to be worried, Kaly thought. He couldn't know how Elizabeth would fare. According to Marika, their nursing instructor taught them about keeping themselves safe. Hopefully, Elizabeth would follow the protocol. She didn't want to see Danny hurt by any potential illness she might contract. And she sure didn't want anyone bringing the flu back to the bakery.

Annie and George were both sleeping when Marika looked in on them. She went to Annie's bedside, pushed her hair back, and put a hand on her forehead. "Her fever is down."

A dark shadow crossed Marika's face that made Kaly's heart drop. She'd been so good at avoiding love. Since Anne Marie died, Kaly tried to protect herself from any possibility of loss. And now she had gone and fallen in love with her daughter. And Annie was sick.

"George has no fever. He might just be tired," Marika was saying. She pulled her brown skirt under her and sat next to him to assess the situation better. "What do you hear from Tommy?" she asked.

"I haven't read his latest letter yet." A lilting sing-song voice offered an optimism Kaly didn't feel. She hadn't known that loving him could feel so good. And now all of that was about to end. Shame seeped out through her cheeks, making her face warm, certain that Tommy's love was a big mistake, as was that of her mother, her children, even the dog. Any day now, they'd all wake up and realize it. Any day now, God would take them all and she'd be punished for her failings.

Kaly wanted to shake off the dark feeling, to sit quietly and read Tommy's letter, but Marika's abrupt tone with Elizabeth bothered her. "What were you thinking?"

Marika gave her a look that Kaly couldn't read.

"You can't think Elizabeth had anything to do with Amelia's death."

Marika shook her head. "The boy still needs his family. I thought Amelia might have talked to her about relatives."

"You sounded jealous."

"There is that." She smiled. "I'm a fool."

"With a perfectly good husband."

"True," Marika said, rolling the sleeves of her sweater up, and looking sheepish. "I'm sorry. At least we know Amelia came to Butte looking for someone special."

"And following someone she once thought was special," Kaly said.

———————

After Marika left, Kaly sat quietly in the room with the children. She pulled Tommy's letter out of her skirt pocket. She placed it next to her cheek, and gazed at the painted pink peonies on the wall, one of the things she had rescued from her crib before moving into the small apartment above the Silver Bow Bakery. Tara had painted it when she was pregnant with Kaly and Anne Marie. She had given it to Kaly last year.

Kaly had also kept the red satin dress. It hung quietly on the wall, a reminder of the life she'd lived. When she married Tommy and moved into the bakery, a lifetime of being an outsider had been swooped up and packed away. But not the red dress. The red dress was hers. That life had been hers, and was part of the mother she'd be. She had to keep it. Otherwise, she knew that shame would envelope her and keep her from loving honestly.

Annie and George had opened her heart and she didn't want to close it.

"It stays." She had said the words so deliberately about the red dress, so confidently that she'd barely recognized her own voice. "It served a purpose, brutal as it was. It brought me here. Not one part of me gets left behind, not the infant left at Miss Anderson's, not the sad ten-year-old who found her sister dead, not the girl who entered the District way too young. They all come with me." That was the agreement she had made with Tara McClane.

Her brother, Dan, had no qualms about any of it. He

simply wanted her in his life. He wanted to get well and get back to work. He wanted to go overseas and fight for justice. He'd joined the military before the mine accident. The poisoned air of that disaster, and his exposure to it, had done something to his heart, and he was no longer considered eligible. He took it in stride. "I'll work here for justice, then," he'd said. But Kaly had seen the grief in his eyes.

The smooth paper of Tommy's letter felt cool against her skin. She turned on a light to read by. The lead from his pencil had been dark but not thick, portraying a serious mood. She took a breath and read.

> *My Dearest Kaly,*
>
> *I hope my letter finds you well. Another month will have passed by the time you read it. I wish I could report day by day. But they keep us so busy here. Right now I'm in the mess tent, soon to be assigned to the hospital tent. It seems my time helping at the Granite Mountain fire was time spent well. They see I am good in an emergency. And there is no shortage of emergencies here.*
>
> *Hopefully I'll be home soon. The rumors fly around camp that the war is soon to end. But how, I don't know. We have no real way to find the news. We know only what they tell us. My commander is a good man who does his best to keep us informed. So far, he's said nothing about an end to this. Still, I have hope.*
>
> *But enough about me. How are the children? Growing and growing I suspect. It will be a full year since I've seen them. I hear the flu is bad here and there. People are dying at unlikely rates. Please keep out of harm's way and stay in. In London they've closed the schools, markets, and churches. They had a fight on their hands closing the taverns. A much stickier matter for sure. Some say it came from Spain. Others say an American soldier brought the germs over. I'm only grateful it hasn't touched our platoon yet. I've had a cold, but nothing devastating.*
>
> *I better sign off for now. Much love to you and the children.*
>
> > *Forever yours,*
> > *Tommy*

Kaly kissed the letter and put it away. The war was over. It had ended in the time it took for Tommy's letter to get to her. He'd be home soon and she couldn't wait.

She had a second letter, one for George. She opened it.

Dear son,

I've not much to say. It's cold here but that is good for the heart. I think of you every day and hope you know how much I love you. I'll be home soon and we'll play some ball. I know your mother is taking good care of you.

Love you so much,
Forever your father

And a third, for Annie:

My little girl,

You are much too young to read this, but I have to say it anyway, I love you beyond the mountains and their wild moon. You make me so happy. That first glimpse of your face changed my life. I'm so happy to have spent those few days with you before I left for the boat. You'll be nearly grown up by the time I get back, having passed a whole year of your life. Please, always know how much I love you.

Forever your father

Kaly folded the letters and put them away, thinking about the time they had shared before he left. It was like nothing she'd ever known. She'd let her guard down and felt real love for the first time since Anne Marie died. Also, when Annie was born, Kaly felt instant love. It was immediate. She would fight off a bear or a tiger or this sickness to keep her child safe. The nagging thought came back to Kaly: Why hadn't Tara done the same? Why hadn't she fought to keep her children safe?

Or maybe she had. At least in her mind. She'd explained it to Kaly several times, but Kaly still didn't understand it. Kaly would continue street work to feed her children if she had to.

But she didn't have to. Tara had given her the chance to

work the bakery and live in the small apartment above it, an opportunity that Kaly had set aside all pride to take. For Annie. For George. He had grown on her with a quieter, simpler kind of love. He was hers as much as Annie. She'd taken him in and wasn't about to let him go.

Kaly got the dog in the deal too, because George wasn't about to let that dog go. The dog was sweet and a good protector. He had soft gray fur, pointy ears and great brown eyes. He watched over George like part of the pack.

Tara came through the door. "The bakery is closed indefinitely, until the flu passes."

"It's just as well." Kaly thought about Annie and George. "They've been sleeping a lot. Should I take them over to Dr. Fletcher's? Or call him to come here?" It was odd to trust her mother's judgment at this late date.

"Keep an eye on them," Tara said. "Most flus affect the young. They say this one is different." She took off her checkered apron and folded it over her arm. "You barely touched your lunch. When you get hungry, I've got pot pies and pasties downstairs that need to be eaten."

"Or delivered to those too sick to get out for food," Kaly said.

Tara shook her head. "I'll send Danny."

"I can't sit here and do nothing." But Kaly knew that she couldn't leave her children, even though she wanted to help.

Tara nodded, as if she truly knew her own daughter. As if she'd spent a lifetime watching her from the shadows, which Kaly now suspected she had. "I'll do it," Tara said. "I'll be careful. I'll wash up good before I come back upstairs."

Chapter Twelve

THE FLU HAD COME back with a vengeance, as if it were furious that people had danced in the streets and hugged each other. Marika had been a fool to think it gone, even for a day.

The war was over. People were happy. But now they were all sick.

Deathly sick. Businesses went quiet again, even the taverns. Every bar had signs posted, ordering people to take their bottles elsewhere. All the stools, chairs, and tables had been removed.

Marika took the trolley south, across Silver Bow Creek, to the cemetery on South Montana Street. A brisk breeze blew through the open windows, cleaning the air. Only one other person rode in the car that day, a young woman who scribbled furiously in her journal. Marika wondered what stories she told. Did she tell of the trains that crossed the Divide from the east, or of the barren granite boulders that covered the pass? Did she tell of Cally Mike, the bum, trying to kill himself? Or of the four dogs following him? Did she tell of the copper kings fighting each other for silver ore? Or did she talk about the miners packed into the cage and being dropped into the shaft, day after day, the flu picking them off one by one?

Marika wanted to tell a happy story. But she was on her way to another funeral, for another stranger, thinking no one should be buried alone. The same dead wagon that had taken Amelia out to the Mountain View Cemetery made its way to the back of the Montana Street Cemetery. A bitter wind blew the sulfur out and around the town, stirring the soot and mixing it with clouds rather than cleaning the air.

If only she could go out to the Columbia Gardens, like she had with Dan, a quiet lifetime ago. In the summertime, wind blew the air clean at the Gardens. Water rippled under a bridge into a tiny lake. The most magnificent pansy gardens lined the hillside and music flowed from the dancehalls. Children hopped the merry-go-rounds, threw their heads back, and laughed.

Snow covered those gardens now, the children of summer tucked away in their homes, waiting for the flu to pass. We are all waiting for this devil to pass, she thought. That's what Marika would've written in her journal.

Winter had already come to the mountain tops along the East Ridge. Snow covered their tips. The pines brightened as the sun came out from behind the clouds and seemed to watch over the barren cemeteries.

She missed the wild beauty of her homeland, where jagged peaks reached for the sky and protected reckless travelers. So many years ago, as a young girl in the mountains of Montenegro, Marika had stood by her mother as her mother watched for Papa's return from the front lines. She had turned to her mother and asked if Papa would come home. Her mother had shrugged her shoulders and crossed her heart. Marika could see the broken lines in her mother's face. She felt the love and wisdom that grew out of those lines and a heart that had been sealed up and broken open.

Papa came home that time. He rebuilt the corral and milked the goat so that Mama could turn the milk to kefir. He dug the rocky dirt up where Mama planted the beans and lettuce. Fresh tomatoes somehow grew in that harsh soil between the boulders. Papa and Mama made *kruske* from the pears at the edge of the property. When they came home from the fields, Marika could smell the wild thyme and the salt of the land. She saw the love in their eyes and her heart sang.

John Hurt drove the dead wagon. The wooden wheels clattered all the way to the far end of the cemetery. She left the trolley and walked to the back of the cemetery where a pauper's grave had been dug. She arrived in time to see the grave diggers pull the wooden casket against their dirt stained trousers. Bits of earth slid into the hole as they settled the box with a touch of kindness. It was as if death had its own life here, specters watching to make sure the workers honored the new inhabitant well.

Not so long ago, Marika had said a quiet prayer for Amelia, from Philadelphia, with a son on the hill. She had been buried alone with her secrets. There had been no family to attend, and no way to get word to her family.

She watched as this new casket slid into the grave. This man, someone's loved one, had expired yesterday from a two-day bout with the flu. Two days. That was a quick demise. She didn't know his name. He'd come on the train to work in the mines and worked one week before missing a shift. He had lived at Audrey James' boarding house. Audrey had sent a runner for the doctor. The doctor sent Marika.

By the time she got there he was unconscious. Marika had stayed with him until he took his last breath. She'd watched his chest wither, as his spirit sat up and took leave. She'd crossed herself and watched him go.

No one should pass from this life to the next without someone nearby to witness their passing. No one should be buried alone. Rules to live by. Rules she hadn't known she'd had.

Standing there with the cold mountain looking down on them she thought about the life this man might have lived. Amelia, too. What life could she have lived. She did know something about Amelia. She'd had that white line around her mouth. She'd fought with Derrick Boggins, a man who'd been to Mama's house for dinner. Amelia had come to Butte in search of someone. Someone special. Some magical coincidence. She couldn't shake the feeling that the magical coincidence had been part of her demise. She thought about that note in Amelia's coat pocket. *J.K., Butte, Montana.* What could it mean?

While the grave diggers buried the miner, Marika stood next to John Hurt and the dead wagon. The horses were well-tamed and needed no whip. She inhaled their rich, earthy smell. She pulled her coat tight against the cold.

"You are still thinking about that girl, aren't you?" he asked.

"It just isn't adding up," she said.

He nodded. "That white line."

"And that smell." A sickly-sweet smell. "So different from that putrid smell of the flu, like something deep in the body rotting. The sweet, the rot, the smells mixed together. It's confusing."

"You think she had help?" he asked.

Marika shrugged. "I might be making up things, but that smell could kill."

"Maybe it did," he said.

She lifted her eyebrows.

"A person could blame the flu for a death and go on his merry way."

"Or her way," Marika said.

Hurt tilted his head to that. "I hate to think so, that she could've gotten better."

"Me too," Marika said. "She was really sick. I watched her suffer."

John bit his lip. "Maybe he wanted to stop her suffering."

The clouds thickened, dropping a gray blanket over the day. The cemetery felt lonely and desolate, and she was glad that John Hurt was there with her. One of the grave diggers hummed as he shoveled dirt onto the wooden casket. His voice was soft and light and barely audible, but it helped her feel the presence of the dead around her. It allowed her own loneliness to soar away toward the mountains.

Marika walked into Mama's house and smelled the rich aroma of beef stew.

"Welcome, *Kceri*," Mama said, using the Serbian word for daughter.

Marika kissed her mother on both cheeks. "That stew smells so good!"

Mama smiled. She took Marika's coat and put it on the only cot in the sleeping room. Before Papa died and before Marika married, they had all four slept in there. A candle burned on the chest of drawers, between a picture of the Mother Mary holding Baby Jesus and a picture of Papa. In the picture, Papa wore a red holiday vest, bordered in gold brocade, over a white ruffled shirt. He wore a black cap with a gold tussle on it. He looked regal, his eyes nearly black and filled with wisdom.

Michael had helped Marko turn the washroom into another bedroom. It would have been improper for Mama and Marko to sleep in the same room now that both Papa and Marika had gone. They had made the small home larger, scavenging wood left over from the temporary morgue built to hold the dead from the big mining disaster.

Marika refused to go into Marko's room, spooked by the knowledge that Frank Hoffman, the man with the flowered bibs, and Bert Brown, Kaly's worst enemy, had all lain on those boards as corpses. They had not breathed their last breaths there, but once there, they would never breathe again. Marika shivered, thinking about it. She believed too much in ghosts to go into that room.

If Marko had ever complained about nightmares or disturbed sleep, or had asked for her help, she would have come in with a prayer to cleanse that room. But Marko was too proud, too much like Papa. He would simply stiff-upper-lip it until he moved out of the house. Then the ghosts would be Mama's problem. Mama wouldn't ask for help either. She would just shoo the spirits away with candles and prayer.

Marika turned her attention from the candle to the main room with its lovely aroma of stew and cornbread. Derrick sat at Mama's table with Michael and Marko. She hadn't expected him again. Michael stood to greet Marika, taking her hand and kissing her on both cheeks.

Michael's hand felt clammy in hers and she let it go. Heat rushed into her face and her heart beat quickly. A chill went through her as the sickly, sweet smell hit her nose, as if a gale from the cemetery had followed her home. Use the branches of wild rose bushes to help the dead move on, Baba had told her.

Derrick bowed his head and put the tips of his fingers together. He was silent for a minute and she could hear him breathing. "Now that I've had a chance to think about it," he said slowly. "Amelia did come to Butte on the same train as I did. I didn't know her, but she had an uncanny way of showing up wherever I tossed my hat. I'd gather my courage to talk to her, and she'd disappear. It was strange, as if fate conspired against us ever meeting." He looked slowly around the room. "And now I guess it has."

"Did she seem sick on the train?" Marika asked.

"Not at all. Whenever I saw her, she was having a grand time," Derrick said.

"But I am confused, she sounded like she knew you."

"She must have mistaken me for someone else," Derrick said. "I've seen it before with this kind of sickness."

Marika remembered that it was a dark night when he brought Amelia to the doctor's office. She'd felt the darkness wrap around them as if he'd brought a shroud with the girl and dumped them both on the doctor's sickbed. The angel of death already had Amelia in his grip. Marika just hadn't known it.

Amelia yelled at him, "What did you do to her?" Marika wondered. He hadn't taken kindly to it when Marika asked him about Stella. He'd gotten cold and silent, piercing her with those eyes.

At one time, Marika had hoped that love could cure all sickness and sorrow, that kindness and care could bring Amelia through this flu, to the other side where she could one day plant pansies with her son. She could walk him to school, his tiny hand in hers. She could ask him each day what he'd learned.

But Amelia was gone. There was nothing she could do about it. Now here sat Derrick, claiming that they'd traveled on the same train to Montana. She would have thought Derrick would deny that he was there that night. If he had, Marika would have suspected him of foul play. But he didn't deny it.

Her mind darted in every direction, first suspicious and then berating herself for feeling that way. Can't a man just be a man, she asked herself, without some dark secret attached? He was here because Michael had invited him. She'd treat him politely. That was her father's voice booming in her head.

But a quieter voice, one as still as hope, said something else. Be careful here, it said. Be careful.

She took the quiet warning to heart and sat next to her husband.

Mama put the stew on the table and cut large squares of cornbread, lifting out a piece for each person. Then she poured milk. She did it all in a timid way. A fearful way, which was not Mama's way. Marika wondered if she was ill.

Mama sat quietly, running her palms under her rust colored skirt, tucking it underneath her. That told Marika she was not comfortable in her own home. Did Mama feel it too? She tried to catch Mama's eye, but she avoided Marika's gaze, asking Michael to say the blessing.

"Any good whiskey to go with that milk?" Derrick asked, stopping the blessing. His sharp chin pointed up. Tiny eyes looked down over his nose.

Marika folded her hands. "After dinner we'll have some *rakija*," Marika said, wondering why she, the girl, had to be the one to speak up. She looked at Michael and waited.

"Bless this food, this delicious stew that Mama made. Thank you, Lord, for providing carrots, potatoes, and a slice of beef for our meal. Thank you for friendship and family and for good health and good work. Bless all at this table, all up on the hill working the mines, and all in the town. Bless the priest. Bless our armed forces and our president. Amen."

"Thank you, Michael," Marko said.

Marika had almost forgotten he was there. She looked over at him as he dipped his cornbread. Evidently, he had no more to say.

Derrick pulled at his chin. He'd taken his small round hat off at the door and she could see the ghost of it pressing his hair down.

"So, you came to Butte from Philadelphia?" She asked what she knew.

"Yes," Derrick said.

"Any ideas about how to reach Amelia's family? Her family needs to know."

"I didn't know her well."

Marika raised her eyebrows. "She sounded like you knew some of the same people from the dress factory."

"It confuses me too. We did work together. But we rarely spoke." Derrick rolled a carrot around in his bowl and then quickly popped it into his mouth. "She just wasn't in her right mind."

"Could the factory help us find her next of kin," Marika said, not wanting to let it go. She looked over at Michael, who seemed to be following the conversation with interest. She looked around the table and all eyes were on Marika and Derrick.

"Perhaps."

"You sound doubtful."

He looked up with tears in his eyes. "It's just that so many have died. There may be no one left to tell her story."

That thought hurt Marika's heart. Perhaps she was over-thinking Derrick. Maybe he was just another miner down on his luck, looking for a job. Just another transient, a bit of a drifter, like so many others who came to Butte.

Then his eyes glowed with a strange, mischievous, almost cruel shine, sending a cold shiver down Marika's spine, pasting her to her chair. She picked up her fork and ate a piece of meat.

Mama looked at Derrick and then turned to Marko. "Will you bring in wood after dinner? The evenings are getting much cooler."

"Sure, Mama," her brother said, brushing his dark hair back away from his face. Grime from the mine lined his brow. He was trying to save up enough money to open his own small shop. He'd gotten on bartending a couple nights at the Casino and was hoping that might translate into something bigger. She couldn't tell if Marko was quiet because he was tired or if he felt the tension in the room. A welcomed guest no one seemed to welcome. Except Michael. Strong-headed, fear-fighting Michael.

"Do you work tonight?" she asked her brother.

"Take out only. They don't need me." He looked worried. The extra money helped a lot, with a little bit going each week into a secret pot for Mama. The two of them had decided to buy their mother a sewing machine as soon as they could. That way Mama could do mending from her own home, instead of having to wait for someone else's machine and only being paid pennies for piece work.

Derrick finished a potato he had mashed into the stew broth. "What a shame, closing down the taverns. Let the people have some fun."

Suddenly, every hair on Marika's arms went up, as if she'd

been standing in the line of lightning. She didn't know where it came from, but there it was again, that sickly, sweet smell, faint this time and quickly dissolving, a whispered memory. This man was wrapped in a smoky veil. Was she being overly dramatic? She didn't care. She did not trust him.

"That girl might have brought it," he was saying.

"Why do you think that?" Marko asked.

Derrick looked at Marika. "She was so sick, right after she got off of the train. She may have had it on the train." He shrugged. "People have been sick ever since."

The idea sank to the pit of her stomach and Marika lost her already frail appetite. "Why didn't you get it. It spreads like wildfire."

He smiled. "I don't know. I had a touch of something in August, but nothing now. I do have a strong constitution."

The way things were going, it looked as if this flu could not give a wit's ass about constitution, Marika thought. But she kept it to herself. Mama would not have her swearing at the dinner table.

"Anyone could have boarded that train already sick," Marko said.

Marika nodded. It wasn't fair to blame Amelia. She was one of dozens of boarders on the train. She gave Marko a narrow-eyed questioning look, willing him to read her mind. She felt certain he saw it too.

Something was off with this man. She looked around the table. Mama quietly ate. Michael happily wiped his cornbread in the last of the stew gravy. Marko studied his plate.

Derrick flashed his strange cool eyes at Marika, daring her to sort it out.

THE WOLF DOG AND
A THOUSAND DEVILS

December 1918

* * *

IF THE WOLF DOG could have traveled back in time and known Amelia in Philadelphia, he would have seen her working hard every day at the dress factory, her sewing machine humming with dozens of others, taking a break when her fingers cramped and her back hurt. He'd watch her marvel in enchantment with Derrick, when he takes up residence at the machine next to hers. But Derrick doesn't pay her any attention at first, his sights set on Noel. She's a dark brunette who arrives alone to the dress factory, looking skinny and ragged. She has a good sense of humor and uses it to keep her distance from others. Amelia doesn't mind. She wants to make money, not friends, so that she and Little Tony can have a good life. Little Tony is beautiful and whole, a little boy to match the best of her dreams.

Amelia brings Little Tony to work, and he finds his way into Noel's heart. Noel volunteers to watch him during her breaks. Amelia hesitates, not knowing the woman. But her affection seems harmless and finally Amelia relents. Tony smiles up at the woman, cooing, waving his little legs and arms when she arrives. Noel smiles at the boy and at Amelia, warming her affections.

Then Derrick starts courting Noel who spends her breaks with the man for nearly a month. Amelia doesn't hide her joy when Noel comes around again. Tony is thrilled that she is back. Derrick is sullen.

When Noel stops coming to work, Amelia figures she's sick with the flu. So many are sick. Unlike many businesses, the dress factory stays open, making masks to protect the people and making uniforms for the soldiers. More and more people don't come to back to the factory, leaving a vast mountain of work for the ones who do. People die by the dozens, according to the newspapers. This flu outdoes anything in modern history.

Amelia gets Noel's address from a supervisor and goes to visit, only to be told by the landlord that she moved out the month before. The landlord, a Mr. Peters, has no knowledge of her getting sick, or of where she went. He only knows that she took very little with her, leaving behind a handful of clothes and a tiny set of baby pajamas.

Derrick then takes up with Rosa, a brilliant young woman who is dark-haired like Amelia and Noel. She's one of the best seamstresses in the shop. Rosa has a flare for design and the owners of the dress shop don't stop her from creating the designs. They don't pay her extra for them, but they do put them on market. It turns out that Rosa's creations sell well. Women love her sense of design, even if they don't know the designs are Rosa's.

But then Rosa disappears.

Amelia looks for her at her home, a room in a large Victorian boarding house. The elderly widow who runs it opens the door cautiously. Amelia explains Rosa and her stunning dresses. The woman's gray curls barely move as she shakes her head in dismay, a sad smile crossing her face, saying that Rosa has gone. That she left without a word. She left her things and the woman keeps hoping she'll return. She's been a great help with the other tenants and she has a way with a wrench and a hammer.

It's eerily similar to what Amelia had heard about Noel. No, as far as the landlady knows, Rosa hadn't gotten sick. She just left suddenly, leaving behind a perfectly good drawing board and several stylish designs.

Derrick looks tearfully at Amelia from his machine.

Almost against her will, she feels badly for him, grief about her husband's passing still in her throat. She shares her lunch hour with him, Little Tony laughing at the man's antics.

Louisa and Mary get sick. Louisa recovers but Mary dies. The funerals are too many. Soon public funerals are disallowed. The papers report the closing of businesses due to a shortage of workers. But the dress company keeps people working. People can't feed themselves without the work. They wear masks and garlic, or lavender, or a bit of rose water, and say extra prayers.

Amelia continues to work. She has no one left to take care of Tony if she falters. She goes hungry many nights so that Tony can eat, and she prays that he'll avoid the contagion. He had it once and that was enough. Perhaps he is immune now.

Louisa comes back to work, weak and pale. Derrick helps her carry bolts of material to the cutting table. Amelia notices the terrified look in Louisa's eyes as he approaches her. She turns away from him and trips. He catches her as she falls. Louisa has trouble righting herself as she tries to avoid his grasp. She's like a caterpillar crawling as fast as it can, but unable to escape the boot stepping down on it.

One day Louisa stops coming to work.

Derrick cries to Amelia, big generous tears, and laments that everyone he loves leaves him or dies. He'll never love again, he swears. Amelia tries to convince him otherwise. Love is good, she says. She and Anthony loved each other. They had laughed and cried, made meatballs and smoked cigarettes. They took Little Tony on picnics and watched him smile at the trees. She has lost Anthony, but it doesn't stop her from loving Little Tony.

Derrick takes up courting Amelia. And Amelia enjoys his company. But after the first week, something odd happens. His eyes turn glazy, and she gets a creeping feeling crawling up her spine. She thinks she is coming down with the flu and panics for Little Tony. She goes to her landlady and begs her to take Tony and care for him if she dies.

Her mother has already passed on. She has never met her father. And she has no siblings. She only has Little Tony and he only has her.

But she has no fever. No cough. No trouble breathing. Just this odd creeping feeling. It's the same fear that she saw in Louisa's eyes, the fear that she imagines Noel and Rosa might have felt.

That's what the wolf dog would see if he'd been in Philadelphia with Amelia: that awful hair-raising sensation flooding her body every time Derrick turned his eyes on her.

But the wolf dog doesn't go back in time. He doesn't cross the continent. He roams the streets of Butte afraid for this boy. The dog prances down Broadway in the December sun, large flakes crusting his head, sniffing the air that stinks of illness. He wanders over to South Idaho Street and up past the hospital, where ambulances run day and night, bringing the sick back to the crowded rooms. Some are taken away in black cars and driven down Montana Street where the dead rest.

The wolf dog trots past the church on South Idaho, where the doors are locked up and candles burn in an outside bin. A woman in fingerless mittens pushes her hair back and lights a candle, putting the wick to the flame of another, sharing the prayer. He runs past the large, airy school that has been turned into a hospital. Women gather there in clean skirts. With earnest voices they offer comfort to the sick and the dying.

They rejoice when a man sits up in his bed and says he's starving and he would like a sandwich.

The dog walks past the Casino and the Copper Tavern looking for soup bones, or biscuits, or even a soft hand to pat his head. He sees the women of the streets, out on the streets. They all rush past him, hurrying back inside the buildings.

He feels the thousand devils in the air, in the snow, on the hoof of a well-trained horse. He can't see them. But he knows when they have passed, and he sees the trail of devastation they have left

The trouble starts when Amelia arrives in Butte. It's not her trouble. She's barely here for it. It's the boy's trouble. He feels poorly, has a cold that weakens his system.

The dog wanders down Broadway Street. Everywhere he goes he smells that odd disturbance coming from the homes. It's the same odor Amelia smelled at the dress factory. He hears random moans, mournful echoes.

He whimpers at the door of the bakery until it opens and he climbs the stairs to the boy, who sits up to pet him. "Shhh, dog," the boy says. "Shhh."

Chapter Thirteen

KALY DIPPED A CLOTH in the cool water and wiped George's forehead. He was burning up. The cloth heated instantly as it absorbed his fever. He coughed relentlessly, struggling to breath. He saw things she didn't see: a spirit in the corner; gray shadows hovering over her, miners and dogs filling the small room. Every time he went into a coughing fit Kaly held him close, feeling helpless.

The wolf dog sat by his side, not uttering a sound. Kaly had no doubt that the dog would absorb the sickness and take it in if he could, to protect the boy. He would die for George. The wolf dog loved him in that crazy, full way that only parents and a dog can love. Kaly loved George, too, with a fierceness she hadn't known she possessed.

A year ago, she had run from love. Every chance she got. She'd been alone and she liked it that way. But, now? She'd fight for George. He would live. She'd will it so. Like she'd done when she was a kid and tried to bring her sister back to life. But that hadn't worked out. Anne Marie had died.

This time, she would not let herself fail.

And this was George—beautiful, angry, delightful, alive George. He would get better. She lay the cool cloth on his forehead, pulled it across his face. Steam lifted off the red mounds of his cheeks. He moaned and pushed at the cloth like it hurt. Tears filled his eyes.

"Kaly," he whispered. "Am I going to die?"

He asked it as if he'd read her mind, seeing the death that she saw. But Anne Marie had been blue. George was pale, not blue. Not yet.

"No, no, no. You are going to live. The doctor will be here soon."

"I hurt," he said.

The dog lifted his head and tilted it toward George. A soft moan came from deep in the dog's throat.

"Where's Annie?"

He was hard to hear and Kaly put her ear close to his mouth. The smell tried to push her back but she wasn't having it. Nothing would push her away from him now.

"Annie?"

He nodded and winced, as if the pain had gripped him at once.

"She is downstairs with Nana."

"Annie will get sick too."

"No. She went with her grandmother as soon as your fever hit." Gratitude filled Kaly. Tara would keep Annie safe. "You've got a fever, but nothing that Dr. Fletcher can't take care of. I want you to drink some water. I'll hold the cup for you and you have to try to swallow, okay?"

Kaly held the cup to him. The water spilled over the sides of his mouth, but he did swallow. She dipped the rag again and pulled the heat from his forehead.

She stopped only to get more cool water. When she returned, he'd fallen asleep. But that didn't stop her. She had to get that fever down. It had to help, she kept telling herself as she waited for the doctor.

Kaly woke up with her head on George's bed, next to his tiny shoulders. A sour smell wafted off him and she hoped it was the sickness leaving his body. At first, she was disoriented. The window was dark. Then she heard the knock at the door and remembered she had sent for the doctor. How long ago was that?

She put her ear next to George's mouth and listened. His breathing was raspy, shallow, and then coming in great gulps. Lifting the weight of herself out of the chair, she listened for her mother and Annie. Why hadn't Tara answered the door? She dragged her stocking feet across the floor and noticed the chill. The fire had gone out while she slept.

Marika was behind the door. She wore a pale pink skirt

and a tan sweater vest, her black hair in a severe bun. In her dark brown eyes, Kaly could see a weariness, and a wariness.

"Where's the doctor?" Kaly blurted. She didn't mean to be rude. But George was really sick. He needed a real doctor.

"He sent me," Marika said simply. She pushed a black leather bag ahead of her as she stepped through the door without an invitation. She went directly to George's bed, took the seat Kaly had been using, and set her bag down. She opened it, pulled out a thermometer, and put it in his mouth.

Marika shook her head when she looked at it. "It's way too high. One hundred three degrees,".

"I've been putting cool cloths on his forehead," Kaly said, relenting and grateful that Marika was there. Fear had exhausted her. George was starting to get that blue tinge to his skin. She was terrified of losing him.

Soft humming came from a room downstairs. Tara was singing to Annie, calming her, maybe putting her down to sleep. Once Annie recovered, they had agreed to keep her in a separate room from George. They had agreed that Tara would keep Annie safe while Kaly helped George get better. What irony, Kaly thought, leaving her daughter in the hands of the mother she'd never had. Life was the strangest thing.

"I gave him some morphine for the pain. It should help his breathing too," Marika was saying. "Will you get another pan of cool water and a fresh cloth? We'll keep working to get this fever down."

Kaly felt herself almost separate from her body, wanting to dissolve into the air like she had when she was a kid when Burt Brown was on her. She had only herself to save then. But this time it wasn't about her. It was about George and the flu. She needed every ounce of her soul's strength to help him.

Kaly had refused Marika's offer to stay with George while she got some rest, but wasn't surprised when the knock came at the door. The woman was determined, if nothing else. Kaly turned her head toward the knock, but then ignored it. She didn't need Marika right now. She had been a great comfort, but she could do nothing more for George, nothing that Kaly couldn't do. Besides, the room had to be filled with germs. The illness was a heavy, dark specter. This cursed flu had no discretion. Young, old, rich, or poor, the illness didn't care.

The knock persisted and then got louder.

Finally, Kaly gave in.

Beth stood there with a bouquet of dried sunflowers, the very last of the fall foliage.

"It is December, you know," Kaly said. "How long have those things been around?"

Beth shrugged and handed the long stems to Kaly.

"You can't come in," Kaly said, sounding harsher than she meant to, but wanting to warn her friend away. "George has got the flu."

"Well, don't beat around the bush. Get right to the point." Beth smiled and her smile felt good to Kaly. She had been so scared. She took a deep breath in the momentary reprieve. In her black wool coat, black felt hat, and soft blue dress, Beth looked beautiful. She had loosely pinned her dark curls up under the hat and several had fallen gently around her face. She was lousy with hairpins and it worked well for her. The soft wisps of hair accented her high cheekbones and sweet eyes.

Beth stepped inside.

Kaly stepped in front of her. Her own ragged dress, stained with George's sweat and bits of blood that had spilled from his mouth, sagged on her shoulders. She worried that the monster had woven itself into the fabric. "You'll get it," she said.

"I've got syphilis," Beth replied. "Bert Brown's departing gift. I'm dying anyway. Let me help."

"I won't be the one to kill you." Kaly was adamant. She would not kill her best friend. Beth had taken her in, given her a home, bought her a dress, and taught Kaly the maneuverings of the Red-Light District. Kaly had tried to warn Beth about Bert Brown, but Beth loved the man anyway. But this was different: she could stop Beth from coming in.

"I'd rather die of this sickness than the pox. It'll be faster, less painful, and far less humiliating," she said. "If he survives, he's going to need you."

"He's going to live," Kaly said with as much conviction as

she had ever mustered. "I'm not leaving his side."

"You're as likely to get it as I am. Let me tend to him while you get some sleep. You look terrible."

Kaly had been up well over twenty-four hours, taking care of George. She stepped aside so that Beth could come in. "Stay if you want, but I'm not leaving until his fever breaks. It came down while Marika was here earlier, but then spiked again this evening."

On the couch, George twisted and groaned.

Kaly rushed to him with Beth right behind her. The wolf dog lifted his head off his paws, looking at George and then at the women. Kaly put the water glass to his mouth. He swallowed and some water spilled down his chin again. But maybe this time he took in a little more of it. She could still feel the heat radiating off of him.

She could hear Annie cooing to Tara downstairs, and Tara cooing back. Kaly sniffed the air. Her mother had made chicken soup. It was comforting, hearing her daughter from a safe distance. As hard as it was for Kaly to forgive her mother, she was relieved and thankful that Tara had pressed for a relationship. Kaly would not have wanted Annie in this room. Without Tara, she would have been faced with an impossible choice: take care of George or protect Annie.

"He's like a little oven," Beth sat at his side. "I can feel the heat from here."

Kaly nodded toward the open windows. A stiff breeze pushed the curtains back into the room like sheer red arms, angry and desperate to get free. "I'm trying to keep the room frigid, but he's still so hot. There is some chicken broth on the stove that should be cool by now. You want to try giving him some?"

Beth nodded.

Kaly brought it to her and sat down next to her.

When George fell back to sleep, the women shifted their chairs a bit away from him, so as not to wake him with their voices.

"Two of the girls at Miss Lottie's have died," her friend said. "Miss Lottie is really sick. She got better and then sick again. This time, they don't know if she is going to make it.

The girls want her to go to the hospital, but the hospital is full and she is low priority."

"Don't worry," Kaly said. "Nothing could kill that woman. She's too mean."

Beth laughed and took off her coat, letting the rest of her curls fall to her shoulders. "True," she said, her voice soft, like she only half believed it. And even if she did, she maybe didn't like the odds. "She'll just scare the bugs out of her."

"Does she know you have the pox?"

Beth shook her head.

"You have to tell her. You can't go back there when this flu ends. You know she'll want you working."

"Not once she knows the money is missing."

"Yeah. That's another problem."

Beth lowered her voice to a near whisper. "Kaly, since I found out, I haven't been entertaining men. I know it would be a death sentence to them." She looked wistful, lost. "But I don't know how many I infected before I found out."

"What have you told Miss Lottie?"

"That I'm sick. Sometimes, I negotiate with the men and do other things...things that won't infect them."

"You have to tell her."

"I will. Eventually. I'll have nowhere to go when she kicks me out."

"You'll stay here with us."

Beth nodded, that wistful look deepening in her eyes. "Annie is downstairs?"

"With Tara." Kaly caught Beth's disapproval when she called her mother by her first name. "Forgive me if I hold a grudge," she said.

"Forgive bull. You want revenge. I know you, Kay."

"Not revenge. I can't get over the fact that she only claimed me when she wanted me to talk Dan out of joining the army. She didn't even come forward when Anne Marie was murdered! I just can't get it to set right, no matter how hard I try."

"Try harder. She must have had her reasons."

"I just need more time."

"People are dying all over town. You might not have

time." Beth moved closer to George and soaked his forehead.

The boy looked up at them.

Beth lifted his head and poured some broth in his mouth. He spit it up almost immediately.

Kaly wiped his chin. She would see to it that he would live. She would not lose him. "How do you feel?" she asked him.

"I hurt," he said, "all over."

He really looked bad. His skin had turned grayish blue. His eyes were gaunt, his breathing labored. He sat up. "I need the bathroom."

Kaly helped him up and walked with him to the commode. The wolf dog followed them. He only left George's side when Kaly took him out to do his business. When George finished, she helped him back to the couch. The dog plopped down next to him. He will live, Kaly told herself again, the conviction strong in her heart. Cool air wafted in, freshening the room.

George will live.

Chapter Fourteen

MARIKA FELT DISCOURAGED AND sick. Not sick like the others, but sick at heart. The sky was dark gray, and this day of December brought a fierce wind with it. The wind picked up at about 4:00 each day, just before dark, the dark smelling of death. This afternoon four more people had come in with symptoms of the flu, a high fever, extreme weakness, difficulty breathing, and the telltale blue tinge to their skin. None of them had the sickly, sweet smell that Amelia'd had, nor the white line around the lips. Marika hoped this was a good sign for those in the sick room right now. Maybe their sickness hadn't gotten so bad that they would die from it.

But four people had died yesterday. There were more than a hundred new cases of influenza. Sixty-six patients were being treated for influenza at the hospital. Thirty-two people died from the influenza in the month of November. And that was after the flu was supposedly gone.

Dr. Fletcher had heard from the Board of Health. People wanted to go on with business as usual. Until they couldn't go on. Some doctors were calling the flu pneumonia, to avoid putting homes under quarantine. Then the Board designated pneumonia a contagious disease, too, which meant that it also required quarantine.

Dr. Fletcher wanted the sick ones out of the waiting room, where people came for common things like a sprained ankle. Miss Parsons and Marika waited for the ambulance to take the fluish four to the hospital. The nurses over there were troopers, but some of them had fallen ill too. That left the hospital short-handed.

They needed a system so that people could stay at home, and still alert the medical teams that someone in the house had the fever. The high fever and the blue lips told the most accurate story. Those people should not venture out into the public. But sick people wanting comfort came to the doctor. It's just what they did. But now coming to the doctor was also helping spread the flu.

She tried to get the feverish ones into the sick room, and then to the hospital. And she did as her grandmother had taught her: be quiet, and hold the sick in holy reverence. Ask for their quick return to health. The nursing classes were good, and she wasn't complaining. But she couldn't help wondering what she might do if she'd actually studied medicine at the university. Dr. Fletcher knew plenty, but it had been years since he'd been to school.

"Will you call the ambulance, please, and see what is taking them so long?" she asked Miss Parsons.

Uncharacteristically, Miss Parsons nodded. Normally she would snap that she only took orders from the doctor. Or she would ignore Marika altogether. Something had softened her. Miss Parsons had once been married to Dr. Fletcher, and although she adored the man, she would tell patients, she preferred working for him to fixing his nightly meals or picking up his socks. One job with any man was enough, she said.

"I'll call them," Miss Parsons was saying, "but they've been slow to arrive all week."

"It's scary," Marika said. "Have you ever seen this kind of sickness before?"

Miss Parsons shook her head. "This is the worst. And I've seen some bad things."

Marika heard the undertaker pull up. He had come for a young man who had died during the night. They had called for an ambulance but it never came. Not that it would have mattered. He died shortly after Miss Parsons made the call.

The undertaker knocked on the back door. Marika opened the door and found John Hurt standing there in his worn out brown jacket. Marika thought him too tired for the job.

They were all too tired for this job at the rate the deceased were piling up.

"What did you decide about Amelia?" Marika asked, after Hurt had loaded up the young man. "Did Amelia die of the flu? Or did she have help?"

He looked at Marika, his crooked nose edged by cautious eyes. He nodded and then he shook his head. "Yes. Definitely the flu. But there is something funny there."

Marika pulled her hair back into a leather tie to keep it out of her face. She tugged her shawl tight against the snow that was blowing down the alley. She thought about the young woman's soft eyes, her beautiful face, and the illness that had turned it blue and ravaged.

Hurt's horses neighed and kicked at the alley snow. Marika crinkled her nose at the raw smell of the them. A wild, alive smell. Soft moans came from the sick room. "They might have a chance," she said. "That's the same thing I keep thinking about Amelia."

"It's possible. A lot of people live through this. But a lot are dying. She arrived just before early October when several people died each day. Her odds weren't good."

Hurt really did look tired, frazzled, worn down. Not that it was her job to assess him. How he handled his difficult work was his business. Still, a little compassion never hurt. "It's been a hard day," she said.

"It has been a series of hard days. Every day the bodies pile up. Then those who were crying one day come in on the dead wagon the next day."

Marika turned her face to the wind, letting it wash over her and dissolve the smell of the young man in the dead wagon. "We don't know how to stop it," she said, wondering how the women in the Tenderloin ever keep themselves or their customers safe? How could they keep their children safe? And what would happen to the children if their mothers succumbed to the flu? "People are stubborn. They don't want to close their businesses."

John Hurt tapped his hat down. "It's a good idea, just not enforceable." He called out to the horses, and they pulled the wagon down the alley.

Marika stepped back inside and went back to hoping that the ambulances would get there soon.

———————

Later that evening, Marika brushed her hair out of her eyes and looked sideways at Michael. He waited, holding his cards close to his face, his glasses on the table. She smiled, shook her head, and lay down a full house, queens and kings. He put down four aces. She grimaced.

"Fine," she said. "Take your pennies. I'll make dinner."

"Don't be a sore loser," Michael said, all smiles.

"Easy for you to say, Mr. Lucky."

"No luck, just skill. My grandfather was a gambler. It's in my blood."

"What about the gamble you took with me? You're not disappointed, are you?" Even though Marika ran hot and cold with Michael, she wanted him to love her. She felt comforted in his presence. With this flu in town, comfort was the thing she needed most.

He hemmed and hawed, yawned, stood, and pulled her close. She felt his belt against her stomach. "You were the best bet I ever made," he said.

The heat rose through her legs, between her thighs, into her chest and neck. Her face felt warm and she pressed it into him, turning her ear to hear his heart beat.

"I couldn't be happier," he murmured, wrapping his arms around her and pulling her tighter, as if he just couldn't get close enough. "This," he whispered, "is true luck."

A soft, glowing sensation moved through her body, knowing that however much she loved him now, she would love him more later.

Someone knocked on the door.

Marika looked at Michael and shook her head "no." Then she instantly regretted it. It could be news about George. She hoped it wasn't bad news, and said a quick prayer.

Michael shrugged his shoulders and let her go. When he opened the door, Marko and Mama stood there with their hands full. Mama wore a full-length embroidered apron over her green dress, and a warm coat over that. She took off the scarf and coat, both wet from the light snow. Her dark hair was pulled into a tight bun at the nape of her neck.

Marko's mouth was turned down, his brown eyes peering out from under bushy eyebrows. He looked like he'd been dragged through the neighborhood for his dinner. With his dark eyes, wide flat nose and full lips, he already looked so much like their father. He'd been so annoying as a kid, making strange noises just to get a reaction out of her. She'd yell at him to stop it, or storm off in a fit, unable to control him, unable to control herself.

The truth was, she missed that boy. Since their father died, everything had changed. He was no longer a boy, and she was no longer the big sister that he was hell bent on disturbing. Throw in a rapidly spreading flu, and everything had changed again.

"You haven't eaten yet have you?" Mama asked. "We've got some delicious sarma here. It'll go bad with just the two of us."

"She went crazy grinding up the pork and beef, seasoning it and rolling it into enough cabbage leaves to feed the neighborhood," Marko said, turning his affectionate grin on Mama.

On Marika's second thought, he looked enough like their mother to see whose son he really was, as her parents used to argue when he misbehaved. "Did you see what your son did?" Papa would ask. "He's your son," Mama would counter, Marko looking back and forth at them to see who would win the argument, all attention taken off of him for the moment.

She felt a twinge of jealousy at the closeness that he and Mama had developed since Papa died and Marika married.

"Michael can eat for the whole neighborhood," Marika said. "And I'm starving."

Michael smiled at her and then at Mama. "You brought the sarma to the right place," he said.

"I'll set the table." Marika went to the kitchen cabinet and pulled out four heavy white plates. The room was now full of the scent of sweetly spiced meat and cooked cabbage. It was a kind, wonderful aroma that Marika remembered from their early years in Butte, and from the old country.

Mama had often made sarma back at home in their Black Mountains. She had made it for the family and for the village feasts. She made it for weddings and funerals. The smell brought a memory so sweet, Marika could almost hear the red kites whistling above the cooking fires.

After they ate, Mama asked about the flu. "How many now?" There was a catch in her voice. She folded her hands in her lap, as if holding a lovely wish that she wouldn't let go.

"Three today," Marika whispered. She could hardly bring herself to say it. Ever since the Board of Health had announced multiple deaths in a day, she had resisted the count. No. It was impossible. But not impossible, because a tragic number of deaths had taken place in October and November.

"I've talked to the store owners," Marko said. "People want their lives back."

"We are trying to keep people alive," she said, including herself with the perceived villains, hoping it would calm Marko. She thought of George, hoping he was through the worst of it. She worried about Marko being out and about, or down in the tunnels. She didn't want him anywhere near sick people.

"Well, I'm going stir crazy with so little to do," he said.

"Chop some wood for us. That'll burn some energy." Marika laughed, using her age-old tactic of getting her brother to do her chores.

Marko stood up, shrugged, and asked, "Where's the ax?"

"Really?"

"Yes, sister. I've got to do something."

"You don't need to do that," Michael said.

"Let him go," Mama pulled out a sweater she was knitting. A red ball of yarn slid off her lap onto the wooden floor. "Otherwise, he'll drive me crazy at home."

At home. Marika got another twinge of jealousy. She wanted to step back in time so she could fight with Papa, be annoyed by Marko, and help Mama cook.

When Marko finished, he was still antsy. "Mama will teach you to knit," Marika said with a sly smile, knowing that a boy would not knit a rope if his life depended on climbing out of a mining shaft with it.

"Mama?"

Mama shook her head in resignation. "Sit down. I've got an extra pair of needles here and some yarn." She put the knitting needles in his hands and taught him to cast on the stitches. "Not like that. Like this," she said, again and again.

Marika laughed and he glared at her.

"Cover your mouth," Michael whispered. "You might embarrass him and he'll stop."

Marika laughed again. "Marko, am I embarrassing you?"

He just glared at her again, a dark cloud passing in his eyes, annoyance more than anger. It felt funny to be on this side of annoyance. She suddenly understood the impulse to want to create more of it. Now, she realized why Marko had made more annoying noises when she asked him to stop. It was fun to be the annoyer. She shook her head and laughed again.

"Really, though, I think it's grand that you are learning to knit," she said. "You'll have hats to last the winter. And with this flu passing through town, blankets will be needed."

"See," he said, giving her a slight nod. "It's not such a silly idea now, is it?"

Michael's brow furrowed as he looked at her.

"You should've left more wood for him to cut if you didn't want him knitting," she said, picking up the dinner plates, putting them in the sink, and pouring heated water on them.

When Marko finally got the stitches cast on, Mama taught him a simple knit stitch. He held the needles as if they were some kind of foreign creatures, stiff little snakes that crawled into his hands unwanted.

"How can you wield an ax with all your might, but barely touch the knitting needles?" Mama asked. "They won't bite. Just twist one in over the other. Do it several times, stitch the piece together, and you'll have a hat."

Marko worked at it, getting a few rows on and tearing them out, starting over, getting a few more rows on, and tearing them out again. Finally, he had the beginnings of a good hat. Mama's extra yarn, a soft yellow ball, rolled out from under his chair.

Marika shuffled the deck, the cards fluttering through her hands like soft wings. "Get ready, husband, to get your butt kicked," she said. "I can see that my luck has changed."

Chapter Fifteen

KALY LOOKED FOR A letter from Tommy, but nothing arrived. It made her worry. She wanted him to know about how sick George had been. The sickness had touched Annie early on but left quickly, leaving her whole and just as curious as ever.

Kaly chewed the edge of her pencil, staring across the room. If only she could sit down with Tommy and tell him about George. It seemed cruel to tell him about George's sickness in a letter, especially since the boy hadn't fully recovered yet.

She focused on a new painting of lilac flowers that had hung on the wall. Tara had painted it in rich purples and greens while George was in the worst of his sickness. Tara had used a large piece of cardboard, since she didn't have a canvas. She had the paints and brushes, but no foundation. That seemed so much like Kaly's life: paints and brushes, but no foundation.

"Dear Tommy," she wrote and stopped. He has a right to know about George, she told herself. Maybe she could begin by telling him that she hadn't gotten sick herself.

She put the pencil down and walked over to where Annie was crawling on the floor under Tara's feet. George was drawing quietly, copying the lilac flowers and putting shadows where they hadn't been in the original picture. Annie crawled toward Kaly and laughed, giving her mother a huge smile just as the sun finally broke through the sooty air. Kaly wiped her daughter's nose with a clean rag, and Annie scooted away. Pulling herself up to stand next to the couch, Annie tossed a ball off the cushion and plopped back down to the floor. She rolled the ball to Kaly, who rolled it back. It was a simple game of trust. I roll it to you and I know you'll roll it back.

It was something so simple and pure it made Kaly feel like maybe their world had begun to right itself. Maybe things would be okay.

"Dog," Annie said.

"Over there with your brother," Kaly told her and pointed toward George, who was now drawing the dog, his pointed nose and ears, his fluffy tail, his dark, watchful eyes.

"Brother?" Annie inquired.

Kaly nodded, pointing again.

"Not feeling well," Annie said.

"Oh no, baby girl, he is much better."

"Go." Annie pulled herself to standing again, walked a few steps toward George, and fell down. "Mama, go to brother?"

George put down his pencil and held his arms out to her. Annie smiled and took off toward him. He caught her just as she fell again, laughing as he hugged her. She laughed and squished his face between her little hands. The wolf dog stood and rubbed his head into both of them, finding the place where he could get the most pets.

Kaly's heart broke in the best way, toward joy and pure appreciation. This is what I'll write to Tommy, she thought, picking up the pencil again. This shared love is the perfect thing to write in a letter to someone so far from home at the end of a war.

After she fed Annie and George some of Tara's chicken noodle soup, and Tara went back to her own apartment alone, Kaly put both children to bed. George didn't argue, but Annie wanted to stay up. She cried and screamed until she fell suddenly asleep. Kaly wondered how she could go from wild and violent one moment to completely peaceful the next.

Beth knocked on the door and came in quietly. "Two sleeping beauties," she said, pointing toward the children. The wolf dog lifted a lip to her and Kaly stopped him right away.

"You do not growl at her," Kaly told the dog in a stern voice.

He dropped his head, but his eyes followed Beth to the chair where she sat down.

"Tea?" Kaly asked.

"Please," Beth said. "I still don't feel great."

"Did you get the flu?"

"No, it's the pox. It makes me feel slightly under the weather all the time. The mercury treatments have helped others. I might try that."

Kaly shrugged. She didn't know much about the treatment, except that it turned a person's smile silver. If anyone could carry off a silver smile with style, it was Beth. Not only that, but it would announce to any informed person that sex with her was downright dangerous. It would keep men from forcing themselves on her. Finally, she'd be protected.

"I keep thinking about home," she said.

"Miss Lottie's?"

"Pfff, that's no one's home. No, my mama's home back in New York."

"New York?" This was the first Kaly had heard about her friend having a mama and a home. She had thought that Beth was orphaned at a young age, like Kaly and Anne Marie.

"My father was a good man until he drank. Then the devil came out in him. A dark, dirty devil. He got thrown in jail for beating my mama. I went to see him while he was there, but he wouldn't talk. Just stared at the wall, like he could crawl inside of it and never come out. After six weeks they let him out and he jumped off the bridge into the Hudson River."

"I'm sorry," Kaly said.

Beth shook her head. "Don't be. He was too mean to come home, and he had nowhere to go. I was nine years old and saw him take that last step."

"You followed him?"

Beth nodded. "I didn't know he was getting out that day. It was happenstance that I stopped by the jail for a visit and saw him walking. He didn't see me. I thought we could find a cheap café and have dinner together. I was happy to see him walk free."

"You never told me."

She waved a hand toward Kaly. "So much had happened by the time I met you."

"If you had a home, why did you leave?"

"Mama remarried, a man even meaner than my father. I

guess she had a hankering for mean men. I don't blame her. As a widow, she couldn't make enough money. She took in laundry, but that barely kept us from getting evicted. She needed my stepfather's income."

She looked up at Kaly, as if to see whether she was still listening. The tea water boiled and Kaly filled the teapot. She took two fragile cups with roses painted on the sides from the shelf and put them on saucers. Kaly didn't want Beth to stop talking. It was as if Beth finally trusted her, now that she was facing her mortality. "How old were you when you left home?" Kaly asked in a gentle tone.

"Twelve, going on a hundred." She laughed. "Mama and James had a baby boy. I took him out to the train yard each day to gather coal that had fallen from the cars. Sometimes, I'd climb up on top and knock a little extra off, so we'd be sure to have heat in those icy cold winters. The little tyke, Theodore, Teddy for short, sat aside and watched while I climbed the train car ladder. He was so sweet. I loved to pick him up and kiss his belly. One day, when I climbed down, he wasn't there."

Kaly sat still, afraid to breathe. She didn't want to know what came next. The story had formed a beat of its own lodged in her throat.

"He had wandered down the tracks. I looked and looked for him, some sign that he was alive somewhere. I walked all night between the rail yard and the river, calling his name. I just kept walking."

Kaly wanted to hold Beth and tell her that she was only twelve, a child in charge of a child. That it wasn't her fault. But she knew Beth too well to try that. Kaly understood what had just happened between them. She couldn't fix this, couldn't make it right for Beth. She could only be a witness to it.

She listened to the winter gusts rattle the windows while Annie and George slept, knowing that her children were safe, that George had begun to heal.

Finally, she spoke. "You are afraid you are dying."

Beth looked at her, tears in her eyes, something Kaly had rarely seen. "I pretended that my parents didn't exist. It would hurt less to leave than to stay, knowing what I had done."

Kaly nodded. "Have you ever told anyone before now?"

"No," Beth said, and let the word hang in the air. "I won't live long."

"Syphilis doesn't kill quickly."

"It's not that. The girls down on the line are getting sick right and left, and some are dying. I'm weak from the pox. I have no fight left, Kay." She lifted her eyes, a tiny bird looking up from the nest, milky eyes begging—not for food, but for understanding, for absolution.

Kaly stood to get the tea. She brought it over and fixed Beth's cup with just the right amount of sugar and milk. Then she fixed her own. Instead of drinking it, she reached across the small table for Beth's hand. It felt fragile and too warm in hers.

She sat there holding her oldest friend's hand, far into the night, long after the moon had come up and the wind had stopped blowing.

Chapter Sixteen

MARIKA DARED NOT GO into the house, a small brick structure with a wrought iron fence surrounding it. The place looked desolate and sad. The curtains were closed, but Marika knew what was inside. The monster. The flu. It was a sad state of affairs that had overtaken Butte. Tragic. No one knew what to do about it. Nurses and doctors wracked their brains and their bodies taking care of the sick ones, only to have them die. Then the caretakers died too.

The wrought iron fence looked like a solid defense against intruders. A dog could live in that yard without having its territory invaded by deer or cougar, or a bear or another dog. But there was no sign of a dog, no barking, no rushing feet toward her, no curled ball at the corner of the house. It was as quiet as the dead air in the mines must have been. The stunted trees had lost their needles. No chipmunks or squirrels climbed the branches. A hushed blanket of snow covered the yard.

It was her job to go into that house. Marika hated it that she had grown used to death, expected it. Still each death sent a panic through her, a sense deep inside of a life ending too soon. In all of her years of wanting to be a doctor, she hadn't expected this. She hadn't known that people would die daily from a disease with no cure. This flu took their strength and their breath. It turned them the color of the winter sky pummeled with clouds.

Marika wanted to make people better. She wanted to soothe them and take the sickness from them, to send it deep into the bowels of the monster it had crawled out of. But she had no comfort to offer the people of Butte. She had no comfort to offer the loved ones that they left behind.

She could not calm their fears. They all knew someone would be next. Everyday people died. Amelia had been a harbinger of all the things to come. This flu had come to Butte, looking for its next victims. And found them. And it all started about the same time that Amelia and Derrick arrived on that train. But it didn't end there. Marika knew she couldn't blame Derrick for hundreds of deaths. But she wanted to blame someone and there was just something wrong about him.

He had a cagey look about him that stirred a primitive fear in her. She'd seen him, stalking, scouring the town, demanding that some person acquiesce to his desires. She'd seen the glint in his eye when he brought Amelia to the door, too sick to survive.

Of course, the flu wasn't his fault, or anyone's. Still.

Marika studied the brown house. It stood alone in the field at the edge of town, not too far from the black head frame of one of the mines. Beyond the house, snow covered the Columbia Gardens, the beautiful pansy gardens, children's swings, the teeter totters, the boardwalk shops that sold popcorn, and the bench where she and Dan had kissed, the kiss she'd put aside to marry Michael.

Further up the pass, Elk Park cut a path through the mountains to Helena. The Highland Mountains rose on either side of the pass, the sky crisp and blue, dropping the temperature twenty degrees, freezing the land. Snow topped their peaks and covered the valley.

The mountains reminded her of Montenegro. The journey by boat to America felt like a thousand lifetimes ago. Marika yearned to see her homeland again, to take her medical skills, once she studied, to their small mountain village and help with the ill. Had the flu hit people there, too? How many had survived? It had not attacked Marika yet, but it could. It lived to kill. The stench of it was lodged in her nose and throat and would not leave, an uninvited, unwelcomed visitor. Go! She wanted to yell at it. The flu would only laugh. Yell all you want, it would say, I'm going nowhere but here and there. And everywhere.

It was everywhere, up every street, in every shop, in the

taverns. And in this house. She took a deep breath, knocked on the wooden door and waited for an answer she feared would not come. She'd brought soup by yesterday and soothed the miner with cool rags. Al Heaton had not been well. His nephew, Joseph, relieved Marika and agreed to stay with Al until he got better.

Marika knocked again. Nothing. She pushed the door open and was greeted by an eerie silence that crept through the small house. It did not feel welcoming. Something sour wafted out of the kitchen and the dim light was saturated with stale smoke, the walls dingy. She pulled her mask up, a soft white cotton that was getting worn out. Mama had lavender at home that she had distilled down to a fine oil, and Marika had put it on her mask. It helped.

She could leave right now. By the dank smell, she knew what she'd find. Making sure that the gauze cloth covered both her nose and her mouth, she stepped into death's shadow. A soft moan came from the back room. Marika hurried with her medical bag and found Al's nephew sick in a chair. Al was flopped across the bed, without a breath left in him. He had turned the dark blue of the devil, the painful ending evident in the wreckage of his body, his arms and legs flung over his bedside.

Joseph had thrown a couple blankets on the floor in a makeshift bed, where he'd apparently spent the night. Or maybe he'd spent it right in the chair where he sat, frozen in grief and illness. Something spilled on his white shirt and brown, threadbare trousers. Marika could see the stain.

"Come on," she said. "Let's put you out on the sofa." She wanted him out of that room. They would come and get Al's body in the noon rounds. Marika thought it better for him to be in a room where he could breathe the air of the living, not that anyone else was there. She pulled a blanket up over Al and said a quick prayer.

Helping Joseph walk to the living room sofa was not easy. He was a big man who must have topped two hundred pounds. His muscles had weakened and gone slack. He could barely hold himself up. With great effort she got him seated, then lifted his legs and turned him to lie down. A purple afghan lay neatly folded over the back of the sofa. Someone with a deft hand had crocheted it, maybe Al's mother or grandmother, or a wife he left when he traveled west to work in the mines. She pulled it over Joseph.

Finding rags and filling a pot with cold water, Marika set to work calming Joseph's fever. He burned hot, just like Al had done the day before. She could only do what she could do. And that wasn't much.

She'd spent her week waiting for the dead wagon. Now she waited again, wondering who would be next. Mama? Marko? Michael? No. She put the fear out of her mind. She was taking precautions. After the knitting lesson, she wouldn't let Marko and Mama come over, afraid she'd expose them to her germs.

As for Michael, well, try bossing him around. It'll get her nowhere.

He was stubborn and beautiful. He had helped her through so much. And now this flu. It had already taken hundreds of lives. How many more would succumb before it finished with the mining city?

The back door opened and startled her. She looked at Joseph and whispered, "Who is there?"

His eyelids drooped. He didn't answer.

Then a familiar face showed up in the kitchen.

"Oh, I didn't know anyone was here," Derrick said.

Marika's stomach turned.

"Hello," she said. "What are you doing here?"

"They've been letting me stay in the back shed. How is the old man today?"

The old man was dead, but Marika didn't say it. "I thought you were boarding at one of the rooming houses on South Idaho."

"Too crowded with the flu about. Is Joseph around? I just want to thank him and I'll be on my way." He wore his small brimmed hat tipped at an angle. She just didn't like that small brimmed hat.

"In the living room, sick." A terrible stench lifted off of Derrick, making the air thick and hard to breathe.

"Not Joseph! No."

"Why aren't you sick, Mr. Derrick?"

"Just lucky, I guess," he said. "And you?"

"Because I do God's work," she said. "Whose work are you doing?" She knew the answer but didn't say it.

He tilted his head and that hat slid sideways. "You know I work in the mines, like your husband."

"Fair enough." But nothing was fair. And certainly not Derrick Boggins.

"Just so you know, that's the same question she asked me," Derrick said.

"She?"

"Amelia." He took the hat off and pushed his sleeves up. "It's hot in here, yes?"

"What do you want?" Marika felt the hair on her arms stand up. She moved herself closer to the door.

"I told Amelia the same thing you told me. I'm doing God's work. She didn't like it, thought I was making a mockery of God. She thought I took the flu too lightly," he said. "You'll understand sometime soon." His voice was flat, subdued and contained, a cultivated art.

"That sounds like a threat," she said.

He twisted his head and stared at her. She felt paralyzed by his eyes, completely unable to move, even though she knew that was foolish.

"I've called John Hurt. He'll be here soon," she said, and turned toward Joseph, comforting herself in taking care of the man, something she knew. She felt the heat lifting off of him. She wiped his face with the cool rag, drenched the rag again in the cold water, and set it on his forehead. Marika repeated the steps again and again.

But Derrick didn't leave. And that frightened her.

He sat on the other end of the couch from her and pulled Joseph's feet out from under the afghan. They were black. "Not a good sign," he said, then tucked the afghan back around them. He patted them affectionately.

Derrick's foot patting went on and on. It felt like the slow burn of a wet log, the long drawn out moment before a light goes out and a gun is drawn. The stench in the room had gotten stronger, vile. A strong bile rose up in Marika, keeping her fear at bay. Derrick stopped and looked at her. Silence stretched out across the town and the frozen land.

"Did you follow me here?" she asked. No one could tell her if Joseph had given him permission to stay in their shed. Joseph was too sick to talk.

"No need to follow you. You're easy to find," he said.

Face fear. Don't run, Papa had said. But the rules for bear were different than the rules for cougar, and different still for a rabid dog. What were the rules for a man like this, one with a slow, matter-of-fact voice, and cold eyes?

Forget the eyes. Find a route out.

And do it now.

Outside she heard the dead wagon. She dropped the rag in the cool water, opened the door, and stood in full view. In the mountains, leaves might have frozen on their branches, eventually dropping to the ground, the sound soft and light, heard only by the wild things and the wind. But the dead in Butte made not a sound as Derrick Boggins slipped out the back door of Al Heaton's home.

John Hurt stepped up to the door. Marika shook all over. That stench filled her nose. She breathed the poisoned air that Derrick had left behind, the acrid smell of panic that froze in her belly.

"Al?" The undertaker asked, before she could decide to tell him about Derrick. She tried to appear calm, and he didn't seem to notice the change in Marika's demeanor. Or maybe he wrote it off to exhaustion. She would have.

He'd put on a fresh coat since Marika had seen him the previous day. Its stiff material looked new and shiny, and she focused on that, fabric being tangible and something she could count on.

John's son jumped out and opened the back door to the wagon. He looked to be about fifteen years old, but Marika knew him to be eighteen, one of Butte's proud graduates, a smart boy with a quick mind. He wore tattered trousers and a wrinkled white shirt, much different than the polished dress of his father. He pulled a rag up over his mouth and nose while keeping his eyes on Marika waiting for her to answer his father.

She nodded. "I was here last night," she said. "I wasn't certain that he'd make it. Joseph said he'd take care of him. By the time I got back this morning, Al was gone and Joseph was sick."

John Hurt nodded. "How bad?"

"Like the others. He's in there on the sofa right now. I doubt he even knows that his uncle has passed. He's pretty incoherent. Al's in the bedroom." Marika didn't mention Derrick, supposedly staying in the shed. She hugged herself in the cold, grateful for the cold. It snapped her to her senses.

"I'll get someone up here to sit with Joseph," the undertaker said, his eyes scanning the horizon.

"My teacher can come over," John's son said.

Marika raised her eyes. "Elizabeth?"

"Miss Jordan. Yes! She's been to nursing classes since the schools are closed. Our school is turned into a temporary hospital and she has been over there a lot."

"Now?" Marika asked. "I'll wait until she arrives." She wanted to ask one of them to wait with her, but it would take both of them to transfer Al to his final resting place.

———

Marika was sitting on the porch of Al Heaton's small brown house when Elizabeth arrived by trolley. She'd been in and out of the house, checking on Joseph, but afraid to stay. She hated it that an exchange with a man could make her shun her duties more than the deadly illness had in all these weeks.

Elizabeth walked briskly with nimble steps and Marika felt a mix of relief and dread, the clear, cool sting of them colliding in her chest. And then something she didn't expect: a strong sense of protectiveness. Elizabeth could not stay in the house alone with Derrick Boggins prowling the neighborhood.

"John Hurt sent me to relive you," she said and smiled at Marika. The smile faded. "You look tired. He's doing badly then."

Marika nodded. "He's not well. I don't know if he'll make it."

"You can go home and rest. I'll get one of the girls from the Red Cross to come help me. You look like you've had a fright."

Marika widened her eyes at that. A fright. Well, yes, she had. Was Elizabeth that perceptive?

The girl laughed. "Don't worry," she said. "I'm not reading your letters. I'm a school teacher. We spend our days trying to put out fires before they begin. It's on the job training to think on our feet and redirect trouble. Let's go in and see what we can do for him."

Marika went inside with Elizabeth. The awful stench of Derrick had begun to dissipate, but the smell of sickness remained. Joseph moaned and Elizabeth went to him. Marika followed. They started the ritual of placing a cool rag on his forehead trying to fight the fever.

Marika calmed herself, as her grandmother had taught her, feeling safer with Elizabeth there. She had questions and she thought Elizabeth might have some answers.

"The devil certainly turned back on him," Elizabeth said. She took her coat off and pushed her sleeves up. She wore a striped dress and a heavy sweater. "Will you put a log on the fire?" she asked.

Marika had forgotten all about the stove and it had nearly gone out.

When the room warmed up again and Joseph slept, Marika took advantage of the quiet. "Can you tell me anything else about Amelia from Jack Kelly's place?"

"Mmhmm," Elizabeth said and seemed to think about it. Her curls had fallen into ragged waves from the heat in the room. "She seemed afraid, like a wild animal, watching her back. But she talked to Kelly, trusted him for some reason. I caught snippets of the conversations."

"Anything you can tell me?"

"Hmmm. I probably shouldn't. But I guess it doesn't matter now that she's passed." She looked over at the fire and back to Joseph sleeping on the couch. She stood and adjusted the afghan.

"Yes?"

"Well, I might have misunderstood. These things aren't always right when eavesdropping," she said. She gave Marika a shy smile. "But I'm pretty sure she was pregnant."

Something cold rippled across Marika's stomach. She felt

the air thicken. "Any idea who the father was?"

"No. None," Elizabeth said. "But I could see that Jack Kelly felt bad for her. See, she followed a man out here. Someone she really liked at one time, but then things went bad. By the time she got to Butte, I think she was trying to find a safe home for her and the boy."

"Is the boy still with Jack?" Marika asked.

"Not sure. I've moved over to Audrey James. And I'm over at the school or up at the hospital with patients. Or out like this, in someone's home."

Marika felt the sadness sit down on her heart. Amelia might have been pregnant, a brother or sister for Little Tony, that he'd never know. The child was one more casualty of the flu, or whatever, whoever pushed Amelia to the other side.

Marika left Joseph in the hands of Elizabeth and a nurse named Marie from the health department. She had met Marie earlier in the week at a boarding house over on Placer Street. The boarding house was a stiff gray, with the paint rubbing off of the sides. Due to last year's Granite Mountain Mine disaster, it was overcrowded with widows and children. Marika didn't like leaving Elizabeth and Marie, but she was exhausted. And she had other things to do.

She headed for John Hurt's office where the room reeked of the flu's strange stench. The bodies had already been taken out to the cemetery, but the smell remained. Her clothes probably carried the stink too. The whole town reeked of the smell of the dead.

"How many today?" she asked.

"Five this morning and who knows how many more in the afternoon rounds," he said. "I don't have a lot of hope for Al's nephew. He looked as like to follow Al as anyone I've seen."

Marika nodded. It broke her heart for the boy. Hundreds of people were gone. The flu had the town spinning in its juices. People locked themselves away and were afraid of their neighbors. And of course, the quarantine insisted they do just that.

"That girl?" he said.

"Amelia?" She thought of what Elizabeth said. She might have been pregnant.

"I think she was poisoned."

"How?" Marika sounded more surprised than she felt. There was something wrong in the girl's death from the beginning. She wrung her hands in front of her, the raw red skin chapped.

"It might not have made a difference in her death, other than to hasten it slightly, maybe to her favor. She would have died from the flu anyway. But there were traces of chloroform around her mouth."

"That's used in surgeries, to control pain."

"The ring was around her mouth and nose, not under her nose like it might have been for a procedure."

"It wasn't an accident?"

"No."

"But who would kill a dying woman?" Someone who didn't want her to suffer? But no one knew she was going to die. No, the person who poisoned Amelia was playing God.

"Didn't you say someone delivered her to the doctor's office?"

"Derrick," she said. The building rumbled from a dynamite explosion in one of the mine tunnels, making her legs feel weak on the uncertain ground.

"He probably thought he saved her," John Hurt was saying.

Marika thought of Derrick's flat, subdued tone of voice, his cold eyes and the way that she felt paralyzed by his stare. She shook her head. "Or not," she said.

THE WOLF DOG HOWLS

January 1919

* * *

IN THE BEFORE TIME, before the flu comes to Butte, the wolf dog, or one of his ancient relatives, might follow Amelia around Philadelphia. There are empty streets where the vegetables rot on carts, where stacks of papers sit unread, and the fish market is as slow as a growing tree. He would see the fear in Amelia's eyes when yet another girl comes back to the garment factory, having recovered from the flu, and goes missing three days later.

Stella.

Amelia goes to her flat and bangs on the door until the landlord lets her in. They find Stella laid out quietly on her bed in a white nightgown, the covers pulled up to her waist, her gray hands on top of the covers at her side. She smells strangely sweet and her eyes are open. But they have lost their light. The dull, milky orbits stare out at nothing. Amelia feels unable to move, and the landlord calls the police.

Stella and the odor of death fill the room. The police arrive with an ambulance crew. But it is too late. The doctor states that she probably died of the flu. But Amelia knows she had already recovered from the flu, worked three days and then disappeared into her bed. Here. Alone.

Later, when Amelia tells Derrick, he drops his head. There is maybe a slight upturn to his lips. He says words of sympathy, but the words float uselessly off. They sound like the nothing that they are. Or maybe they sound too much like a quiet glee. Amelia notices his cold, uncaring attitude, and she says so.

He accuses her of being jealous. She questions herself, wondering if she is making it all up. Is she making up this sudden urge to break all things off with him, to never again let him near her son? What about this fear for her life? And worse, her fear for her son's life? She doesn't know. Derrick sounds so reasonable, but he gets so angry when she stands up to him. His chest grows and his voice carries the edge of disgust. One more false move from her and he will leave her forever, he says, taking her last chance for happiness.

She breaks off the engagement.

Days later, she boards a train to Butte, following Derrick. Why, she doesn't know. To warn others? To stop him? Stop him from what? She has ulterior motives, a secret that she tells no one.

The train is full of soldiers from the tents where the germ has spread, and dozens have died. They'd said prayers, hoping to escape their own demise. If the wolf dog could have been there, in that before time, he might have seen the tiny creature that jumped from one sad soldier to the dress of the girl. He might have stopped the danger from entering his town. He could have kept his boy from faltering and lying sick in a bed above the bakery, trying to recover.

Now he wanders through the Copper Camp and howls. He sings at the bakery door, a mournful wail. When the bakery door opens, he stifles a moan so as not to wake the sleeping boy, trying to keep the devil at bay.

Chapter Seventeen

JANUARY HAD A WICKED chill to it as Marika caught the trolley car toward town. The windows were wide open. The brittle Butte wind blew hard against her face. The sulfur in the air burned her eyes. Her mind was spinning a million miles a minute. New Year's Eve had come and gone, and she'd barely noticed. Mama had made a special dinner but there was no room for celebration. So many had died. Every day Marika worried about Mama, Marko, and Michael. Only by some odd element of grace, they had escaped the flu so far.

She crossed herself as the wind threw snow through the open window into her face. They passed several men in work clothes, women in heavy coats, and the more ragged women of the streets looking for a bit of help to feed themselves. Drifters slept in alleys, sure to freeze. The whole town had iced up. Their only hope was to get back to the saloon for another pint, warming themselves as they loitered in dark spaces where the law might not find them.

A woman with a pink silk skirt flowing out under her wool coat passed by, her feathered hat forward on her head and tipped to the side. One of her dainty hands held it on. Marika spotted Derrick on a bench, snow swirling around him as he watched the woman. She pulled the trolley cable and the car stopped for her. She disembarked.

"You know more about Amelia than you are telling us." She blurted the words out, throwing her suspicions into his face. Her tone felt violent and strange, even to her. Here, in the open air, the fear she'd felt at Al Heaton's place the other day dissipated. Standing in the street, where others strolled, boosted her courage.

He looked at her askance and nodded slowly.

"It bothers me, thinking of you on the same train, without an explanation, as if it was all just happenstance."

A shadow crossed his face. "It's not your business, but I'll tell you so you can put your mind at rest and leave me alone," he said. "We were engaged to be married. I broke it off and she went crazy. She wouldn't leave me alone, so I left Philadelphia. She followed me."

Marika bit her lower lip and narrowed her eyes at him.

"You don't believe me. But it's true. She wouldn't take no for an answer."

"Is the child yours?"

"He's the reason I asked her to marry me. He's a joy, even though he's the offspring of some other man. But Amelia was impossible. She was jealous, always checking up on me and accusing me of things that were insanely criminal. I think that she felt no one should have me if she couldn't." He gave Marika that flat, soft smile. "I warned her that it was dangerous to follow me, that she risked catching the flu. But she wouldn't listen."

"Yet, in spite of the danger, you traveled."

He waved a hand at her. "Pfff. I've hardly been sick a day in my life. I have a kind of magic." He smiled again, this time a half smile with scaly lips that crusted at the corners. Something slithered off of them and a chill went through Marika. She knew that kind of magic. It was no magic at all, just deceptively cruel deeds.

Baba had taught her to stay clear of it. Worms crawled under Marika's skin. It didn't take a sensitive person to recognize the bitterness in this man. She thought of a dark night in Montenegro under the shadow of Durmitor, when a man had killed his brother for the love of a woman. It was love turned into a weapon.

Get far away, she told herself. She shook her head. Still, she thought, this was not an ancient feud. This was a young woman in America. And if she had followed Derrick from Philadelphia, after he had broken off their engagement, there wasn't harm on his part in that. She was just a smitten girl who couldn't believe her bad luck.

She wrestled with herself, trying to decide how much to tell him. "She didn't die of the sickness," Marika finally said, even though she did die of the flu. Marika had witnessed every breath of her demise. She knew she was wading into dangerous territory with Derrick, places and topics she had no business telling him. But she thought he should know. He knew Amelia. They'd been engaged to be married. The streets trembled with an eerie stillness, listening closely.

Derrick looked at her from hooded eyes. She caught the glint of a sparkle in them. Was he laughing about her death? Did he think Marika a fool? Was he gleeful, having gotten away with something?

"No?" he said, with a pitch to his voice and a slight tilt to his head.

Clouds moved in and a dark gust blew down the street, pasting her skirt to her legs and blowing her hat back so that she captured it with a hand to her head. The cold air lifted her skirt at her knees, chilling her thighs. Dirt and debris skidded across the snow as a crow landed on a nearby rooftop and cawed at the street.

"Amelia was killed," Marika said. There. The words were out. Even if the official word of her death was the flu, something was wrong.

"How say you?" The question carried a laugh in the rhythm.

It irked her. Deputize me, just give me the power, she thought, her brain racing, and I'll put him in jail myself. But she had no power.

"She had been poisoned, and that poison weakened her system, making it impossible for her to recover from the flu," she said. "We are looking into it. I wonder where that looking will lead us." She hoped the air of mystery frightened him, like he had frightened her at Al Heaton's place. She hoped it left him wondering if they were on to him. A nagging thought pushed its way into her mind. She couldn't just accuse someone of murder with a feeling. But it was such a dark feeling. There had to be something to it.

"You are an interesting woman." Derrick stared into her eyes, looking through her, as if all the power of the whole world belonged to him.

It paralyzed Marika, made her very afraid. It pulled her into that eternal nothingness. Into the devil's land.

He stood up and walked away, leaving her blithering nonsense to the crow, counting the seconds until she came to her senses.

Shaking Derrick's darkness off, Marika strolled toward the supermarket, where she veered away from the produce section. No apples or any fruit or vegetables at the open market. What if she chose an apple that a sick person had just picked up and put back? She would not let the flu ravage her, too. She left empty handed and hungry.

She held her breath as two gray horses pulling a dead wagon clopped by, the wheels spinning snow toward her. She lifted her skirt and stepped into the alley that led to Kaly's apartment. Following her, the crow landed on the awning above the door, tilting his head in her direction.

Kaly answered the door, her hair falling to her shoulders. Beth sat on the couch. She had an untouchable beauty, with her soft curls and rich blue eyes. Today she wore a light blue skirt and waistcoat, her black boots polished to a shine.

"How are you feeling?" Marika asked her.

Beth shrugged her shoulders. "I have the pox. I can't feel no good."

If one disease doesn't get you the next one will, Marika thought, instantly horrified by her jaded attitude. Had she been infected by Derrick? Or had she seen too much death this last year and a half? Did Derrick see her utter failure when he looked through her?

"I am sorry to hear that," Marika said, "They are searching for cures."

"Yeah, when hell freezes over they'll give it to the likes of me."

"Bethy, don't talk like that," Kaly said. "We'll get you the medicine when they find it. Won't we?" She looked at Marika.

Marika saw the desperation in Kaly's eyes. She had already lost so much. Kaly would not want to lose Beth too. But the sad truth was that Beth would likely be too far gone to be helped by any medical discovery.

"Tell her," Kaly said. "A remedy could be found any day. The scientists want to cure this blight on the nation, on any nation. Meanwhile there are things you can do. Like Mercury. And sweating helps. And isn't there an herb for it?"

Marika shrugged. "Wild pansy, but Dr. Fletcher says it doesn't really work."

"Well, he's not exactly the hopeful sort." Kaly lifted her chin. "Bloodletting?"

"Hasn't been used in ages. And it's an old wives' tale, again at the word of Dr. Fletcher. But he's right." Marika couldn't believe she was quoting Dr. Fletcher and agreeing with him!

"No matter, the plague will get me first," Beth said with a laugh.

"Scientists are working on it." Marika wanted to comfort both women by sounding confident and reassuring. There was no harm in feeling hopeful. "And I heard that cases of the flu might be lessening some."

Kaly nodded. "I'm not worried about Annie and Tara. They both seem to have recovered. And George is getting better day by day," she said. "More than anything, I'm worried about myself. If I get it, who will take care of Annie?"

Marika nodded. She had no words of comfort here.

"George will find a way to a life filled with good stories," she continued. "But Annie's not old enough to know she'll need to tell a tale."

"We'll keep her safe," Marika said. In the old country, Kaly would be considered Marika's sister, her sister by her father's brother. Would that make Marika another mother to Annie? And for the first time she realized that Baba was also Kaly's grandmother. "She's got family. We'll give her stories to tell."

She thought about Amelia, with no family to contact. "I wonder what stories Amelia would have told. What was her life like in Philadelphia?"

"That young girl who has a son over at Jack Kelly's boarding house?" Beth asked. "Go ask Jack. He loves to talk. He draws people in and they tell him everything. Talk about a guy with good stories to tell!" Beth lifted her hand in a gesture that said, there you go. I just solved your problem.

Kaly laughed. "Leave it to you to fix things. You've always got an angle going."

"Well, like a great gambler once told me: Everyone, even you, will take an edge when they can," Beth said.

"Can you go see if he can tell you more about Amelia?" Marika asked Kaly. "What brought her out here with a child? It's such a dangerous trip."

"I'll see what I can find out," Kaly said.

"Maybe he knows where to find her family," she said. Out of the corner of her eye, she saw Beth watching Kaly, a glint in her eye. She felt sadness crawl up her chest to her throat. Beth knew the long road of syphilis. Beth's beauty would disintegrate in its grip long before her heart stopped.

Chapter Eighteen

WHAT PEOPLE MOST REMEMBER about the Copper Camp is the way the townspeople welcome strangers. They'll feed you, buy your beer, and give you shelter. As the snow pelted Kaly's face, she understood that Jack Kelly would have taken Amelia in and would now have a yarn to tell. He'd tell her story with care, guarding her secrets and spilling the engaging details, including murder, mayhem, and ghosts.

Pulling her wool coat tight, she leaned her head into snow. For once, she was glad for the face coverings they all had to be wearing to ward off the flu. It was warm and shielded her face in a comforting way, something she hadn't expected.

The boarding house, built of brick and wood before the turn of the century, looked like a secure fortress in the gale. Kaly stepped up onto the front porch, its white paint blending with the blizzard. She felt like she did last year when she knocked on Miss Anderson's door, wanting something. Here she was, again, seeking good will.

Perhaps Jack Kelly did know something about Amelia. She didn't know why she cared, except that she had seen too many women die too young. Women of the line had families somewhere who might never know when or how their daughters died, or where to visit their graves. It bothered her that so many women of the tenderloin met their ends alone.

Jack Kelly answered the door, tall and burly, his red full beard poking out from under his blue cloth mouth covering. The cloth was rough at the edges and looked as if he might have sewn it himself. Kind green eyes looked at her over the top of it. "Well, Lassy," he said in a deep, rich voice. "What brings you out in this storm?"

"I'm searching for more information on Amelia. I was here about her before."

"Sure. I remember. I'm still looking for a home for her boy." He looked toward the sleeping room.

"How are you feeling? Miss Anderson said you'd been over at her place sick."

"Oh, that woman," he said. "She shouldn't be telling others my business. I'm fine. Just a little cold, that was all."

"You took Little Tony with you over there?"

"Ah, yes, what else could I do? I couldn't leave him here."

"But you brought him back?"

"The boy pitched a fit every time I tried to leave without him. Big tears, worse than the boy's poor departed mother. You try telling that boy 'no.'"

"Speaking of his mother," Kaly said. "Did you talk to Amelia much?"

"Indeed," he said. "That one liked to spin a tale."

Kaly tilted her head in a question. So, someone actually had heard the woman's stories before she died. A whistle blew at one of the mines and Kaly wondered that the mines still ran, with so many sick miners. The town seemed to have a constant flow of workers ready to fill any gaps.

"I just offered her a cup of tea or two," Jack was saying, "and she was off and running. She was a talker, upset. Oh, but where are my manners? May I offer you a cup of tea?"

The wood fire filled the kitchen with a gentle warmth. She could see why this man's rooms were always full. He took her coat and put it on a chair, and she sat at the table. The flower-print wallpaper made Kaly wonder if a woman had lived there at one time.

"My wife's idea," he said as if reading her mind. "I have no need of such fancy things, but I keep it because it makes me feel close her."

"Has she passed?"

"Two years on now. Bless her soul." He crossed himself.

"I'm sorry."

"We all go sometime. But, you're here about the young laddy's mother?"

"Yes, I thought perhaps you could help us find her family,

tell them she's passed on. And tell them about the boy here with you, too."

"That boy plum wore himself out this morning, crying and crying for his mother. I gave him some boiled oats and honey. He finally fell asleep." Jack poured the hot water into a flowered teapot. "My Jeanie's favorite." He motioned to the steaming teapot and put two matching cups out. "No need to get rid of perfectly good things."

"She must have been lovely."

"That, she was."

"How long was Amelia here?"

"Not long. A couple of days. She seemed perfectly healthy to me. I never would have thought she'd meet her maker so soon." He rubbed his beard in a thoughtful way.

"Do you know what brought her out west?"

"She was trying to solve a mystery. Had to do with a man."

Of course. "Did she come west with a man?"

"You could say that. Although it's the 'with' that's not quite right. She followed him out here. They worked together at a dress shop back east. She went on some picnics with him. To hear her tell it, he started out kind and generous, and so concerned about her and the boy. The boy's father had already died of the flu, leaving poor Amelia on her own to figure a way to care for the child.

"She loved making dresses. Loved the fabric and the colors. She would go on and on about her love of turning a flat piece of material into a skirt or a waistcoat. She had a talent for it. She said she did and I believed her.

"Well, she liked this man, thought he might be something special. Then one day, out of the blue, he ignored her and the boy at work. See, she would bring the boy to work with her. She had no one to watch him. She felt happy about the man and his attention to the little tyke. Then this fellow withdrew and stopped talking to her, she thought she'd done something wrong and wanted to fix it. But the man wouldn't say a word to her.

"That raised her ire.

"But then a woman went missing from the garment factory. Or, the way Amelia said it, another woman went missing. A steady employee just never showed up for work one day.

Never showed up anywhere."

"She thought he had something to do with it?"

"She did. But then she figured she was jealous, was blaming him because she'd been spurned. I told her he shouldn't-a treated her that way."

He poured the tea with sugar and cream, and put it on the table. Taking a seat at the far end of the table he took his face covering off. The light from the window made the red in his beard shine.

"He started spending time with another woman at work, and she went missing too. He said she'd gotten sick with that terrible flu that had been going around. But he had an odd smile when he said it. Amelia noticed. It was strange to her, him smiling about something like that. People had been getting sick and dying by the dozens."

"Did this other woman show up again?"

Jack shook his head. "And there were others before those two. Amelia knew something was wrong. She began to count her lucky stars that he had abandoned her."

"She thought she could go the way of the others."

Jack nodded. "She knew he wouldn't stop. He chose the women without families or support. They must have thought the Good Lord had blessed them and finally sent them someone to love, only to have him turn on them, and send them back to the Good Lord Himself.

"Her suspicions ate at her until she followed him. He had said he was going to visit a sick friend. He didn't tell Amelia, rather he told a mutual friend of theirs and that friend told Amelia. The girl thought Amelia had been pining over the man for too long and wanted to put an end to it by exposing his affections for someone else."

"Amelia didn't see it as affection?"

"Nope. The woman was indeed sick, that much she knew. When she got there the curtain had been pulled back from the window to let the light in. Light and fresh air are thought to help cure this sickness.

"From the shadows Amelia watched as he put a rag over the woman's mouth and nose, clearly causing her demise. The woman fell immediately to the floor. No one else noticed or said a word about it if they did. Later, Amelia was told that the woman died of the flu."

"She knew better."

"Ah, she did. And that is what brought her to Butte and such finality. She wanted to stop the man from ever hurting anyone again.

"Instead, the flu stopped her."

Kaly thought on that. If what Jack said was true, the women had been killed for nothing, for something as normal as falling for a man. "Her obsession with him had put her on that train," Kaly said. "That's most likely where she got the flu. Bad air circulates on trains." She took off her mask and sipped her tea. Beautiful, red and blue flowers lined the inside of the cup. A quiet spirit settled near Kaly, and she felt a soft haze cross her cheek. Jack's wife, she thought.

"I don't know so much about that," he said. "She could have brought the sickness right from the east. The human body is a mystery to me and, I guess, to most people."

The blizzard had picked up and snow pelted the window, which rattled in its frame. Kaly did not look forward to going back out there. This warm kitchen, this tea, and this burly man combined to make her feel safer than she'd felt in a long time. George and Annie were safe, too, with their grandmother.

Even with this violent illness, the world would go on. Those who struggled to survive might succeed or they might not. Just a simple action, such as following a man west, or drinking on a train, could make that difference. An impulse, or a fraction of a second, decided who lived and who died.

"Thank you for helping me. I'll finish my tea and take my leave. You've given me a lot to think about." She listened to the window rattle and knew that, sooner or later, she'd have to walk out into the fierce gale that was assaulting her town.

Marika sat at Miss Parsons' large desk, Dr. Fletcher's heavy medical book opened in front of her. She wore what struck Kaly as a doctor's office uniform: white blouse, simple dark skirt, and pinned back hair.

"Good morning," Marika said. "Brave of you to come out in this weather."

"When duty calls…" Kaly shook off her coat in the entryway.

"Did you find out anything?"

"She worked at a dress factory."

"So, Derrick told that much of the truth," Marika said.

Kaly cocked her head at her.

"That couldn't have paid much," Marika was saying. "What happened to her husband?"

"He died of the flu. Jack Kelly still needs to find a home for the child."

"Was he complaining?"

"No. In fact, he had taken Tony to Miss Anderson's. He was sick and went over to The Big House to recover. The child went with him."

"She didn't try to keep the little boy?" Marika asked.

"She may have tried, but Tony put up such a screaming fit each time Jack tried to leave him, that the poor man just brought him back home."

"Maybe he thinks that's how he'll see his mother again. Has anyone told him that she's passed on?"

Kaly shook her head. Jack Kelly said he hated to upset the boy. An unexpected sadness welled up in her chest. "The boy needs a home," she said.

"You're glad you decided to make a home for Annie, aren't you?"

"I am."

"But…?"

"I would never have been able to do it if my mother hadn't shown up and offered me a job and an apartment."

"You have Tommy, too. He'll be home soon."

"I hope so! But what about all the women who find themselves pregnant with no magical mother that steps out from the shadows to offer shelter? Their children have nowhere to go. And now, a large burly man is left in charge of a small boy whose mother made a fatal mistake."

"Mistake?" Marika cocked her head and lifted her hands in a gesture that asked Kaly to tell her more.

"Following a man out here."

"So again, Derrik told the truth."

"I don't know," Kaly said.

"She must have been desperate, to spend what little money she had on train fare. I wonder when he learned she was on the train with him."

"Frightened more than desperate," Kaly said. "And it wouldn't have been easy to hide herself and her child from someone. Little boys aren't a quiet sort." Except when they are sick, she added to herself.

"Derrick said they were engaged, he broke it off, and she followed him to try to get back with him."

"If this Derrick," Kaly said, "is the same man that Amelia told Jack about, he's dangerous."

"But why follow danger, why not just let him go?"

"She told Jack that the women the man dated got the flu and disappeared or died. Amelia had gotten suspicious and followed him. She saw him put a rag over a woman's mouth. She collapsed. Later, she died of the flu. But Amelia wasn't so certain. She thought he had something to do with her death, and that he'd do it again. She wanted to stop him."

Marika eyes widened. "Why kill someone who is already dying?"

"An angel of mercy?"

"Or so he perceives himself."

Kaly watched Marika tap her finger on the desk, the rhythm soft and pure. They didn't know if this Derrick was the same man who had frightened Amelia, and that was what plagued Kaly. She'd been falsely accused so many times. It was no fun. "Maybe he did feel pity toward the woman," she said. "Maybe he was helping her sleep through it."

"I have seen Dr. Fletcher put people out for surgeries or to set a broken bone."

Kaly nodded.

"Maybe he was trying to be kind by sedating her. This flu is brutal. For some, it's an extended agony. Maybe he did think that he wanted her to sleep through the worst of the suffering. Maybe he wasn't trying to kill her."

"We don't know what she actually saw," Kaly said. "We

are hearing the story from her to Jack to me. A lot can change in the distance that story has traveled."

"But Derrick delivered Amelia to the doctor's office that night."

"It fits with a show of care."

"A show. Exactly. Something pretend."

"Others could be in danger." Kaly held Marika's eyes. Most people underestimated cruelty, giving others the benefit of the doubt. But she could see that Marika understood brutality. A surge of sisterly camaraderie overwhelmed Kaly, almost bringing her to her knees with missing Anne Marie.

Chapter Nineteen

MARIKA KISSED THE ICON of Mother Mary and blessed herself, thanking the Lord for keeping her safe all of these months. So many had fallen ill, but somehow, she and her family had been spared from suffering the flu. Knock on wood. Just for good measure. Not that the Lord was too busy, but just that she didn't mind helping Him out by accepting a little old-fashioned luck.

Walking toward the East Ridge she thought of the mountains in Montenegro and the blue green water of the Tara River. She recalled the day Papa, Mama, Marko, and she had visited Ostrog Monastery and St. Basil. Dressed in the traditional cloth of red velvets and golden trim, they had traveled on horseback for days to Danilovgrad and beyond.

They reached Ostrog in the early evening and stood at dusk on the side of that cliff during Vespers, the sky turning pink. St. Basil, wrapped in Holy cloth, cried his sacred tears. He'd been resting there peacefully since his death, many years ago, but he still cried tears that blessed the world. After Vespers, the priest rubbed the tears on Marika's forehead. She felt an unworldly peace.

They camped at the base of the cliff that night, saying their prayers with extra fervor. Marika remembered how safe she'd felt, with the saint watching over them. Gone were any worries about wolves, mountain lions, or poisonous snakes. Nothing could touch them, surrounded as they were by blessings. Marika slept as if she were sleeping in the hands of God.

The next morning, they crossed back over the mountains and gathered the fruit to make *kruske,* the pear brandy that the old ones taught the young ones to drink. One shot in the morning to start the day. One shot to ward off illness.

Marika wondered if the traditional brandy could ward off an illness as wicked as this flu. Tears rimmed her eyes and her breath caught in her throat as she wondered what was happening in Montenegro. Would there be anyone left to sing the songs for those who'd left and never returned? Could St. Basil's blessings reach this far west?

To Marika, the church on South Idaho had felt almost the same as the one in her homeland. Especially at Vespers and during Sunday morning Liturgy. But now, when they needed it most, there was no open church to pray in. Like so many other places, the church had been shut down to help stop the flu's spread.

And there was no saint in Butte to weep for the sad souls bound to mortality.

Dr. Fletcher stood at Miss Parsons' desk, pale and grim. Miss Parsons had her head in the medical book and barely looked up as Marika entered. The tension in her brow was obvious. Her strict face fought for control, as if sadness might spill out at any moment, and she couldn't, wouldn't let that happen.

"Good morning," Dr. Fletcher said. "I've got a job for you."

"Okay," Marika said, glad to be of use. Anything was better than feeling helpless.

"There is a sick family over on Gold Street. Go make sure they have water, blankets, and food. Do what you can to keep their fevers down."

Marika stifled a gasp. "How many?"

"Five."

"Will anyone else be there?"

The doctor looked over the top of his glasses at her, his face stony. "Everyone else is out tending to other families. Or they've taken sick themselves. The contagion has slowed down some, but not enough to matter."

Feeling a deep well of dread, Marika picked up her skirt and turned back toward the door. Witnessing death had become her forte, seemed to be all she was good for. She waited like a caged animal for the flu to slither between the bars and open its poisonous mouth to her.

Dr. Fletcher and Miss Parsons must have felt the same, but they didn't say it. Miss Parsons had just missed two weeks of work. Dr. Fletcher had spent every afternoon over there with her. When she did finally show up again she was pale and fragile, barely weighing a pound.

Marika couldn't bring herself to think about the flu on the walk over to Gold Street. She preferred to think about the weather: the stormy clouds, the bright sun and below zero temperature, the snow on the mountain, the snow blinding her in a fierce wind. She could do nothing about the weather, but build a fortress against it. She could do nothing about the flu. But...nothing.

That day on Gold Street she lied to the mother, and tended to her, until she joined her family on the other side. From Gold Street she went to a Slavic home near the church where a young son managed to cross the flu's threshold alive, and ready to eat good soup. A shop owner, a bartender, a boxer, and two dozen miners all required food delivered to their quarantined homes.

She went down to the Cabbage Patch where the devil's own king threatened her with a club if she didn't leave. They'd take care of their own, he'd said. She went to Dublin Gulch to tend to a sour faced woman full of stories, until the stories disappeared and there was nothing more Marika, or anyone, could do for her. She went over to the Finlen Hotel where several guests had fallen ill. And, just for good measure, she stopped by the Washington School that they had closed to students and opened for patients.

By the time she got home, and shook herself out of her coat and her soiled work dress, she was mad. Furiously mad. Not wanting to be there mad. She wanted to be on the side of a cliff, on the side of mountain. Or in a cave would be better. Just roll a stone over the opening and let me rest, she thought.

"What is wrong?" Michael asked.

"This God forsaken town is what's wrong," she blurted. "Nothing to do here but drink or pray, and now not even that. Churches are closed and taverns are deadly." She was falling fast, and she knew it. But she didn't care.

Michael reached out a hand. "Come here," he said.

"No, don't touch me." She pushed it away. "Everywhere I go, everyone is sick. And I can do nothing. Their dreams are all slipping away. And now my dreams are fading fast. I'll never be a doctor. I was a fool to think I could be." Forget this place. Forget this stupid home with this stupid man, and the whole stupid idea of love.

She grabbed her coat and left. It was below zero in the Mining City that night, and if Michael tried to come after her, she didn't know it. Blinded by rage, she made her way to the Silver Bow Bakery. Maybe Tara McClane had a bottle of whiskey. If she did, Marika intended to drink it, all of it.

She stormed into the kitchen, only to be stopped short by the sight of Dan in an apron covered in flour.

"Are you the new chef?" Marika asked. He looked less than exquisite. "Oh no, don't tell me. You are the new baker." She laughed at her wit.

He shook his head. "I couldn't join the military. The mines aren't safe. Nowhere is safe. I have to do something. Everyone, even you, has to eat." He smiled that half smile at her and her angry heart jumped. She would not be soothed, she told herself, but she would laugh at his expense.

"Elizabeth says I look charming in baking dust."

"Elizabeth?" Marika raised her eyebrows. "I was in nursing classes with her. We sat with Joseph Heaton together." *She gave me the brilliant news that Amelia had been pregnant*, she thought, punching another nail into her bitterness.

"She said so."

Jealousy swelled in Marika's throat. But why should she be jealous? She married Michael. Why should she care? About any of them? They were all going to die. She'd be the last one standing, she was pretty sure.

"Are you okay? You look sick suddenly." Dan cocked his head at her and smiled. Was he tormenting her? Did he see her sour mood? Get out of here before you completely make a fool of yourself, she thought. But she didn't leave.

"Your girlfriend," she said. "And I could care less."

"Sounds like jealousy to me. You are long married. Did you forget?"

How dare he just call it out like that? How dare he taunt her?

"I'm not jealous," she said. The words had a mean tone and she heard it. Good, she thought, I'm tired of being nice. But she felt no comfort in her meanness. She hated that he had a girlfriend, hated herself for being so immature. Hated that she was married. Hated it that she would never be a doctor. Would she ever face reality? "Well, okay, I am," she relented. "But it doesn't matter what I think or feel. I have no power to affect or change anything."

He took off his apron, walked over and pulled her into his arms. "It's okay," he said. "You have a good life with Michael. You made the best choice for you. I want a good life too." He'd missed her point completely, but she didn't care. She put her head on his chest and cried. She hadn't realized how the year had taken its toll on her. She'd been trying to be brave for so long that suddenly all of her fear, her umbrage at the unjustice of it all, just spilled out.

Pulling herself away, she wiped her tears. "I have to go home," she said, leaving the bakery and completely forgetting why she had come.

―――――――――

By the time Marika got home, her fingers felt frozen stiff. She could barely walk as the cold had penetrated her boots and chewed at her toes. Tears froze in her eyelashes. Michael greeted her, and the stove, which had been stoked, warmed her with welcome comfort. She was glad to be home. Home was where she belonged.

She wanted to tell him that she was sorry. But she was tired of apologizing for herself, tired of being good and trying to be helpful. In all honesty, she didn't want to get rid of her sour mood, but it had leaked out of her anyway.

"Can we forget my fit?" she asked. She didn't know how long she could go on without her husband and she hoped she'd never find out. She wanted to be here, she did. But her rock hard will had nearly disappeared, into the ethers never to return. She knew she couldn't survive without it.

He walked around the table and pulled a chair close to her. He'd cleaned up and smelled of earth and good spices. "I didn't know where you went," he said. "I was scared."

"I went," she said, "to find a bottle of good whiskey and drink the whole damn thing." She sluffed her coat off onto the chair and ran a hand through her wet hair where the snow had melted into it. "I went to forget my sorrows and this deadly flu. I went to feel sorry for myself."

He rubbed her arm with his knuckles.

"But I can't hold a grudge long, not even against this sordidly bitter town, and its wretched flu, as much as I want to. Do you know that hundreds have died in a few months?"

Michael nodded, and took her hand in his. This time she didn't pull away. "And I've been useless?" She felt the tears fill her eyes. They were not tears of sorrow, although they could have been. They were tears of anger, and the anger spilled out of her for a long time that night. Until finally they went to bed. Michael covered her with a warm blanket and pulled her into his arms, and she thought, someday, she might find sweetness in the world again.

——————

The next day, Marika took the trolley to work. The temperature was below zero and the windows were wide open on the cars, freezing her to the bone. A young child sat in the lap a of big man with frost on his red beard. The boy, maybe two years old, cried and hit at the man, clearly wanting down. It was a struggle of wills and Marika wondered who'd win. She'd place her money on the boy.

The man looked over at her and said, "He's a rough one, this kid. Strong as hell."

"You look like you can hold him," she said.

"When he gets his ire up, he wants what he wants."

Marika laughed at that. "Don't we all!" She still felt last night's ire deep in her chest and she didn't want to go to work today. Except for the freezing cold, she was tempted to stay on the trolley until quitting time. Not that there'd been a quitting time once the flu arrived.

"Name's Jack Kelly," the man was saying. "Everyone calls me Jack. And this here's Little Tony."

That set Marika's spine straight. "Amelia's son?"

The man lifted and eyebrow. "Did you know her?"

"Marika Jovich. I work at Dr. Fletcher's office." She could see the recognition light in his eyes.

"Ah," he said, with a nod. "You were with the boy's mother, then." He looked at the boy, who had quieted down. Tony looked back and forth between them, as if to solve some great mystery.

The trolley stopped and she saw a crow sitting on the brick bank building across the street, toughing out the winter, like the rest of us, Marika thought.

"Mama?" Tony looked up at her, a hopeful look in his eye. When no one answered he pushed against Jack again, trying to get down.

"I haven't the heart to tell him." He glanced over at Marika.

"He doesn't know?"

"I have these," he said, and held up two letters and his hands wobbled. "They were in her things and I didn't know what to do with them."

Marika suddenly felt like she was in an old novel, something risky and dangerous. "Are they addressed to anyone? We've been wanting to tell her family."

"This one's got Little Tony's name on it. But he's too young to read. And it didn't seem right, me opening it and butting into her private stuff." His eyes shifted and he looked worried. He pulled the boy tight, hugging him into submission. "I thought I'd bring them to that girl at the bakery. She seemed to take an interest in his ma."

The trolley started up again, jerking Marika back into her seat. It passed right by Dr. Fletcher's office by the time she realized she had missed her stop. She nodded. "I can take them to her, if you'd like. I'm her cousin."

Jack Kelly pulled the letters into the hug with Little Tony, as if they were small animals he, also, needed to comfort. He seemed to be thinking about it. "No," he said finally.

"I better take them over to her. That way I can get some of Tara McClane's good cooking." He turned further toward her and his eyes glinted. "A man needs good home cooking once in a while."

Marika bit her bottom lip and leaned back in the trolley seat. "Go in the alley door," she said. "I hear it's always open."

Chapter Twenty

SNOW HIT THE GROUND in blowing sheets as Kaly and George reached the apartment with the wolf dog. They were soaking wet when they got inside. He'd been feeling much better and this was his first time out. Kaly knew he still felt weak, but at least he was up and moving. And he was eating. That boy could eat. And so could his dog.

She unwrapped a big bone and handed it to the dog. If she could get the wolf dog to sit still at the door, Kaly could dry him off.

"*Andjo*," George said.

Kaly cocked her head at him. "What?"

"Andjo. It's the Serbian word for Angel. Andjo Luk. That's his name," George said. "Angel Wolf. He kept me safe when I was sick."

Kaly stopped wiping the dog down. "When did you start learning Serbian words?"

George shrugged. "I heard Mrs. Jovich say it."

"Marika?"

"Yes, she said he was an angel. And I knew it was true as soon as she said it. He was in my dreams and every time I woke up he was sleeping right next to me."

"Andjo it is then!" The wolf dog bit the towel Kaly held in her hand. "Go get your own towel and dry yourself off," she said to George. "Change your clothes too. And then check on your sister and tell your grandmother that we are back." Having been half a loner most of her life, Kaly was still baffled by this whole business of family. "And take Andjo with you," she added, snagging the towel out of the dog's mouth.

"Remember the prayers we said in the church that day at

Mr. Lailich's funeral?" George had gone with her to Stojan Lailich's funeral. Stojan, Marika's father, was her uncle.

Kaly nodded.

"I saw God when I was sick. He sent Andjo to save my life." She knew he'd been delirious. But. "You saw God?"

"Yes, He told me about Andjo," George said with finality, calling his dog to follow him downstairs to find Annie and Tara. He stopped abruptly and turned to Kaly. "Can we go to the church and light a candle for him?"

The dog? What a kid. "I wish we could. The churches are all mostly closed because of the flu. As soon as this passes and the churches open again, we'll light them for everyone who has recovered, including you. And we'll light them for everyone who has gone back to the angels."

That seemed to satisfy him.

Kaly was astounded by his gratitude to the dog, never mind that she stayed awake for nights on end soaking rags to calm his fever and watching him breathe. But she understood. The white dog had been her angel all those years ago at The Polly May when Bert Brown attacked her. He sat on her until she left her body and floated into the clouds with the white dog. They sat there together, waiting for Bert Brown to finish. When he finished, she returned to her body, found her way through that snow-filled day only to find her twin sister, Anne Marie, stone-blue dead.

"Here," George said when he came back into the room. He handed her a white candle, surprising her for the fourth or fifth time in less than an hour. "We can light it here. Mrs. McClane gave it to me."

"You asked her?"

"She said it was no bother. She said God will see the candle no matter where we light it."

Kaly went into the kitchen and got out a small bowl. She scattered rice around in the bottom of it, set the thick candle in the center of it, and handed a match to him. As George lit the candle for his dog, Kaly made a promise to herself to try harder to forgive Tara. It was time. She did feel immense gratitude toward her mother for giving them all a home. Especially now.

Kaly's old life had been simple. It had revolved around pain and money.

Just then Kaly heard a man's voice downstairs. She scooted out the door, leaving it open and saw Jack Kelly and Little Tony. Tara put Annie on a blanket on the floor and Tony joined her. As she watched her daughter play, offering spoons to Tony, a powerful love broke like a big wave crashing against all the rocky losses she had ever suffered and her heart broke open. When Annie looked up and smiled at her mother, Kaly wanted to rush downstairs, pick her up, and hold her tight. Instead, she watched the beginning of Annie's first friendship.

Tara sat down at the booth with Jack while the two little ones sat on the floor. Kaly couldn't hear what they said, but the conversation was animated, lively. Jack passed something across the table to Tara and she put it in her apron pocket.

Back in the apartment George sat on the floor with Andjo. "I should be able to go out by myself," he was saying. "I've already been sick and recovered."

Overnight, he had gone from being a child to being a mature boy. Had the flu affected his brain in such a wonderful way? "Here is something you can do." She pulled Tommy's letter from a drawer. "Read your father's letter and write back to him. He'll love to hear from you."

Tears welled up in his eyes as he took the letter. "Will he really come home?"

Kaly didn't know the answer to his question, didn't think he was old enough to know how hopeless she'd been feeling about ever seeing Tommy again. But she knew that he'd resent her if she lied to him. A deep sense of shame overwhelmed her. How could she raise these two children well?

"Yes," she said, her voice soft and firm. "I hope with all my heart that he'll come home to us." That was the best she could do.

"I don't want to lose another dad."

"I know, son," she said, "I know."

"I've been thinking." Tara arrived in the doorway with Annie on her hip. "We need a plan of some sort."

"For?"

"For them." Tara lifted her eyebrows toward the children. "In case something happens…"

Kaly was suddenly fuming. She knew what Tara meant. Who would take care of the kids if neither Tara nor Kaly lived? Here Kaly was trying to protect her children and Tara flung her fears at them all like a wet old rag.

Andjo whined. He wanted to go back outside.

"I'll take him out," George said.

"I'll go with you," Kaly needed a minute to calm down. She grabbed her coat and a rope for the dog, not that he needed it.

Andjo ran up and down the alley, coming back to them, and throwing his head toward the street, telling them to follow him. When they didn't he bowed down and stuck his bottom into the air. Kaly and George looked at each other and laughed.

"What a dog," Kaly said.

"Hey. Don't call him that. He's an angel." George smiled. "Andjo. Come Andjo!"

Andjo promptly ignored George and ran down the alley again, this time disappearing around the back of the bakery. A couple of nurses walking down the street glanced up at them and went back to their chatter.

"Do you think Miss Anderson is okay? And Julian?" George asked.

"I'm not sure. But I'll try to find out tomorrow. I'll ask Marika."

"*Hvala*," George said.

"Where are you learning to talk like that?"

"From Marika. She's from Montenegro."

"But you're not from there."

"But your father was. So we should learn. It means 'thank you.'"

She tilted her head at him. "You are a mystery, sweet child. You are welcome."

"Do you think I could go help Miss Anderson?"

"What do you want to help her with?"

He shrugged. "I'm not sure. I can help with chores and things. Maybe the children could live with her again and she wouldn't have to do all the work herself. I heard the nurses talking about the children left behind by parents who had died from the flu. They have nowhere to go."

Kaly shook her head. George paid such close attention to the world around him. He was the exact opposite of what she'd been at his age. After Anne Marie was killed, Kaly had pulled inside and gone mute. She was ten years old and refused to utter a sound for a year. The world had been dead to her, just like her sister. But Kaly was alive. Finally she had to open her mouth and speak again.

"I can help her," George was saying.

He would help her, too. Kaly knew. "Not now," she said. "We don't want to risk you getting sick again. When this sickness passes, she'll be happy to see you and that will be help enough for her."

The afternoon sky had turned a brilliant red from the smelting dust in the air. In the glow from that sky Andjo came running back to them.

Before the sickness swooped down onto the citizens of Butte, the town was loud and raucous all times of the day and night, lighting up every saloon on every uptown street. Booze would flow. Musicians would sing, and miners would dance until they fell down.

Now, devastated by illness, Butte was a ghost town.

———

When Kaly, George, and Andjo got back upstairs, Annie was busy walking back and forth between the couch and Tara. She had the biggest smile as she walked. When she saw Kaly her eyes sparkled. She pivoted and waddled toward her, nearly losing her balance as momentum carried her forward.

"Mama," she cooed. Her sweet, melodious voice melted Kaly's heart. She caught her in her arms and Annie rubbed her cheeks against Kaly's. Annie put her hands on the sides of Kaly's face and squished her mother's face, as if she were a big pillow.

Tara handed Kaly a small white dress. "She'll need this."

Tiny roses in every color dotted the soft cotton. Tara had sewn wooden buttons down the back of it, and made the tiniest of buttonholes.

"Thank you," Kaly said. "It's beautiful."

A whiff of something rich and delicious saturated the room. Kaly caught it and her belly rumbled. She smiled.

"Sarma rolls," Tara said.

"My favorite. About that one thing," Kaly said. "I'll ask Marika and Michael if they will take these two, should something happen to you and me. But nothing is going to happen to us, right?" She fluffed Annie's cheeks and knocked George, who was sitting nearby, with her shoulder.

Tara smiled, and that warmed Kaly's heart. For a minute, they had made each other happy. Here, in the midst of all of this heartache, with an angel dog, a wise boy, and a little girl, a mother and daughter had found their way to each other.

─────────

The next morning Kaly went to check on Beth. George wanted to go too, but she told him no. She told him that he needed to stay home and rest to fully recover.

"I have fully recovered," he said.

"The answer is still no," she said.

She didn't want George seeing her friend's demise. Since she hadn't been around in a week or so, Kaly assumed the worst. It was Beth's habit to be intermittently absent. And it was Kaly's habit to worry. She couldn't know if Beth was truly sick or if Kaly's way of thinking had gotten the best of her. Better to play it safe.

Tara agreed to watch Annie and George while she was gone.

"I know I was not a good mother to you," she had said last night after the children were in bed. "I'm sorry. I'm trying harder with Annie and George."

Kaly had not responded to that. She had nothing to say, but now she wished that she would have acknowledged her mother's apology.

"I'm sorry," Tara had said. Yes, me too, Kaly thought as she made her way to the Red-Light District. But she didn't want to think that way. She wanted to stop making her mother wrong for something that seemed to be out of her control at the time. Tara didn't have options. She did what she thought would keep Kaly and Anne Marie safe. Right now, she told herself, there is enough to worry about, without dragging the whole, long past into it.

Crib windows were shut, curtains pulled, and doors closed. Some doors were boarded over. The closed up quiet of the District and the debris in the street made Kaly feel edgy and out of sorts. It sent pin pricks down her arms. She looked around for danger. Finding none she knocked on Beth's door.

Beth answered it in her nightgown, her hair down and disheveled. She seemed weak, as if her legs could barely hold her up. And there was the blue on her lips, and the sour smell.

The breath caught in Kaly's chest. All the breaths she had ever breathed with Beth hung in that sour air. No fire had been lit, and the room was cold.

Beth crawled back into bed.

"You've caught it," Kaly said.

"It's this or the pox. I'm dead either way. Syphilis will hurt for a lot longer."

"Could you just stop being brave for one minute?" A sad dread crawled up Kaly's spine. A deep sickness shot straight to her stomach almost doubling her over. She knew Beth was right. She didn't want to know it, but she knew it.

Beth shook her head. "I've had no room for weakness in my life. I've always had to find strength to pass by one heart-ache to the next." She started coughing. The sound came from deep in her chest. A wild ocean rolled around in there, loud and booming.

"Shhhh," Kaly said. "I am here. You can rest now."

Beth shook her head again. "Did I tell you how my Ted-dy died?"

"You don't have to. You told me he disappeared."

"That's only part of the story."

"Think of good things right now. Put your heart at ease. The past is gone." She had just told herself that very thing on her way to see Beth.

"I remember it like it just happened, I remember the train yard and that train. I was twelve, he was two. I should have pro-tected him, should have heard that train coming instead of be-ing bunged up in my own mind about my step-father's cruelty."

"Beth, I beg you," Kaly said. "It's too late now. Let your

mind rest. You need your rest."

Beth was having none of it. She had a story to tell and, like the train, her story was coming fast. The engineer hit the brakes, and they screamed. It was the saddest sound she'd ever heard. Teddy probably died before the train stopped. Beth walked the track looking for his young body.

"I should have been watching him," she said. "I loved him. He was my child, in the way that only a child can have a child."

She paused for a coughing fit, her face turning blue. Curling up into a tiny ball, pain creased her face until finally it went slack and she took in a new breath. "Teddy is my angel now, watching over me here on this bed, me, sick and dying, and Teddy, so bright and young. He is waiting for me in the heavens. He's not mad. He was never mad. He wasn't even afraid. He was just shocked that he could be here one minute and gone the next.

"I hopped on a flatcar. I sat there in the blazing sun, my face as cold as the steel tracks, silent as the hot air around them. The shock that never wore off. I never cried my grief. Shame dripped from my very pores. I was too young to have a child that lived. But he had lived. Teddy came into the world, huge and crying, pulling on my leg, wrapping himself to me like a piece of wet gauze.

"That day he crawled away? I thought about how his father, my mother's husband, kept trapping me and hurting me, even after Teddy was born, even with Teddy in the room. I'd scream and no one would come. I tried to tell my mother, but he called me a liar. That day that Teddy disappeared, instead of watching him, I was planning revenge. I was thinking about killing my step-father.

"Maybe the life went from Teddy in a flash of light, instead of being squeezed and bled from him year after year. There is much he might have seen and been, my brother, my child." She looked at Kaly with milky eyes, under heavy eyelids. "He never could have known that I was his mother. My mother insisted she'd raise him as her own. And she would have, given the chance, a chance I took from all of us.

"She didn't even ask me who his father was. She didn't ask

how a ten-year-old could have a child. She didn't ask about the bloody panties. She just took him to her chest, like a child she'd born.

"I rode that train away from the land of betrayal. But the worst one, in the end, was my own. I betrayed my own son by taking my eyes off of him and putting them on the cruelest man I had ever known. That man wasn't even there, but his evil followed me like a heavy cloak while my Teddy's love got wiped out by that train.

"Letting my child die from neglect born of anger is not something I can ever forgive myself for. Now, I can barely breathe, and I don't deserve to have him rescue me. Yet, here he is, as bright as the sun, as white as the pure light of Jesus. I have warm hands to fall into.

"I found his lifeless body beside the tracks. I picked him up and took him on the flatcar with me, placing him in my lap, my skirt spread out beneath both of us. I looked at the blood on his face and willed his lungs to bring in air. With my own breath, I pushed air into them. But it was too late. His lungs had collapsed. His heart had stopped, although mine beat fast enough for both of us.

"Someone, I don't know who, took him from me at the first stop. I imagine they buried him somewhere on that green hillside. It was a small town with a small train station, a place that opens up to accept your grief, and then closes over it like the nighttime petals of a flower, a town I could never find again.

"And now I'm dying. I can feel my lungs collapsing. And Teddy comes floating across the train tracks to find me, to take me home with him." She finished her story with a rasping breath and went quiet, the air around her going still.

Kaly thought about that story for a long time after Beth passed. She sat at her friend's bedside, holding her hand. The light faded and the air grew cold. Beth's beautiful quiet spirit lifted up out of the room to a mysterious green hill where her son had so long ago been buried.

Chapter Twenty-One

MARIKA WOKE UP IN a sweat. The black wolf had visited her. He'd looked at her with glowing green eyes, pawed the ground, and growled. He demanded she follow him through the thick woods, ripe with old guttural sounds, and the smells of a thousand ancestors. He bared his teeth and paralyzed her with his eyes. She stood completely still, unable to move. When she finally turned to go, the wolf chased her, and she ran hard, stopping on a plateau above the huge creature.

What do you want? she asked. He told her to pay attention. The forces of nature were not to be ignored. Dismiss them and they will crush you. But no, she said. I have a mind for study, a heart for healing. She wouldn't be crushed. The wolf came so close, it nearly smothered her with its great body. She could smell the wet earth in his fur, hear its heart beat. *Use them,* the wolf told her, letting out a haunting howl, and trotting off across the land, leaving her desolate and alone.

She got up and got dressed, washed her face and tried to wash the dream away. It left her feeling shaky and confused. She needed to do something to burn off this dread she felt, and set out for the doctor's office.

When she got there, Dr. Fletcher was in a grim mood. Marika had never really seen him sulk before. He looked up at her from the chart in his hands, shaking his head.

"Go home," he said. "There is nothing any of us can do here but offer comfort. And little good that has done."

"But things are better," she said. "The number of people coming down with influenza has decreased."

"Your time is running out," he said. "The odds are against you now. You'll get sick. You put everyone you love in danger."

Marika realized the doctor wasn't sulking. He was resigned.

"I haven't gotten sick yet," she said, tugging her mask tight. She'd been washing it every night and the material was beginning to wear thin. She'd ask Mama to make her a new one.

Miss Parsons looked up from the medical book she'd been studying. Between Marika and Miss Parsons, the heavy medical book had found a permanent home on the desk, right next to the scissors and pencils. Everything a curious office person could need. "We've been boiling the blankets before we use them again, to help stop the spread. Seems to be helping."

"I'll do that," Marika said.

"Exactly what I was thinking," Miss Parsons said.

"Let's build a fire." Marika wouldn't give up. Not yet. Many more of those who came to the doctor's doorstep or to the hospital were going home, instead of to the cemetery. That was success.

They built a blaze behind the clinic and put a grate on the flame and a pot of water on the grate. Smoke singed the air, throwing off a musky smell, a back alley offering, a hazy prayer.

"That doesn't look much like doctoring to me," Dan Mc-Clane said.

Marika's heart leaped, flaming hot like the fire. She rarely saw him these days, and now twice this month. Just the sound of his voice could still make her weak-kneed, and bring her straight out of her senses.

"Hello." She dropped her head. Couldn't she think of anything more clever than that to say?

"It's Elizabeth," he said.

Right away, Elizabeth. For Pete's sake, couldn't he just be slightly gentle about the woman. Let her name be the fourth or fifth thing he said, instead of the second? Marika was horrified at her own jealous reaction at the mention of his Elizabeth. She'd been helpful with Joseph Heaton.

"She is sick," Dan said, his shoulders slumping. His lower lip trembled. "Can you come help her?"

Marika looked at Miss Parsons. "Yes," she said. "Of course."

"Is the doctor available?" he asked.

This set off a whole different fury in her. "He just went over to the hospital," she said.

Miss Parsons' eyes widened at that.

"Well, he did," Marika said in a huff, grabbing her medical bag.

———————

Elizabeth rented a room in a two-story brick building at the end of Broadway. She was on the first floor sleeping soundly, most of the covers were on the floor. The blankets that were left on the bed were tangled around her legs. She'd clearly been tossing and turning. She looked terrible. The brown patches covered her face. Her breaths were shallow and raspy. None of this was a good sign.

Marika's jealousy turned to shame as she sank onto a nearby chair and put her hand on the woman's forehead. It was very hot. She and Dan began trying to cool her down.

The sun came through a small dirty window, casting a gray light on Elizabeth as she opened her bloodshot eyes. Strands of her curly hair were pasted to her pale cheeks.

Marika tucked a blanket under her shoulders. "How are you feeling?"

"Not good," she rasped. "I hurt all over."

"Try some water," Marika said, pouring water into Elizabeth's mouth, spilling a little, but getting some of it down. The woman was able to swallow some of it, which was a good sign.

"Just keep the thermometer under your tongue, okay?"

Elizabeth nodded, and Marika saw the strength it took for her to accomplish this simple task. She pulled the thermometer out and read it. One hundred four degrees. From the medical bag she pulled a solid amount of quinine and mixed it with some water. The quinine would help bring her fever down.

"Try this," she said.

Elizabeth took the medicine well, but moments later went into a coughing fit. Marika cleaned her mouth with a dry rag. The rag came back with dotted red. She had coughed up blood. The rag would need to be burned or boiled.

Marika hoped that soon the quinine would set in and Elizabeth would sleep.

The night carried on with blood spotting her ears, and a feral shivering. Her fever came down and spiked, until it settled at a mildly warm 102. Watching her, Marika felt her own lungs tighten and freeze. She'd seen people who had died in one night. She didn't want this for Elizabeth. Or for Dan.

The girl stirred. "It's come down," Marika said in a soft, calm voice, "but you still have a fever. I think you are going to be okay."

Suddenly, she remembered the black wolf from last night's dream. It had chased her and she ran hard from it until she stood on a plateau of land above the huge creature. Her grandmother had said the wolf, especially the black wolf, was a messenger. He came to bring peace. Thinking of her grandmother's words, Marika felt a quiet calm come over her. She knew that Elizabeth's fever would pass. Someday the flu would pass and the people would return to the streets of Butte. Someday all would be well.

Elizabeth moaned and turned away. "Danny?" she whispered.

"I'm here," Dan said and came closer. "I'm not going anywhere. Unless you want some of my mother's famous chicken noodle soup."

A slight smile appeared on Elizabeth's lips. "That might be good," she said.

"Should I?" he asked Marika.

She didn't understand his sudden lack of confidence. And then she knew. While he was good at doing whatever needed to be done, he was fragile in the world of the heart. And he had fallen in love with Elizabeth.

Marika gazed at the girl who was ghostly thin. Translucent eyelids fluttered and closed.

Again, Dan looked at Marika, eyes pleading for her to tell him what to do.

"Yes," Marika said. "Be quick and the soup will be here when she wakes up." She put another cool towel on her forehead.

He stood up.

"Dan?" Marika said without taking her eyes off of the

girl. She heard him pause at the door. "She will wake up." She hoped it was true.

Using the very scientific method of counting on her fingers she listed the steps she'd taken. Gave her water, quinine, and rags to cool her fever, talked to her in a comforting manner, encouraged Dan to come back with chicken soup. What was left to do? Feeling totally helpless sitting in the wooden chair next to the young woman, she knew that Elizabeth could lose her life. Or she could live. Marika crossed herself and prayed.

Elizabeth was still asleep when Dan came back with the soup. Marika tried to keep the worry out of her voice. "The flu has worn her out," she told him.

"I'll put it on the stove to keep it warm," he said.

He hadn't been gone long. Mrs. McClane must have had the soup already made up. Perhaps she figured that was the only thing she could do to help people. Give them good food. Just feed them and keep them healthy, now that the County Health Board had loosened the restrictions somewhat.

Marika and Dan sat quietly through the night with Elizabeth. Michael hadn't liked it at first, but when Marika explained how sick Elizabeth was and that Dan loved her, he relented.

Late in the night, Elizabeth threw up blood. Blood lined her ears and nose, and her feet had begun to turn black. Marika all but gave up hope. But then, as the morning sun rose up over of the East Ridge, turning the sky a soft pink, the same soft pink had begun to return to Elizabeth's skin. Her cough had subsided. The blood at her ears and nose dried and fell away. As the morning passed the brown patches on her face lightened and disappeared.

Marika was flooded with gratitude. On the way home, she stopped outside the church and lit a candle. The sanctuary was a small outside structure that had been built for prayer while the churches were closed. A dozen candles stood tall in the sand at the bottom of it. Marika added her thanks to the glow.

She thought about the death that she'd seen in

Montenegro, helping her grandmother in the hospital tent. She thought about last year at the Granite Mountain Mine fire, where 168 men died. She thought of Frank Little and the senseless brutality of his death. And now this flu had stolen the lives of hundreds of men, women, and children. Influenza had come the long way across the sea, or from the east coast, or from the south. It had crossed the Rocky Mountains to the streets of Butte, Montana, virulent and powerful, like nothing anyone had ever seen.

Cold evening light flooded the room as Marika opened the office curtains. The beautiful pink sky had come and gone, but it was a beautiful morning that had allowed a young woman to live. The back room of Dr. Fletcher's office looked out on the alley where the dead wagon had arrived over and over during the last months, and the alley was empty. The room had been turned into a temporary holding place as Butte's hospitals and morgues overflowed with the sick and dying. And the room was empty.

Amelia. Elizabeth. One died. One lived.

Who chose?

This lament belonged to the random work of the wind, the shift of the sky, the paper boy who walked left instead of right, the last drop of water given over to the horse in the pasture. She could call it anything. Because nothing made sense. This deadly disease came from nowhere but the sweat on the drifter's fingertips, the rich man's fork, the priest's holy robe, the dirt of the mine.

This devil had no discretion, only insatiable hunger. It preferred a young man or woman in full health, but it would take a child or a ninety-year-old or a sickly teen. It didn't care. It had plowed a wide path of death and destruction through the town.

As she looked out the window, Marika wished for more talent and knowledge, for an education to match her desire. A woman doctor from Helena had gone to the northern town of Whitefish when the flu struck. She had not lost one single patient. The same could not be said in Butte. The final count may well be near a thousand.

Amelia's brown wool dress had dark blood stains on it. If Marika had been less hopeful, she would have known that Amelia didn't have a chance. The demon started there and moved fast, knocking down almost everyone who dared to cross it. Whoever pushed Amelia through death's door probably prevented an extra night of suffering. It could have been a wild mercy.

There was a light tap on the office door, and Kaly walked in.

She looked as ragged as Marika felt. It had been a rough time for both of them, apparently.

"Beth died," she said in a small, flat voice.

"Oh, no," Marika replied. She remembered Beth had said she'd rather die of the flu than of the syphilis, that it would be a merciful death. "I'm sorry."

"I don't want to go home," Kaly said.

Marika slowly sank into a chair. "Annie and George won't know why you've disappeared. They'll only feel your absence."

"They'll be fine," Kaly said. "And what about you? If you don't rest, you'll be next." She looked out the window toward the dark sky of the East Ridge. "I don't think I could stand to lose you too." Tears welled in her eyes.

Marika drew a breath to cover her surprise. Kaly hadn't been affectionate, even after learning that they were cousins. And Kaly was right. She'd been lucky. Being on the right side of the Mining Town's luck meant only slightly less grief than being on the wrong side of it.

"It would take two of us to do the work you do." Kaly smiled and tilted her head, a teasing expression Marika had grown used to.

"Kay," Marika said. "Amelia?"

She waited for Kaly's nod.

"She did have the slight blue marks at her neck."

Kaly nodded her head. "She was strangled."

The words were matter of fact, like a dozen young girls had been strangled. And they had been. But this was different. This was long fingers stretching into Amelia's life when she was already dying.

"Influenza had her in its grip," Marika said, "but so had something else. She'd been poisoned too. There were traces of chloroform around her nose and mouth." Marika pushed her hair back out of her face.

"He wanted to make sure she died. But why?"

"Playing God?" Her voice lilted up, as if Kaly could answer the question.

"With a real mean streak."

"And no conscience."

"Doesn't sound much like God," Kaly said.

"It's so senseless. We've all seen enough death."

Marika shook her head as if shaking it off, sorry she had started this conversation, giving too much limelight to the cruelty, feeling so badly about Beth, eager to change the subject. "How is Annie?"

"That one is strong as a horse, crawling all over the apartment. She's restless, like everyone else. Town's like a trapped coyote about to chew its leg off."

"It's too much for all of us," Marika said.

They sat there in the quiet of the doctor's office for quite a while before Kaly pressed her lips together and put her hand into her pocket. "I have something to show you," she said. She put two envelopes on the desk. One had Little Tony written on it. The other was blank. They had both been opened.

The softness of her voice washed over Marika. Fields of sage grew south of town and sent the subtle aroma of dirt and smoke into the air. The Indians used sage to clean the land and the space around it. On the side of the cliff at Ostrag Monestary, in Montenegro, the priest used incense to bring blessings to the land, and release the impurities of the pilgrims who had traveled there. In this western mining town, alley smoke rose in through a crack in the doctor's window, offering absolution.

"Amelia's letters?" Marika asked. She had forgotten all about them.

"Jack found them in her things," Kaly said, "and brought them to Tara."

"And she gave them to you." She took the letter out of the unmarked envelope and read it out loud.

To whoever reads this,

If you are reading this. I am probably gone. Please take care of my little Tony. He needs someone good and full of love. He's a wild one, but with care and understanding he'll settle down. He won't know what happened to me and he shouldn't.

You might think the flu has got me, and I think it will. I've watched so many die. But it's also possible that foul play is at hand. It's not fair that Tony should be punished for deeds his mother did or didn't do. Please surround him with your wisdom and help him grow into a good man.

All my love to him, always,
Amelia

Marika looked up at Kaly, who was watching her intently. "Audrey Riley was right. Amelia knew that someone was after her. But she came to Butte. Why? Why Butte?"

"Read the second letter," Kaly said.

My Dear Little Tony,

Someday, you will be old enough to read this and I want you to know how much I love you. Since you are reading this, I am not there. I have a wonderful surprise for you. Jack Kelly, the man I left you with, is your grandfather. Mother, out of some misplace shame, never told him about me. So, he doesn't know. It's a secret that you don't have to keep. If you need something, ever, go to him. I can see already that he is a good man.

All my love, your Mother

Marika looked up at Kaly with a tiny little gasp. "The magical coincidence. She was looking for her father." She thought of the note she'd found in Amelia's pocket. *J.K., Butte, Montana.* Jack Kelly, Butte, Montana.

"While trying to stop a killer."

"Does Jack know, yet?"

Kaly shook her head no.

The two women sat there, in mutual befuddlement,

wondering what all the wild winds of the east had brought to the Copper Camp.

———————

Marika went home to Michael, and felt a deep sense of belonging, not wanting to think of Amelia, or Little Tony, or Jack Kelly. She didn't want to think of Beth's death and Kaly's grief-stricken face. She just wanted to be right there with her husband. Her body felt so right with him, so opposite of the sick feeling she'd had all that day. She wondered if she was coming down with the devil flu. So far, she'd been strong.

She thought of the last time she'd seen Derrick. His eyes had swarmed over her in some knowing way, like he had dominion over her. Nary a smile to his lips. That strict face haunted her.

"Come here," Michael said.

He ran his hand across her brow and down her cheek. "You are here now, with me." He kissed her forehead and pulled her close. She melted into him, molding her body to his, letting her tears flow down his chest.

———————

Marika cleaned the back room. Now that flu cases had slowed down in earnest, the room would no longer be needed to house the sick and dead. Dr. Fletcher and Miss Parsons had both gone home. "Exhausted," they had said in unison.

Very much like when Amelia showed up last fall, just as she was about to shut off the light and turn the lock, someone knocked on the door.

Derrick stood in the fading light with a bottle of *kruske*, pear brandy.

"What do you want?" she asked.

He held the bottle up. "To make it up to you. I know you think I brought the trouble. I didn't." He made his way in and set the bottle on Miss Parsons' desk, pulled two shot glasses from his pocket, poured the brandy, and handed one to Marika.

Against her better judgement, she took it. The brandy was pure and light going down. It hit her stomach, and the grief of the last months dissolved a little. Just enough for her to remember that the sun would continue to rise long after this flu left. The constant barrage of sick people had made her harsh and judgmental. Had she judged Derrick too harshly?

She smiled at him. Not knowing what he wanted seemed irrelevant. He poured another drink for her and she took it.

"But we're here now." He stepped close to her and she could smell the *kruske* on his lips. "Perhaps we can find a way to help the town."

"That time is already gone," she said, sipping her *kruske*. It burned her throat going down and that felt good.

"So many misunderstand me," he said.

She leaned back against Miss Parsons' desk. The room felt cold and stilted.

"All I ever wanted," Derrick was saying, "was to bring joy to them and to end their suffering. But they didn't value me." He moved closer to her, put his arm around her, and pulled her close. "You can change that. You and me can cure this pain."

She slid out from under his arm, hiding a small terrified gasp. The room tilted. Shadows crowded and swirled in the dust motes, pressing the air like a vice, making her head hurt.

Their. Multiple.

"How can we?" she asked. She tried to keep her voice steady, all emotion shut down, her brain working overtime. "Nothing we can do tonight."

"Oh, but we can." He took his hat off and set it on Miss Parsons' desk, brushing her arm with his hand, and turning his gray eyes on her. "I don't really need a hat inside, do I?"

Marika felt that electric paralytic trance. As if it were its own being, it tried to take hold of her. "I have to go," she said.

"I'll tell you about Amelia." He poured another drink for her, eased back slowly, against Miss Parsons' desk, next to Marika, his shoulder nearly touching hers.

Something in the angle of his head, his thick, droopy eyelids, the vague, senseless look on his face, sent a sharp warning signal through Marika. She picked up her drink and sipped it. "Go on," she said.

"I loved Amelia. We were going to be married. She was the

most beautiful girl I had ever seen. Far too beautiful to suffer." He drank down his *kruske* and refilled his glass, a sudden cruel glint in his eyes, turning them on her. "Beauty should not have to suffer bad luck. You should not have to suffer bad luck. You haven't gotten sick, but it's only a matter of time."

The alcohol made her too woozy and she felt her chest tighten. She realized what was coming next. She heard the crows outside the window and wondered when someone would notice she was missing.

"You are beautiful." He touched her shoulder. "You don't feel good, do you?"

She didn't feel good. And she felt very afraid.

He ran his hand down her cheek. "It's okay. You'll sleep now. The flu can come on so quickly."

"You did it, didn't you?" Marika said. But it wasn't really a question. "You killed Amelia."

"The flu killed her, but I did help her along a bit," he said. "She wanted to break off our engagement after promising me her life. I only took what she promised me.

"I watched her on the train, drinking with those soldiers. I saw the one with that blue tinge to his lips looking at her. I encouraged him to go talk to her, light her cigarette, share a drink with her. It didn't take much. This flu is such a friendly thing.

"She felt me watching her. I could tell by the startled look in her eyes when she'd turn around and no one was there, just me hiding in the shadows. And to think, she came after me, trying to hide herself and the boy, as if I wouldn't know what she was doing.

"I saw her get that first inkling of the flu, the lost step, the slumped shoulders, exerting a great effort to pick up her legs and move. She had watched the others get sick and she knew the signs.

"It took very little to push her over that edge. I came out of the shadows and offered to walk her to the doctor's office. She tried to resist, but the flu had weakened her and I had the chloroform. Before I knocked on your door and handed her over to you, I covered her mouth and nose with a rag, just a touch, just enough to keep her weak." He pulled his hand out of the pocket of the large coat he wore.

"And Stella? What did you do to Stella?"

"Ah, she was more difficult. Stella had a stubborn streak. She was suspicious and wouldn't be charmed. But in the end, I convinced her."

"The rag?"

"Just a touch. She was already sick." He gave Marika the icy eyes and disjointed smile, a smile that had no joy in it.

"I haven't promised you anything," she said.

Derrick shook his head. "But you have. Each day I see how you look at me. I see the love in your eyes. I see how you long for me. That longing is your promise. The flu will take you or I will. Wouldn't you rather have it be me?" He stepped closer and trapped her in his arms.

Her sides burned where he touched her, his grip firm and unyielding. "You are right," she said. "I am not feeling good. I should go home now. Michael will be waiting for me."

"Oh, no. It's late for that."

"Not too late. We could just talk about it another time. Come back over to the house for dinner." She was buying time, trying to sort out a plan. But he wasn't having it. There was no time. He tightened his grip on her. She tried to push him off, but he held steady. She looked around frantically. The drink had weakened her. "Michael will know," she said. "He'll come after you."

"Michael will be grateful that I took good care of you in your last minutes." He held the rag in the air like an emblem of surrender.

Hers.

"No one will come for you," he was saying. "They'll all think you are simply helping the sick. Which in a way, you are. I don't feel so good, either." He smiled a yellow-toothed grinned at her. She could smell the sour film on his tongue.

Behind her, Dr. Fletcher's large medical book sat on Miss Parsons' desk. Marika freed a hand, picked it up, and swung it hard against Derrick's head.

He flinched and lost his hold on her.

She slammed him again. And again. She grabbed the scissors from Miss Parsons' desk and ran as hard as she could, out the door and down the street to the Red-Light District.

Marika ran harder than she'd ever run before and she didn't look back. Her lungs and legs burned, as the icy air blew past her. She clutched the scissors. Let him come after her. Let him catch her. She would cut his throat.

Chapter Twenty-Two

KALY LOOKED IN THE closet. She had nothing to wear. Dust had settled on an abandoned spider web in one corner. She knew she should clean it right now, instead of waiting. Waiting for what, she didn't know. She grabbed a broom and knocked the dust and the spider web away.

She finally settled on the green taffeta dress, one of three that she now had in her closet. Tara had made it for her for George's birthday, saying that she should have an Irish-green dress. Kaly had loved it then and loved it now. But, being the bitter abandoned daughter, she hated to admit it. But being the loved, grateful daughter, she delighted in the dress. She held it close and swirled around the room with it, then spread it out on the bed. It was perfect.

"Hurry," George said from the other room. "Annie wants to crawl around in her new outfit. She's getting it dirty."

"Well, stop her," Kaly said.

"Try to! She's too stubborn."

"Where is your grandmother? Ask her to help you."

"Downstairs, baking," George said. "We're open again, remember?"

As if Kaly didn't remember. "Of course. Well, I'll just be a minute." And a second later, "What is she baking?"

"Sweet breads for the troops. I wanted to help but she won't let me. She said I had more important things to do today."

Kaly smiled at that and opened the bedroom window. "Yes, you do," she said, letting the soft folds of the dress hang to her ankles. She twirled and the dress flew around in the breeze. Crows lined the top of the bank building, cawing at each other, taking flight and landing again, chattering at each other, as if they knew something special was about to happen.

The buildings looked over the land, stretching an open palm out to the snowy peaks of the Highlands. Houses dotted the valley as the town shifted away from the black metal head frames. The miners that lived in those houses took the trolley or caught rides with friends back up the hill for work. But not today. Today all things stalled, for just a little while, as the flu faded and the soldiers returned from war.

Kaly sat on a hard, wooden bench at the train station, where she could see Homestake Pass. The train tracks stretched all the way from the east, across the hard tack ground of the plains, and through the rough boulders of the pass, the winter sun watching it all. The wooden station floor, spotted with mud tracks, attracted Annie's gaze. Kaly resisted her tug of war. She wanted down, of course. Her chubby legs poked out from under the soft white dress with tiny white roses that Tara had made for her. Kaly had knit a soft white sweater to go with it.

Whoever would have thought that she, Kaly Shane, Kaly Monroe, would have embarked on such a project with her mother? Not Kaly Shane. That's for sure. But this Kaly Monroe was a very different creature from Kaly Shane. Her crib in the Alley seemed foreign. Her life had changed so much. Her husband, Tommy Monroe, would be on the next train arriving at the Butte station. She could at least keep his daughter clean for his arrival.

George sat beside them, his feet flat on the floor, his palms on his thighs. He shook his head "no" and smiled half a smile at Kaly. "She'll make a mess of it," he said. A janitor had been through with a broom earlier, before the crowds of Butte people gathered to wait for loved ones. The janitor had made little difference. Silt and dirt crossed the boards like old friends.

Kaly nodded at George, while holding Annie tight. "When did your sister get so strong?"

"Ask her," he shrugged. He had buttoned his coat to his chin and wore a small brimmed brown hat. Both made him look very proper for a ten-year-old boy who might at any other time be out playing in the snow.

Kaly knew he was nervous. Last night he'd been a million questions a minute. What is he like? What if he doesn't remember me? What did he do there? Did he get hurt? Until finally, what if he doesn't want me?

Kaly had told him that Tommy loved him very much, and that he would always be his son. That calmed him enough that he finally fell asleep. The rest might have done him good, except that he woke early a frantic mess, cleaning the kitchen, making the beds, picking up Annie's toys. He wore poor Andjo out, racing around the apartment behind him. The wolf dog seemed to be the only one without a jangle of nerves at the moment. He lay quietly at the foot of the bench, inches from George's already large work boots.

Kaly thought about Marika's sudden appearance at the bakery door last night. She had narrowly escaped from Derrick Boggins, running to the Red-Light District, where the women surrounded her and asked no questions. People had strolled down the street, oblivious to Marika's plight. Horses neighed and cars rolled on by. Smoke had lifted out toward the flats while Marika sat in the crib next to Kaly's old crib. A woman she didn't know sat on the bed, knitting and singing a dance tune that Marika had never heard before. Another woman sat outside on a bench, humming the same tune.

"I felt safe with them," Marika had told Kaly, who knew exactly what she meant. The women of the line smelled danger a mile away. They protected their own and those in their midst. No words, just pure, sweet, animal protection.

"Am I making it all up?" Marika had asked her.

"No," Kaly had replied. "You've just been in the presence of evil. We must stop him. Let's go tell the sheriff. And you tell Michael when you get home."

But the sheriff had dismissed them, as if a killer in their midst was nothing to think twice about. After all, the killer flu had been in their midst since early September.

"But this is a man," Marika had said, had pleaded.

The sheriff had nodded. "We'll get to him. We have a lot more to worry about right now," he said. "Don't find yourself alone with him again." As if Marika were to blame. That sent both women into a rage that they could barely contain.

They had raged to each other all the way to Marika's house, where they nearly fell down in stupid laughter, exhausted and wondering if Michael would listen. But if Michael took them seriously and went after Derrick, Marika had a whole new worry. What if her husband killed Derrick? He would face trial and go to prison.

Annie's squirming brought Kaly back to the present.

"Mama," she said. "Down." She smiled that crazy, beautiful, charming, please-give-me-whatever-I-want smile at her mother.

"No, baby. You stay on Mama's lap."

"Kaly," Annie tried again, laughing and patting her mother's arm.

George looked at Kaly with a raised eyebrow.

This time, Kaly shook her head. That would get Annie nowhere fast. Kaly did not like it when Annie used her first name. She started to say so when a shrill whistle and the screeching sound of iron wheels on tracks silenced her. Annie went completely still. George stared wide-eyed at the metal creature come out of the east.

Tommy was coming home.

The platform filled with people pushing each other, trying to get to the front of the crowd. Bright reds and pinks blended with the dark blues and browns of Sunday bests. Two brave crows sat on a wooden railing near the benches, watching, sunshine glinting off their feathers. They were curious bystanders, waiting to see what would happen, and to see who would get off of the train, and who would have been left behind in the trenches.

Kaly felt pulled in two directions. Her body wanted to run to Tommy, to touch him, and feel his belly pressed against hers. But she also wanted to shrink away and hide. She knew the dangers of loving someone too much. Yet, here she was with children attached to her, and a dog. And this was Tommy, a man, her man. Couldn't she please slow down her beating heart?

She'd felt that pulsing between her legs with each new letter she'd read. The warmth reached up into her chest, her body tingling. She hadn't told George last night, but she had the same worries he had.

What if Tommy didn't want her?

Now, with the train pulling in she could barely keep from throwing herself at the huge metal train, to find the answer once and for all. Act mature, she told herself. You have children, she told herself. But what was maturity anyway? And hadn't she been acting mature since she was about ten years old? So, go ahead and revel in your giddiness, she told herself, giggling.

George looked up at her, his hat tilting, and giggled too. Annie squished her cheeks between the palms of her tiny hands and let out a delighted shriek.

Beyond her daughter's brown curls Kaly saw the crowd milling around, waiting. They chattered, like the crows. They all knew something good was in the air. She couldn't decide what to tell Tommy first. How much she'd missed him, or how the flu had ravaged the town… Or about Marika's sudden face at her door last night.

Kaly's head spun. The train whistle blew. Smoke billowed into the air as the engine screeched to a long, drawn out halt. The doors opened and people piled out of the cars. Up and down the tracks, men in stiff black suits and women in colorful dresses with feathered hats ducked through the open door and spilled onto the platform. Some of them carried their luggage and others waited to collect large trunks.

Tommy was not the last person off of the train, but he might as well have been. Each new person who disembarked, and was not him, sent an arrow of panic right through her heart. She was certain she would faint as she moved closer to the open doors. She steadied herself on a nearby railing, causing the crows to take flight. Annie leaned out of her mother's arms and reached for the crows' tail feathers.

George never took his eyes off of the train door.

"Kaly!" Tommy yelled across the platform. "George, my boy!"

He looked tall and slender in his uniform and so handsome, an angel from above. They ran to him, her with Annie in her arms, George with the dog at his side.

George got there first and Tommy picked him up and swung him. Then he pulled the boy into a hug that lasted forever. Without letting go of the boy, he pulled Kaly and Annie close, kissing his daughter until she squealed with laughter. He put his head in Kaly's hair. He kissed her neck, her cheek, her lips, holding all of them close for the whole world to see.

The dog whined at their feet and sat so properly, waiting his turn. Finally, Tommy reached down and patted his head and rubbed his ears. "Hey boy," he said.

Then he stood and pulled everyone close again. Kaly's skirt billowed in the breeze, their love floating in the folds of the fabric and settling in her bones. She cried and held them all so tight, tighter than she had ever held anyone before.

Chapter Twenty-Three

THERE WAS A GRACE in knowing what happened to Amelia. Marika comforted herself with this knowing. A young girl, working hard, making barely enough to keep her child alive, meets a man who promises her all good things in life, a home, safety, security, a bed for the child, full cupboards, love. Love.

Instead, she finds he lied. He charmed her like he had charmed the others. And she was taken in, just like the others. The man walks away patting himself on the back for the ruse he'd pulled and how he had single handedly kept it a secret. Thank God for the flu. And he walks away free to feign love another day.

But Marika wasn't having it. She'd gone to the sheriff. When he laughed at her, she went to her husband.

"He killed her," she said, the words floating in the air between them. She loved Michael and he had been consistently with her. But this was different. This was his friend. Michael might not believe her.

She sat across the table from him. Escaped smoke from the stove coated the air. She felt warm here with Michael. The times she'd felt safe in the last two years had been fleeting, and they had all been with her husband. He was the balm that soothed her heart. His skin next to hers calmed her in a way she'd never imagined possible. Besides Mama and Marko being healthy, he had been the one good surprising thing in her life this year.

How could Papa have known? How could he have read into her soul that she would find peace in the midst of heartache with this man? How could he have possibly known that

Michael would be so good for her?

She sat down at the wooden table Michael had built. He had made four chairs, two extras, one for Mama and one for Marko. They had all sat on them and played some mean games of poker, with Michael consistently beating the others. Tucked away in the bedroom, Michael treasured two smaller chairs. "For the children," he'd said so innocently that it almost slipped by her.

"But medical school," she'd said when she caught on.

He smiled that sweet smile and took her to the chest of drawers, where he'd pulled out a wooden box, which he had also made. He set it on top of the dresser and opened it. A flood of money spilled out.

"After medical school," he had said, closing the lid without looking at her. "I've been saving for it. This will get us there. Maybe you can talk to the other women doctors in Montana and get an idea what to expect."

For once, she could find no words. She threw her arms around Michael's neck and pressed her head into his chest, wetting his shirt with her tears.

She would do the work. She'd earn every moment of that year studying and learning all that she could push into her brain. She felt her grandmother's blessing rise up and cross the wild sea, all the way from Montenegro to this Montana mining town.

She was going to medical school.

But first.

"He killed her," she said again.

Michael nodded. "Tell me."

"Derrick killed Amelia. She died of the flu, but he pushed her over that edge."

"You are sure?"

"He admitted it. He tried to kill me."

Silence slithered through a cracked window. The light bulb swung on its thread, making the light falter and shine on Michael's face. Marika had no idea what he would do with the information, but she saw the knowing twist in his dark eyes. A slow calculation turned his eyes black and narrow, a wolf's howl escaping his throat.

He stood to go. The sun had not yet come into the winter sky. Even though the new fire crackled and hissed, the room was cool. Marika did not want him to leave her yet. Not with Derrick out there and maybe nearby, knowing that she knew.

"Amelia's son?" Michael asked.

"He is safe. Jack Kelly is working graveyard at the Orphan Girl. He left the boy with Miss Anderson to watch. Tara has agreed to take him, to raise him, so that he can grow up in a family, with Annie and George. Kaly will help and Tommy was all for it. 'The bigger family the better family,' he said.

"Jack Kelly agreed, but only if he can also stay in Little Tony's life."

"Can Derrick get to Tony?"

Marika's heart sank. She hadn't thought of that. That Derrick would want to kidnap or hurt Amelia's son hadn't even crossed her mind, or that he might do it out of spite to get back at Marika. She had figured Derrick was nothing but a cruel drifter who would quickly plan his move to the next town.

"Let's go." Michael grabbed his canvas coat from the wall and handed her wool coat and scarf to her.

Pulling it on felt dangerous. She knew nothing about stopping a killer, or snatching a child from a kidnapper.

Far up on the hill a siren shrieked, signaling the shift change. Was it really morning already? Miners would soon return to Miss Anderson's Big House for a warm meal and a good sleep. A mist rose up from the flats as the sun once more peaked over the East Ridge, turning the sky a pearly pink.

On any other day Marika would have savored the glory of the sky spreading out across the land. But not today. All that beauty stood in stark contrast against the menace the boy faced, if Michael's hunch was right.

He called the sheriff's office. He waited a long while. "No answer," he said as he hung up the phone.

They walked quickly, the bitter air biting their faces. Marika pulled her scarf up over her ears and tucked the long part into her coat. It wouldn't be long before she overheated from the fast pace of the walk. Until then, she'd be warm.

Michael knocked on the door of The Polly May. The knock was firm and solid, not too frantic. "I don't want to scare anyone," he said, "or wake more than we need to."

Of course, he would think of others. She hadn't realized how much of a chess player Michael was, always thinking three moves ahead. Less than an hour ago, Marika had sat across the table from him and said, "He killed her." Now, Michael was protecting Amelia's son.

Miss Anderson answered the door, her white hair a rat's nest, her nightgown long and faded. "Yes," she said. She cocked her head as if to say, "What are you doing at my door before the sun is up?"

"Miss Anderson," Michael said. "May we come in?"

"We can explain," Marika said.

"I hope so." As they entered the Big House, Marika noticed that she wore no shoes, and stepped lightly on the rich, soft Oriental carpet. Many photos of young children hung on the walls. Some of them smiled. Some of them had dark eyes filled with fear.

"Is Amelia's son Tony here?"

"I'm not in charge of him. I've only got him until Jack is off shift. You probably heard I'm not fit. I hope that's not what you are checking up on. I've done nothing wrong."

Marika shook her head. "You are not in trouble."

"But the boy might be in danger," Michael said. "Can we see him?"

"In danger? In danger how? Jack Kelly is a good man. He'd mean no harm to anyone. I've known him for years. He's been taking care of the boy, even though he keeps saying he's not capable."

"Can we see him?" Michael asked again.

Miss Anderson walked over to the stairwell and stood at the bottom. The same oriental carpet climbed up the stairs. "Tony," she yelled up the stairs. "Tony." As if a young child would answer her and deliver himself to her.

Just then a loud bang came from the alley.

Marika looked at Michael for an answer.

"The fire escape," he said. "Wait here."

He was gone before she could argue. And she was quick to argue.

Outside Derrick ran down the alley with a crying bundle

in his hands. Small legs kicked at his thighs. "Down!" a tiny voice cried.

Michael was on Derrick before he could reach the next block.

"Call the sheriff," Marika yelled to Miss Anderson, and ran to grab the boy from the pile they had all landed in.

The police siren disturbed the serenity of the early morning light, and anyone left still asleep in the Big House.

Marika had the boy in her arms. He looked baffled as he poked her nose.

"Mama?" Tony asked. Marika didn't have the heart to tell him that his mother had passed away. She hoped someone had already done that.

"We have a good home for you," she told him instead, "with a sister and a big brother and a dog. And all the good food you could ever want."

"Papa?" he asked.

"Yes, Mr. Kelly will be there too," she said, wondering how often she made stuff up that actually came true.

The police took Derrick into custody. This time the sheriff listened to Marika. She hated it that it took Michael to get him to listen. What the hell was wrong with a woman's word?

But Derrick was in jail, and the boy was safe. Maybe now justice would be done.

Maybe now Amelia's spirit could rest easy.

Marika brought the boy back to the Big House. Miss Anderson had gotten dressed and combed her hair. Jack Kelly had arrived and stood next to her. He still had his work bundle under his arm.

Tony reached his hands out to the man.

Jack took him and held him tight. "I'm sorry, little guy," he said.

"Papa," the boy said. "Not sorry."

"Tara McLane will be by to get him later today," Jack told Marika, tears welling up in his eyes. "I'm going to miss the little guy."

Marika and Michael held hands as they walked at a much slower pace than they had raced to The Polly May. Marika breathed in the Butte air. It was sharp and acrid, but smelled just like home.

She thought of the money Michael had saved, and of talking to the women doctors in Montana, and of applying to medical schools. When they returned to Butte, she would be older, wiser, and of service. Her heart swelled to think of how she would miss Mama and Marko. But it would be okay. They had made it through the flu, the mining disaster of last year, and Papa's death. Michael would be with her and she would write home every day.

She squeezed his hand and pulled herself close to him.

"*Hvala*," she said. She hadn't even known all that her own heart wanted.

THE WOLF DOG RUNS WITH THE WIND

Spring 1919

* * *

THE WOLF DOG RUNS to the East Ridge, where the mountains make a natural barricade, and back to the boy. The flu has gone and the boy is free. He is determined to gather strength and feel his joy again. The town opens and flourishes again. There are jobs and people flock to the Copper Camp. The city regains its heart and life carries on.

There are less of them. More parents are needed to replace the ones who have passed. The children cling to pant legs and long skirts. They find food at their tables, and fresh sheets for their beds. At night, someone reads them a story.

When they ask about their parents, the room goes quiet.

Or maybe someone talks about the long-ago flu that lifted their parents up, like rich, wonderful spirits, beyond the brilliant mountains. There, they eat strawberries and run through fields of wildflowers. The air flows freely through their lungs like love and no one will ever hurt them again.

The light-haired woman with the green eyes dances around the bakery, swinging the baby, smiling a huge smile for the soldier back from the war. He laughs with the boy and the dog barks at his happiness. At a booth, her mother sits with another young boy, feeding him a cheese sandwich, and teaching him simple words: butter, girl, dog, boy, love. Papa.

"Papa," the boy says, and touches the red beard of the big

burly man next to him.

The people of Butte cheer in the street. Hip hip, horray. Hip hip, horray!

The war is over, the flu is past, the danger is over.

They feed the poor, take care of the sick, help the crippled walk. They shelter each other, pour wine and whiskey, pat backs, kiss cheeks and foreheads and lips. They swing around and around, their skirts flying in the air and their hats taking wing.

We will live, they say, having made their way around the black tip of suffering. It's a soft whisper at first, and then the chant takes hold. We will live! We will live for those in the graveyards at the far end of town, for those who won't see their children grow up, for those whose mothers wept.

The wolf dog pushes his head into the boy's open palm. Together they cross the land, walking over the copper tunnels and the opium dens. Together they stroll past cafes and taverns and churches with their doors wide open.

The boy will grow to be an old man someday, long after the wolf dog has gone to the mountains for the last time. He'll look back at the glory of this day, blessing the dog and himself, blessing those who gave way to a tiny devil who stole their breath.

The wolf dog watches the boy dance with his father in the soft haze of spring, and he runs circles around them. He watches the people flood the streets with chatter and laughter. Relief and joy fill their eyes. Like one body, like a dream of angels, like some beautiful ghost, the town's grief rises out of the mist, and floats up to heaven.

Author's Note

* * *

IN THE FALL OF 1918 influenza swept the nation and came to the mining town of Butte, Montana. Butte's population was estimated at about 90,000 residents at that time. Between September 1918 and the winter of 1919 influenza killed approximately 1,000 people in Butte and Silver Bow County. About eight people a day died in the month of October alone. *Beautiful Ghost* is a work of fiction. I have taken great liberties with the events, the town, and Butte's history. Any mistakes in fact or representation are entirely my own. All characters are figments of my imagination and are not meant to portray any actual persons, alive or dead.

ACKNOWLEDGEMENTS

* * *

I WOULD FIRST AND foremost like to thank my editors and publishers at Open Books, Kelly Huddleston and David Ross, for their support and their belief in *Beautiful Ghost.* Without them, this book would have remained a dream far into the future. A huge thank you to Maggie Plummer for jumping in to help me when I most needed it, for her editing, and for helping me find the heart of this story. This is a much better book than it might have been without Maggie's help. Thank you, Susan Sage, for being a beta reader and taking on the challenge at a late notice!

Thank you to Janelle M. Olberding for her amazing book *Butte and the 1918 Influenza Pandemic (Disaster).* She states that her book was "a work of love" and I believe her. She did the hard research on the 1918 Influenza Pandemic in Butte, Montana, making it much easier for me to write *Beautiful Ghost.* Thank you to Jane Little Botkin for her wonderful book *Frank Little and the IWW: The Blood That Stained an American Family.* She touched the hearts of so many in Butte with her book. Her book inspired the Frank Little parts of *Beautiful Ghost.* Thank you to PBS Montana for their engaging and informative documentary *Butte, America.* Thank you to everyone who gave me feedback on *Copper Sky.* I've taken it to heart and, hopefully, incorporated some of that feedback here.

A big thank you to my brother, Ed Marsenich, for helping me with early research and for his enthusiasm about this book. Thank you to my brother, Bob Marsenich, and sister-in-law, Karen McMullen, for giving me a place to write and their ongoing faith in my writing efforts. Thank you to Jan Myers for giving me a place to write and for supporting my writing efforts with her amazing photography. Many thanks to Ellen Leahy Howell for taking the time during our hikes and backpacking trips to share her knowledge and wisdom about the 1918 influenza pandemic in Montana.

Thank you to Marty Phillips for going to the Butte Archives with me, a place to get lost in! And thank you to Ellen Crain and the Butte Archives staff for pointing us toward the information we needed. Thank you, Judith Bromley, for my author photo. Thank you to Carrol Carreau for always being there. Thank you to Women Writing the West and Western Writers of America for supporting my writing. I've made many friends along the way and am very happy to be a part of both organizations.

All my Butte stories begin with my family and early friends. They shaped my life, my language, and my stories. They taught me to love. To them I am forever grateful. A giant thank you to the people of Butte for their incredible resilience, for finding a way through the seemingly impossible, and for their very bright and generous hearts. Without them, this story would not have been possible.